*Acclaim for* NELLY ROSARIO's

Song of
the Water Saints

"An electrifying debut. Powerfully written, meticulously imagined, and arresting to its core, Nelly Rosario's novel is a flame for the mind and heart, the sort you are endlessly grateful for."  —Junot Díaz, author of *Drown*

"Effortlessly intermingles three generations of women, dropping unadorned dialogue amid spare and lovely prose."                                      —*Entertainment Weekly*

"Rosario does an excellent job conjuring the colorful, vibrant scenes of Caribbean life."  —*Los Angeles Times*

"Every small scene that Nelly Rosario writes reaches toward a larger truth out in the world, and also a smaller, more intimate truth. . . . There is a physicality in the language that speaks of an angry, human spirituality and the struggle to be alive."  —*The Oregonian*

"Lush and assured . . . each brief chapter reads like a snapshot of a soul."                        —*Time Out New York*

NELLY ROSARIO

# Song of
# the Water Saints

Nelly Rosario was born in the Dominican Republic
and raised in Brooklyn, where she now lives. She
received a B.A. in engineering from MIT and an
M.F.A. in fiction writing from Columbia University.
She was named a "Writer on the Verge" by the *Village
Voice Literary Supplement* in 2001. *Song of the Water
Saints* won the 2002 Pen Open Book Award.

Song of
the Water Saints

# Song of the Water Saints

## NELLY ROSARIO

VINTAGE CONTEMPORARIES

*Vintage Books*

*A Division of Random House, Inc.*

*New York*

FIRST VINTAGE CONTEMPORARIES EDITION, SEPTEMBER 2003

*Copyright © 2002 by Nelly Rosario*

The Library of Congress has cataloged the Pantheon edition as follows:
Rosario, Nelly, 1972–.
Song of the water saints / Nelly Rosario
p. cm.
ISBN: 0-375-42087-8
1. Women—Dominican Republic—Fiction.  2. Mothers and daughters—
Fiction.  3. Dominican Americans—Fiction.  4. Dominican Republic—
Fiction.  5. Women immigrants—Fiction.
I. Title.
PS3618.O78 S66 2002
813'.6—dc21                              2001036035

**Vintage ISBN: 978-0-375-72549-4**

*Book design by Johanna S. Roebas*

www.vintagebooks.com

Printed in the United States of America
10  9  8  7  6

Song of
the Water Saints

# SCENE AND TYPE #E32

WHITE BORDER-STYLE POSTCARD
COUNTRY UNKNOWN, CA. 1900
PRINTED BY: PETER J. WEST & CO./OTTO NÄTHER CO.
HAMBURG, GERMANY

*They are naked. The boy cradles the girl. Their flesh is copper. They recline on a Victorian couch surrounded by cardboard Egyptian pottery, a stuffed wild tiger, a toy drum, and glazed coconut trees. An American prairie looms behind them in dull oils.*

*Shadows ink the muscles of the boy's arms, thighs, and calves. His penis lies flaccid. Cheekbones are high, as if the whittler of his bones was reveling when She carved him.*

*The girl lies against the boy. There is ocean in her eyes. Clouds of hair camouflage one breast. An orchid blooms on her cheek.*

# Song One

# INVASIONS · *1916*

Graciela and Silvio stood hand in hand on El Malecón, sea breeze polishing their faces. Silvio hurled stones out to the waves and Graciela bunched up her skirt to search for more pebbles. Her knees were ashy and she wore her spongy hair in four knots. A rusty lard can filled with pigeon peas, label long worn from trips to the market, was by her feet. Silvio's straw hat was in Graciela's hands, and quickly, she turned to toss it to the water. The hat fluttered like a hungry seagull, then was lapped up by foam. Silvio's kiss pinned Graciela against the railing.

It was a hazy day. The hot kissing made Graciela squint against the silver light. Beyond her lashes, Silvio was a sepia prince.

—That yanqui over there's lookin' at us, he murmured into Graciela's mouth. He pulled out his hand from the rip in her skirt. Graciela turned to see a pink man standing a few yards away from them. She noticed that the yanqui wore a hat and a vest—he surely did not seem to be a Marine. When she was with Silvio, Graciela forgot to worry about anyone telling on her to Mai and Pai, much less panic over yanquis and their Marine boots scraping the cobblestones of the Colonial Quarter.

Passion burned stronger than fear. Graciela turned back to Silvio.

—Forget him. Her pelvis dug into his until she felt iron.


Graciela and Silvio were too lost in their tangle of tongues to care that a few yards away, the yanqui was glad for a brief break from the brutal sun that tormented his skin. With her tongue tracing Silvio's neck, Graciela couldn't care less that Theodore Roosevelt's "soft voice and big stick" on Latin America had dipped the yanqui the furthest south he had ever been from New York City. Silvio's hands crawled back into the rip in Graciela's skirt; she would not blush if she learned that the yanqui spying on them had already photographed the Marines stationed on her side of the island, who were there to "order and pacify," in all their debauchery; that dozens of her fellow Dominicans somberly populated the yanqui's photo negatives; and that the lush Dominican landscape had left marks on the legs of his tripod. Of no interest to a moaning Graciela were the picaresque postcard views that the yanqui planned on selling in New York and, he hoped, in France and Germany. And having always been poor and anonymous herself, Graciela would certainly not pity the yanqui because his still lifes, nature shots, images of battleships for the newspapers had not won him big money or recognition.

—Forget the goddamned yanqui, I said. Graciela squeezed Silvio's arm when his lips broke suction with hers.

—He's comin' over here, Silvio said. He turned away from Graciela to hide his erection against the seawall. Graciela watched the man approach them. He had a slight limp. Up close, she could see that his skin was indeed pink and his hair was a deep shade of orange. Graciela had never seen a real yanqui up close. She smiled and folded her skirt so that the rip disappeared.

The man pulled a handkerchief from his vest pocket and wiped his neck. He cleared his throat and held out his right hand, first to Silvio, then to Graciela. His handshake swallowed up Graciela's wrist, but she shook just as hard. In cornhashed Spanish the man introduced himself: Peter West, he was.

Peter. Silvio. Graciela. They were all happy to meet each other. The man leaned against the seawall and pulled out a wad of pesos from a pocket in his outer jacket. His eyes never left Graciela and Silvio.

—¿So, are you with the Marines? Silvio asked in an octave lower than usual, and Graciela had to smile secretly because her sepia prince was not yet old enough to wear long pants.

The yanqui shook his head.

—No, no, he said with an air of importance. His thumb and index finger formed a circle around his right eye. Graciela looked over at Silvio. They wrinkled their noses. Then more cornhashed Spanish.

With the help of a Galician vendor, Peter West explained, he had accumulated an especially piquant series of photographs: brothel quadroons bathed in feathers, a Negro chambermaid naked to the waist, and, of course, he remembered with the silliest grin Graciela had ever seen, the drunken sailors with the sow. In fact, the sun was not so mean to him when he wore his hat and jacket. And fruit was sweet, whores were cheap.

Graciela reached for the pesos before Silvio did; after all, Peter

West had thrust them in her direction when he finished his convoluted explanations. But he quickly pulled the pesos away, leaving Graciela's fingers splayed open.

With the promise of pesos, Graciela and Silvio found themselves in the Galician vendor's warehouse, where Peter West had staged many ribald acts among its sacks of rice. How happy they had been to help this yanqui-man push together the papier-mâché trees, to roll out the starched canvas of cracked land and sky. Silvio straddled the tiger with its frozen growl while Graciela pried open the legs of a broken tripod to look in its middle. When West lit the lamps Graciela and Silvio squealed.

—¡Look, look how he brought the sun in here!

Silvio shaded his eyes.

—This yanqui-man, he is a crazy.

Graciela's whisper rippled through the warehouse when the fantasy soured. The pink hand tugged at her skirt and pointed briskly to Silvio's pants. They turned to each other as the same hand dangled pesos before them.

—¿You still want to go away with me, Mami, or no?

Silvio's whisper was hoarse.

Graciela's shoulders dropped. She unlaced her hair and folded her blouse and skirt. In turn, Silvio unbuttoned his mandarin shirt and untied the rope at his waist. Graciela folded her clothes along with his over a pile of cornhusks. In the dampness, they shivered while West kneaded their bodies as if molding stubborn clay.

They struggled to mimic his pouts and sleepy eyes. Instead of wrestling under heavy trees by Rio Ozama, or chewing cane in the fields near bateyes, or scratching each other's bellies in abandoned mills, or pressing up against the foot of a bridge, they were twisted about on a hard couch that stunk of old rags. Bewildered, they cocked their necks for minutes at a time in a sun more barbarous than the one outside. Their bodies shone like waxed fruit, so West wiped them with white powder. Too light. So he used, instead, mud from the previous day's rain.

"Like this, you idiots."

Where his Spanish failed, West made monkey faces, which finally made Graciela titter—only to reveal gaps where her teeth had been knocked out in a fall from a cashew tree. She found it difficult to sweetly gaze up at the beams of the warehouse as he had instructed. Her eyes remained fixed on the camera.

Then Graciela and Silvio watched in complicit silence as West approached the couch and knelt in front of them. Graciela's leg prickled with the heat of his ragged breathing. One by one, West's fingers wrapped around Silvio's growing penis. He wedged the thumb of his other hand into the humid mound between Graciela's thighs. Neither moved while they watched his forehead glitter. And just as they could hear each other's own sucks of breath, they felt piercing slaps on their chins. West ran to the camera to capture the fire in their faces.


As promised, the yanqui-man tossed Silvio a flurry of pesos. Graciela rubbed caked mud from her arms while Silvio, still naked, wet his fingers to count the bills. Graciela wondered if he would hog up the money, then go off to porches and storefronts to resoak her name in mud. As she wiggled her toes into her sandals, cigar smoke made her bite the inside of her cheek.

—Me amur, ¿qué pase?

This time the knotted Spanish was in Graciela's hair, the grip on her shoulder moist. Before she could demand her own flurry of colored bills, a crash echoed throughout the warehouse. Glass and metal scattered across the floor. The photographer ran toward the crash and in his frenetic efforts to salvage the film plate did not bother to strangle Silvio.

Graciela and Silvio ran from the warehouse and hid behind barrels along the dock, suppressing adrenaline giggles.

—You liked it, she said.

Silvio made a fist, then pointed to the pockets of his shorts.

—¡Gimme my earn, you! Graciela hissed. She clutched at his pocket. A puff of hair flopped over her eye.

—You liked it too, he said.

They wrestled, the strange arousal they had felt in the warehouse pumping through them again.

—I'll hold it for when I come for you, Silvio said in between breaths.

Graciela had to trust Silvio. She tied up her hair into four knots and ran to the market, where she should have been, before Mai sent her brother for her. Silvio kept his head down to try to hide the recently-paid-man brightness in his eyes. He should have been home helping his father with the coal. Graciela and Silvio did not know they had just been immortalized.


Absentmindedly, Graciela plucked four pieces of yucca for barter from the vendor's selection. Silvio's narrow back had disappeared into the market crowd in a swagger that thickened the dread in Graciela's throat. She was about to hand the vendor a lard can's worth of pigeon peas, only to realize that she had left it at the warehouse.

—Devil's toying with my peas.

Graciela bit the inside of her cheek. She turned away and fled.

—¡Ladrona! the ever-suspicious vendor yelled into the crowd, but today, as usual, no one listened.

Away from the mass of vendors, fowl, and vegetables, Graciela's chest heaved under the stolen yucca and her hair unraveled again.

Once her stride slowed down, she banged her forehead three times with the heel of her hand. ¡Sugar! She was supposed to buy sugar, not yucca, which already grew in her father's plot. Graciela sucked her teeth, almost tasting the molasses hanging heavy in the air from the smokestacks eclipsing the hills.

—Graciela, your mai looks for you.

A woman with the carriage of a swan and a bundle balanced on her head walked from the nearby stream. Her even teeth flashed a warning as she stepped onto the road.

—Mai's got eyes all over me.

—You be careful with those yanqui-men ahead, the swan woman responded with a finger in midair. Then she walked toward the whistling ahead, bare feet sure and steady.

Graciela shaded her eyes. Tall uniformed men in hats shaped like gumdrops sat on the roadside. They drank from canteens and spat as far onto the road as they could. Graciela squatted in the dense grass to see how the fearless swan woman would move safely past them. The yanqui-men's rifles and giant bodies confirmed stories that had already filtered into the city from the eastern mountains: suspected gavillero rebels gutted like Christmas piglets; women left spread-eagled right before their fathers and husbands; children with eardrums drilled by bullets. Graciela had folded these stories into the back of her memory when she snuck about the city outskirts with Silvio. The yanqui-man in the warehouse seemed frail now, his black box and clammy hands no match for the long rifles aimed at the swan woman.

"Run, you Negro wench!" The soldier's shout was high-pitched and was followed by a chorus of whistles.

A pop resounded. Through the blades of grass, Graciela could see the white bundle continue down the road in a steady path. The woman held her head high as if the bundle could stretch her above the hats. Another pop and Graciela saw the woman drop to the ground. The soldiers milled around the screaming and thrashing in the grass. Some already had their shirts pulled out of their pants.

Behind the soldiers, Graciela scrabbled away in the blades of grass. By the time the pack of men dispersed, they had become olive dots behind her. The yucca grated inside her blouse. Twigs and soil lodged in her nails. Half an hour later, with all four hair knots completely undone, Graciela was relieved to catch a glimpse of donkeys and their cargo, vendors with their vegetable carts, a rare Model T making crisscross patterns on the road.

The air was tight as she pulled herself up and ran past neighbors' homes. No children played outside. Graciela did see horses — many horses — tied to fenceposts along the way. She could not shake the urge to yawn and swell her lungs with air.

The main road dropped into a dustier, brushier path, leading to the circle of familiar thatched cabins. Two horses were tied to the tree by the fence. Graciela could not hear her mother yelling to her younger brother, Fausto, for coal, or the chickens clucking in the kitchen. Fausto was not sitting on the rickety chair making graters from the sides of cans, saying, —Mai was gonna send for you, stupid harlot.

Instead, from the kitchen came the clatter of tin. As Graciela moved closer, the stench of old rags flared her nostrils again. Inside, Mai knelt by a soldier whose fists entangled her hair and had undone the cloth rollers. Fausto, a statue in the corner. A man wearing his mustache in the handlebar style of the yanquis calmly asked Mai where her husband hid the pistols and why he was away in the hills. Mai's face was marble as she explained that her husband had no weapons, he was a God-fearing farmer, and there was her daughter at the door with yucca from his plot, see how dirty she was from working so hard with her beloved father, come Graciela, come bring the fruits of his sweat so these gentlemen can see how hard we work.

Graciela stepped forward with thin, yellow-meat yucca she was too ashamed to say her father had harvested. The interpreter shoved Graciela against the cold hearth and jammed his face against hers.

Must be cane rum coloring his bloodshot eyes, she thought, Devil toying with her peas again, trying to stick pins in her eyes to make her blink.

— Pai don't got pistols, he only got cane rum, Graciela said.

Her eyes still on the man, Graciela pointed to a shed outside. The man twisted the ends of his mustache. With the same fingers he clamped Graciela's nose and held it until there was blood, which he wiped against her blouse.

— Now you've got my aquiline nose, he said, then sucked the rest of her blood from his fingers. This overeager display of barbarism fueled in Graciela more anger than fear. Mai, Graciela, and Fausto watched as he helped the yanqui-men load their horses with bottles of cane rum. Before taking off, they rinsed their hands in the family's barrel of fresh rainwater.

．　．　．　．　．

The mandatory disarmament of the city and its outskirts left a trail of new stories that would find their way back to the eastern mountains. By 1917, the country fell prey to young American men relieved that their incompetence had landed them in the tropics instead of Europe, where fellow soldiers had been dropped into a bubbling World War. For the next eight years these men sparked a war, equipped with sturdy boots, uniforms, and rifles, against machetes, rusty revolvers, and sometimes bare feet. It was a battle between lion and ant. And when an ant pinched a paw, the lion's roar echoed: in Mexico, Panama, Cuba, Haiti, Dominican Republic.

A passionate creditor, Woodrow Wilson, demanded that the country's debt dollars be paid back in full while World War I shook across the ocean. At roughly 23°30' north longitude, 30°30' west latitude, Graciela and Silvio could not distinguish the taste of gunpowder from salt in the air of El Malecón.

. . . . .

Graciela's swollen nose stung as she peeled away the yucca's husk. Yellow and gray veins tunneled through the tuber's white flesh.

—¡Sugar! I send you for sugar, and you take the morning with you, Mai said, panic still twisting her voice.

For a moment Graciela wished that the soldiers had worked harder on Mai, had left her eyes swollen shut so she could not notice Graciela's unraveled hair.

Of course Graciela could never reveal that in the two hours she had been gone the seasalt was good against her skin, and so was Silvio, and that she was even able to earn some extra money . . .

Mai blared about hard-earned peas, and money for coal, money for shoes, money for sugar, about what green yanqui soldiers do to girls with skirts aflame, how lucky they all were to have been spared. Mai whacked her daughter on the back with a cooking spoon, squeezed the tender cartilage of her ears, wove her claws into Graciela's knotted hair. And Mai sobbed at only having her own flesh and blood with which to avenge humiliation. Excuses for the lack of peas, or money, or sugar on the table were postponed until the following day, when Pai returned from the bush with better crop and a heavier whipping hand.

Pai did emerge from the bush with better crop, but with hands too blistered by a week of harvesting to draw out confessions. He unearthed the pistols from under the water barrels and, with a furrowed brow, oiled them in the privacy of the outhouse. Graciela was perversely relieved by his preoccupation with who had snitched him out to the yanquis, and she carried on with her household chores, rag-doll dramas, fights with Fausto. Whenever she thought of Silvio buying tamarind balls with their money, Graciela bit the roughened inside of her cheek.

—Get yourself a whipping branch, Pai said days later to Graciela after he had devoured an avocado. He sat in front of the house repairing his only pair of shoes while she reluctantly climbed the cashew tree. As she handed over a thin branch, Graciela saw where mercury still stained the cuts on his hands.

—I told you to get a thicker branch, girl, he said.

After she had chosen the branch and wet it as he had instructed, Graciela followed Pai to the back of the house; Mai had already laid out the rice and stood a few feet away with her arms crossed. Without being told, Graciela removed her dress and knelt on the grains.

—You beat her good so she learns, Mai said to Pai. Then she disappeared into the kitchen, where Graciela could see her spying between the wood planks.

The first strike of the branch burned across the back of her thighs.

—Cry hard, girl, and satisfy your mai.

Pai thrashed the dirt around them. Graciela kept the smirk that she knew could make Mai's voice turn to pieces of breaking china. Finally, Pai cut the branch across the soles of her feet and hurled it to the bushes. Exasperated, he set a brand-new lard can full of peas on her head.

—Girl, you stay there till you lose that insolence.

Rice grains cut into her knees and the can of peas ignited a migraine. Still, Graciela would not confess; nothing she could have said would put her in a favorable light. Better to withstand the bursts of pain in her knees than to tell of her travesties with Silvio and multiply the existing worries in the household.

To numb herself Graciela sang songs, counted to ten twenty times, made popping sounds and saliva bubbles, concentrated on the caterpillar by the outhouse. Her thighs pressed tighter to hold back urine. After the breeze had chilled her raw skin, she began to itch where Pai's forgiving whip had left inevitable welts. A bug tickled her ankle. A sneeze crippled her side.

—¡Move and I shoot! Fausto said. He wore a gourd on his head, pointed a long piece of sugarcane at her, and revealed his own gaps for front teeth.

Two lizards copulated behind the barrel of rainwater. And suddenly Silvio waved pesos across Graciela's mind. He had not snuck around to their grove of cashews with his telltale whistle since the day of the yanqui. The clouds above Graciela did not move. In her agony, her anger and longing for Silvio became interchangeable.

Had Pai known of what she did with Silvio, he would have let the whip open her skin. He might have had Silvio hunted like a guinea hen. Might have scared him with a fresh-oiled pistol. Or turned him over to the yanquis.

With the frozen clouds and the sun baking circles in her head and the can of peas tumbling to the ground and the rice grains up against her flushed cheek, Graciela decided she would hunt for Silvio herself and make him put a zinc roof over her head.

# SILVIO · *1917*

Silvio never gave Graciela her share of the earnings. He spent the pesos on spicy sausages, on the winning cock, Saca Ojo, and on his favorite patient whore. Nor did Silvio dare muddy Graciela's name on porches or storefronts. (—You liked it too, he remembered her knowing words.)

Silvio withstood a year of Graciela's demands for a house of their own. He joined the yanquis' new Guardia Nacional Dominicana, where he was outfitted in starched slacks and sturdy shoes. It was an accomplishment, Silvio insisted to naysayers, for a man as dark and illiterate as he to be entrusted with yanqui guns. He was not a traitor, he explained, but a quality man with goals, who had already started wearing long pants. At fifteen, his penis swelled when the same elders who had tattled on him took off their hats in his presence. And when, at the sound of his voice, porch girls fanned themselves faster.

A quality man of goals must also head a household. Silvio agreed to elope with Graciela. One night at last, he blew his tell-tale whistle among the cashews. Like sudden thunder, Silvio invaded her home in his fresh yanqui haircut and pushed aside Pai's machete while Graciela ran past her shrunken mother to gather her few belongings.

Silvio had cleared a plot of land for them. He knew Graciela was disappointed to find that, instead of the turquoise palmwood and zinc house behind her lids, their new place was not much different from the thatched cabins she had left behind.

—This will have to do for now, Silvio said and brushed off dust from the knees of his slacks.

Inhumane military training demoted many an eager cadet back to civilian status. Silvio's own starched slacks, real shoes, and arrogance disappeared after a Marine ordered him to string his own friend Euclides from a mango tree. Euclides, in his zeal for trouble, had stolen the Marine's shoes. Euclides had taken them in jest, Silvio explained to the shrimp-skinned Marine, who, in near-perfect Spanish, had called him in for "a little talk." By the time Silvio tracked down Euclides to warn him, he knew that despite three meals a day and an enviable uniform, belonging to the yanqui police force came with too many problems. As did life with Graciela.

Within a year of their eloping, the fever of Silvio and Graciela's clandestine meetings had dwindled to predictable luke-warm pleasure during siesta and after sundown. Graciela was no longer Silvio's, despite his having her under a roof and being able to hitch up her skirt at will. Just a year ago, she had been completely his when she let him pick off every baby tick that had stuck fast to her ankles from running through a field of grass. And Silvio certainly believed Graciela his shortly before the yanqui-man incident, when she confided about a deadly disease afflicting the women in her family, which causes them to bleed between their legs every month. But the patient whore he frequented recently told him that all women had the disease, and now, more than ever, Silvio felt he had lost Graciela to a world bigger than himself.

But those were crazy moonshine thoughts, because daily life itself seeped into Silvio and Graciela's bodies like cement. As when, throughout their meals, Graciela would chew her food slowly and stare at him with what Silvio increasingly saw as the wide eyes of a cow. ¿What? ¿What? he would yell, hoping she would not bring up again the goddamned turquoise palmwood and zinc house.

Graciela's cow eyes and Euclides' murder convinced Silvio that he preferred the unpredictable ways of the waters to the whims of shrimp-skinned generals and to Graciela's irritating company. Silvio planned to join a fishing fleet that circled the Caribbean. He let his hair sprout out from its yanqui haircut. One night he sat by the fire he had made of his uniform and shoes, and the next morning he kissed Graciela goodbye after a hearty breakfast of cocoa, breadfruit, eggs, and boiled bananas.

. . . . .

On the morning of his first voyage, Silvio had dragged Graciela to her parents' house. Even with his grip, Graciela stirred the dust around them.

—¡Don't need to swallow my own spit 'cause you wanna fish!

—Just for peace of mind, mi cielo, he said.

—Don't worry yourself, Silvio. Not one of your kids will look like you. Graciela punctuated her words with a fisted index finger.

Mai received Graciela and Silvio with crossed arms.

—You're a man of few words, Silvio, but you need to be firm with this one, she said and jutted her bottom lip toward Graciela.

Once Silvio left for the docks, however, Graciela walked back to her own house in another haze of dust, followed by a grumbling Fausto, whom she forced to help file down the series of padlocks. In turn, Fausto ran home to tell Mai of Graciela's hammock-rocking, and the idleness of his sister's broom, the cold in her kitchen.

In the evenings, neighboring women brought Graciela some food. Then they undid the kindness as if slowly unraveling a swatch of silk by a single thread.

—¿That you want to ride on a ship? ¿With feet in lace-ups and those raisins of hair under a hat?

Celeste, Graciela's childhood friend, always spoke the loudest and made the others cackle. She wondered aloud when the trail of daily chores left undone would catch up with Graciela and freeze over her dreams.

—Ah, but you'd wear lace-up shoes too if El Gordo had them for you, Celeste my love. Because Graciela knew how much Celeste would give to bed down El Gordo, who had more ranch cattle than Celeste's impotent husband.

There was also the not-so-pious woman they all called Santa, who brought Graciela lavish goat meat and vegetable dishes. After Graciela consumed her portions, Santa would sweetly say to the women gathered in the kitchen,

—Our dear Graciela's hearth is colder than a witch's breath.

One day, to everyone's surprise, Graciela invited Santa over for a midday meal of mashed plantains, ham, and cheese. Afterward, Graciela offered Santa a rock-candy sucker. Only after Santa had sucked the candy down to a nub, did Graciela say,

—¿Was it all good, Santa?

—¡Oh by far the best I've had!

—Well, that sucker is what my armpit tastes like after a long hot morning at this hearth.

And though Santa did not speak to her for weeks, the rest of the women could not stop asking Graciela how she had managed to cook with the sucker lodged in her armpit the entire time. News of the prank spread, with camps dividing between those who liked Santa and those who didn't, between those who liked Graciela and those who were beginning to distrust her.

Still, the women liked to forget their work as Graciela wrung the rain out of their clouds. When there was no major news to chew on, they could always set their tongues on Graciela and her ways:

—That poor girl's lazier than an upper jaw.

—Show me her pots and I'll show you her bed.

—That fool's wasting her life waiting on that other fool.

For months after Silvio's departure, Graciela rocked in a hammock when visitors were not coming around. Out of loneliness, she would sometimes visit her parents, where she found herself having cordial, yet strained morning teas with Mai and clipped exchanges with Pai, when he descended from the hillside. He would occasionally slip a coin into the pocket of Graciela's apron; from the way Graciela quickly slurped her tea and darted her starved eyes when Mai clattered the dishes, Pai suspected that Silvio had not been sending any fishing money home after all. Pai's concern grew when he realized that Silvio would not be returning any time soon. He then forced a reluctant Fausto to go protect his sister from the "roaming men of low virtue" that had assaulted the city and its outskirts. Just two years younger than Graciela, Fausto had already mushroomed into an animal of a boy who, according to Pai, was built like a yanqui on an ox. Though Pai was giving up a much-needed workhand, he armed his bumbling twelve-year-old son with a pistol and sent him off to live with Graciela until Silvio's return.

—Learn now how to really defend a household, he told

Fausto. Always careful, Pai had already sent word to neighbors to keep watch over Graciela.

Outside on her hammock, Graciela could ignore the disarray inside her home and stare at the wispy cirrus ships in the sky. In the clouds, she wore lace and carried a parasol in the park of a place where the talk was garbled but pretty. Rocking in her hammock, Graciela imagined Silvio on the high seas, sprawled on the deck, maybe looking for her in the clouds. Fool with ideas, she scolded herself. Her eyes closed against the humid breeze.

Forget dirty tongues, she told herself further. They were all over the place: in the town, in the soup, even in her own head. Always trying to stop her from doing what she wanted. She would sit and let her home shrivel if she wanted. It was hers. And if she wanted to wait for Silvio for months, she would. He was hers as well.

Graciela stood up and stretched until she heard a snap somewhere inside her body. Now that Fausto was here, maybe he could help her finish the little plot she and Silvio had started behind the main cabin a few months back.

—Fausto, she called out. He emerged from the kitchen shed, chewing on a piece of lard bread.

—¿Can't you do anything but eat 'round here? Graciela said. Fausto looked down at her, then brushed some crumbs from his lips.

—I got the pistol, so I do whatever I want. Pai says I run this house, Fausto said. From his shorts pocket he pulled out a piece of cheese and brushed the lint from it.

—And if a yanqui were to come here this minute, ¿what the Devil would you do to save us?

Fausto reached into his other pocket, then dropped the piece of cheese.

—¡My pistol! ¿Where the hell is my pistol?

Fausto turned in circles, patting himself on the hips. When he looked up at Graciela, he found himself face-to-face with the pistol's barrel.

—Donkey-face. I dare you to go and tell Pai. You tell him to send Graciela herself to defend me next time. She's a better son than you are.

In one deft move the pistol disappeared behind the neckline of her blouse.

·  ·  ·  ·  ·

Graciela had always been a fool with ideas, everyone said, long before she had waited for Silvio to whistle for her in the cashew grove and take her away.

—Mai, God willing, I'm gonna ride ships. Big ones with tiny waists, she had sung at nine years old.

Mai had not looked up from her ironing. A pair of Pai's underwear lay smoothed out on the table. Graciela stretched the underwear to show the width of the metal whale that could take her to where sky and water met.

Mai looked up from her ironing. A momentary glimmer. Then she saw Graciela's idle hands.

—Ideas, ideas. That head in the clouds won't do your chores or fill your gut.

Mai spat and let the iron sizzle.

And then there were the three Spanish nuns with bunioned feet who had paid everyone in town a missionary visit when Graciela was four. Graciela had snuck behind the kitchen to hear the added s's in Mai's speech, the lisp reserved for rare visitors.

—I have always tried to instill God into this little girl, her mother had said, hands clasped at her chest.

The following week, Graciela found herself in the colonial church, hairline pulled taut with bits of cloth from old dresses. The church's dilapidation testified only to outward neglect; mission work was still going strong. Church beams spread out like protective arms above Graciela. Blocks of sunlight cut into the darkness to illuminate pews, statues, bits of floor. Graciela had the urge to stand inside the blocks of sunlight.

—¿That where Jesus is? Graciela had asked, pointing to the blocks of light.

—Jesus is everywhere, said the nun who called herself Sol Luz and led her toward a small room behind the altar. There were children already there, milling around an object in the middle of the room. They took turns spinning a colorful ball fixed to a metal arc. Graciela pushed and pinched her way through, until her fingers reached the ball, which she learned was called a "globe."

Only after she had sung all the holy songs and gulped down a hunk of stale bread with near-sour milk, was she allowed to return to the globe and turn it on its axis as if it were a rotisserie.

—You are here.

Sol Luz bent close to put Graciela's finger over a speck rising from the globe's surface.

—¿Me? ¿On the head of an iguana? Graciela narrowed her eyes. The iguana head was but a nick on her fingertip. She saw other animals: the haunch of a sheep, a goat, a dog. They encompassed as many as four of her fingers.

—I am from here—España—and came here.

Sol Luz dragged her finger to the left of the dog's leg, across an expanse of blue.

—I rode a ship all the way here, where you are, she said.

—¿Why did you come to this iguana and not go to the dog's ears over there?

Graciela moved Sol Luz's finger in the opposite direction.

—I came to bring Jesus, she said, leaving some spittle on the globe.

¿Why bring Jesus to such a small iguana when there were bigger animals? New questions prickled Graciela's throat before she could finish asking the last; the answers mattered less.

—Ah, the dilemma of mission work, the nun said, as if trying to sort out for herself why she was there on that speck of land with so much misery.

—¿And does anyone live here? Graciela pointed to blue bulls and horses.

—Not always good for a little girl to ask so many questions, Sol Luz said. —No one lives in the ocean. Sure, the Lord created fishes and sea animals, but not the sinful women with fish-tails, or pirate ghosts, or the water saints that you people talk about.

Sol Luz's eyes became fixed stones and Graciela thought for a moment that she looked like a fish.

Each Sunday thereafter, Mai would drag Graciela home by her pigtails.

—¿Can't I bring the globe home with me?

—Ask as many questions about Christ as you do about that pitiful ball, Mai said.

¿But how much bigger could the world be when the head of a tiny animal was her whole world? Graciela's fingers traced mountain ridges and the dips of rivers. ¿Would the people there be engulfed in a shadow and look up to the sky to see the swirls of her fingerprints hovering over their lands?

. . .

Graciela begged Sol Luz to run outside and watch the sun as she ran her finger over their speck on the globe.

—¿See my finger? Graciela's voice echoed throughout the church.

—No harm in humoring the poor child, Sol Luz thought to herself as she walked to the church doors. Indeed, it was unusually dark outside, and with her heart in her throat Sol Luz lifted her eyes. She was ashamed of herself when, expecting colossal finger-tips, she found a heavy cloud hovering over the church. A cool breeze signaled rain, and with a grunt at her own foolishness, she ran back inside.

· · · · ·

When Graciela thought she would pack her rags to break the monotony of her days, Silvio returned for the New Year celebrations. Sea breezes rushed ahead of him to their cactus fence. Fausto returned to Mai and Pai's home when he saw Graciela stuff her knotted mass of hair under a scarf and bury Pai's pistol near the rainwater barrel. Quickly, she stoked the fire for a meal, swept the yard, tried to erase the look of pining she was sure Silvio expected.

Silvio returned with kingfish and squid strung on his back. There was licorice for Graciela in his pockets and Madame C.J. Walker grease to replace coconut oil for her hair. A yellow-ochre tinge lit up his crown from the sun and salt of his travels, making his hair look like the macaroni he told her he had tasted in St. Lucia. Kisses and long stories made her forgive his absence—only to discover later the rash on his groin.

During his first stay at home, he complained to Graciela how the stillness of land, the permanence of the ground underneath his feet made him feel as if his joints were welded together.

—Devil's still dancin' in my head, he said when Graciela's chamomile tea failed to stop the hammer tearing apart his temples. In their bed, Silvio flopped over, long after Graciela had fallen asleep, then his ragged breaths would wake her before dawn. And twice a day Graciela had to send for Fausto to refill the water jug that would cure Silvio's insatiable thirst.

Despite Silvio's uncharacteristic neediness, Graciela was glad to have him back home. She was impressed by the skill with which he prepared barbecued fish, and conch soup, and vinegary ceviches. Unlike hers, his hands stayed uncut when digging out the meat from a crab, which he fed to her in slimy bits. —Try it, you squid, he said, when she refused the seaweed and onions entangled in his fork. A strange man of the sea he had become to the land-anchored Graciela, and it made her proud. No, Silvio was not like all the other dull men in town, with his narrow back, his yellowed naps, his sea speech. But their three weeks of reacquaintance were over—just when Graciela had begun to get used to the extra salt in their food, just as she was feeling proud of herself for not harrowing him about the turquoise palmwood house.

So Silvio came and went with the tides. Twice a month, his weekend stays heated the kitchen with frying fish and boiling plantains. Folks arrived to hear tales of ghost ships abandoned at sea. Silvio told of real and invented ports where the crew stopped to sell their catch. He described his searches for pirate loot at the bottom of the ocean. And when Graciela was out of earshot, he confirmed that white women had the fragrance of the sea and its treasures. When the fish was sold, given away, and eaten; when the travel stories were told, and had worn thin; when people no longer exclaimed "¡Llegó Silvio!"; and when he was ready for brine again, Silvio would tie up his bags.

—Take me, Silvio.

He would put his finger to Graciela's lips, but later she followed him to the docks with her own bags. Each time, sea mates teased Silvio for his inability to wrest himself from his hound.

One afternoon in early February, Silvio departed for the sixth time, according to Graciela's tally. On this occasion, he hopped on the boat and turned to face the horizon even as Graciela waved. Long after the boatful of those leather-faced men sailed around the turn of shore, Graciela lingered by the water sucking salt from her lips.

—¡Thief!

She spat her bitterness into the water, whose currents drew Silvio away and lapped at the seawall; whose depths contained jewelry unhooked from the wrists of the wealthy, whole bodies of metal sea animals with fractured waists, and hundreds of ball-and-chained bones trapped in white coral.

Nausea came to Graciela. That February the goat had not been slaughtered; her rags remained bloodless for the first time since she was ten. No more waiting.

Graciela collected some belongings, and tied them up in the hammock. She wanted to leave the capital, perhaps head north to Santiago, the Heart of the Country. The new life inside her pulled her daydreams down from the clouds. Up north in the pulse of the country, they could build a bright turquoise palmwood house with a zinc roof for their new family. She would wait for Silvio's return, and then convince him, and if he did not join her, she would leave without him, and take up washing or cleaning until the child was born. Then she would make her palmwood house, and call on Silvio to show him that she was not a woman to be kept sitting and waiting idly for her life to happen . . .

Graciela's dreaming also set in motion Fausto's plan. He invited a friend over to help him till the small plot of beans he had been helping Graciela tend. As the boys rolled up tobacco joints, Graciela could hear Fausto's put-on baritone through the breadfruit trees.

—Once Sis leaves, I'll bring that little number down from Villa Consuelo to live here with me, you'll see.

But the moon went through its faces and still no Silvio. Common talk brought greetings from him, which Graciela knew were fabricated by pitying friends.

It was already August—half a year since anyone had last seen Silvio. In six months, the speculations surrounding his extended absence bubbled up like a foul gas. Out of consideration, someone suggested to Graciela that his boat had floated far out to the Mona Canal. There was talk of sharks and trouble with Marines. A lynching. Celeste, as always, offered the possibility of a distant woman, one who perhaps did not squabble as much.

The real story people feared.

—Those butchers left the fishermen hanging in a bunch like a hand of bananas, said Desiderio to whoever would listen at Yunco's.

The local bar was packed with Prohibition-free Marines, and Yunco, always out to profit from fortune and misfortune alike, covertly turned his home into the "locals' local" bar after curfew. Desiderio, a regular "yunquero," had heard the lynching story from his cousin, who had heard it from Flavia the johnnycake woman, who lived with El Gordo, who worked in the sugar mill of the Turks. And El Gordo, who was eating out of Celeste's kitchen unbeknownst to Flavia and Celeste's husband, heard the tale from the Turks themselves.

And the Turks, who seemed neutral enough in matters between Dominicans and yanquis, ran an information exchange out of their sugar mill. They bribed Dominicans for details on the gavillero rebels and any other anti-yanqui activities, then sold it to the yanquis. But to assuage their guilt in aiding the yanquis, they also bought information from yanqui-friendly Dominican spies to distribute freely among the people. It was in this web of information that Silvio's fate became enmeshed:

That one of the fishermen in Silvio's fleet deserted them because of a dispute over money. That he went to the Turks. That the Turks then gave the yanquis detailed information on a fleet of so-called fishermen who made trips to the Caribbean. That these fishermen would swing around the nose of the island to the east instead, where they unloaded weapons for the gavilleros hiding out in the hills.

—This is what I heard myself.

El Gordo pounded his chest in competition with Desiderio.

—And those yanquis then chopped them down from the tree. They say that in El Ceibo pigs were shitting buttons and bits of nails, Desiderio said, proud of his contribution to the grains of information.

—Now no one eats pork in El Ceibo, he added with a wink.

—Things are really bad in the east. Bad like purple gas. El Gordo sighed and took a swig of rum.


By September, Graciela had stopped rocking in her hammock. Her seven-month belly popped one of the cords, prompting her to fold up the hammock and tightly wrap up most of her belongings in it; she prayed she would not have to later unwrap it to wear her black skirt and mourning veil. If Silvio did not return before her labor, Graciela was determined to push out her child, pack up the rest of her things, and head north, wailing baby strapped to her back and all. ¿So what if it was a foolish thought not to wait out the forty postpartum days? Tired she was of waiting for her life to truly begin. A departure would be progress, she was sure. Living in this cluster of ramshackle shacks had not been part of her vision of life with Silvio, and now there were more than two futures to think about. Asking the clouds for mercy and ignoring the vivid memory of a straw hat being lapped up by sea foam, Graciela waited one more month for her own signs of Silvio.

· · · · ·

It was an easy pregnancy, with Graciela sending Fausto all over town on errands. Water bread and not lard bread, she insisted, and Fausto had better make sure to sift any maggots from the sugar if he purchased it from Joselito. When Fausto was out of the house, Graciela would curl up in bed to work on a rag doll for the future baby. Then she cried herself to sleep when its uneven button eyes gawked back at her, one red and tiny, the other black and large.

Everyone who used to laugh at Graciela's ship-and-lace dreams knew that her baby must have been crying in the womb. They also knew that Silvio's body had been found so riddled by bullets, there was more kindness in saying sharks had devoured him.

The day her daughter was born, Graciela had rocked under anvils of cumulonimbus ships. Gray clouds tumbled after each other, herded by winds to where they could relieve their weight. Must be difficult labor, rain, she thought, rubbing her belly. Crows squawked over the waving trees, dipping over her as if flaunting their gift of flight. A blanket of smoke, of burnt ashes in the ominous sky—the death of her Silvio, she speculated. Thunder changed her mind. No, no, their fruit is life, a good sign. In the silver underbelly of one of the ships, Graciela was certain she saw Silvio. Alive. He was sure to return to her that night, she understood.

The air had cooled, causing land crabs to scurry out of their holes. Cashew leaves turned their waxy sides up and field mice ran up the trunks of trees. Fausto stabbed a spot in the yard with an ax, while Graciela shooed the chickens inside the house and closed all doors. The rest of the day she spent adorning her home and combing her hair tangled from the coming rains. Fausto's whistling and the sharp jabs in Graciela's womb kept her awake before Silvio's arrival.

In the October night, Graciela woke to rain dripping into the pot at the foot of her bed. Fausto was curled in a cot, sleeping soundly, despite heavy ozone in the air. Graciela waited for the sea breeze to enter through the creaking door. The tiny voice had echoed again, languishing at the bottom of her spine, then crawling to her forearms, where cold had already tightened the tiniest of hairs.

—¡Silvio! ¿That you?

For the first time she was afraid of what jumped inside her. She wanted Silvio to arrive before the child; for the pain of childbirth to be only in her womb and not in her heart.

—¡Fausto!

He snored louder than the thunder outside.

—¡Fausto! ¡Go get Ñá Nurca!

He snored louder than the thunder outside.

—¡Fausto!

Cold and whirring in her womb ate at her. The night howled when Graciela pried open the door. Rain cloaked her.

—¡Silvio!

Spongy ground sucked at her feet. The sky growled as she broke into a jog. A flash of blue lightning found the ax in the yard, and the nerves of the heavens seemed to converge at its handle. Graciela stopped; her feet were buried in unusually warm mud. The rain was saltier than her own tears. She whiffed a sharp sulfuric odor, then the undeniable smell of excrement. Graciela crossed a flooded ditch, wading to her shins in sewage.

The small cement house was a refuge at the end of the road.

—¡Ñá Nurca! She beat on the door until the elderly midwife opened and, without a word, led Graciela into the house by lantern light.

—Like the Devil himself you smell, Ñá Nurca said.

—And I'm about to have Juan the Baptist himself, Graciela yelled with the jolt in her womb. Used to the hysteria of life-givers, Ñá Nurca cupped Graciela's face and complained that Graciela should have sent word with Fausto to the yawning servant girl.

—Go boil water and prepare the birth bed, for the love of God, Ñá Nurca snapped at the girl.

Graciela's moans were muffled by the crackling of the skies. Ñá Nurca's teas and tinctures opened her womb, sending Graciela to the tenuous membrane between life and death. In the velvet behind her lids, she saw Silvio's muted face, then that of a child's.

—Come back, woman, come back, Ñá Nurca said to Graciela.

The servant girl, accustomed to the trials of childbirth, gathered the soiled cloths as fast as she could. Ñá Nurca's gnarled hands massaged Graciela's body relentlessly in an attempt to coax out new life with her own.

By morning, as the storm subsided, the bleating of Graciela's labor had alerted the neighbors. The elaborate word-of-mouth network eventually drew Mai away from her duties. With soup and clean linens she appeared at Ñá Nurca's— not before boxing Fausto's ears for having slept through the night.

That afternoon, Graciela's baby was born, healthy, kicking furiously out of the muting pillows of her mother's warmth. Ñá Nurca wrapped the afterbirth in a cloth for burying and saved the umbilical cord for Graciela's safekeeping. She joked about the child's big fists as she wiped her with warm water.

—Mercedes, Ñá Nurca, call the chichí Mercedes, Graciela mumbled.

—¿This little hurricane with the name of mercy? Ñá Nurca

said, noting again the unusually large fists and discovering a mole on her toe.

Ñá Nurca swaddled Mercedes in a fresh blanket before putting her to Graciela's breast. The child latched on tightly to her mother, not letting go even after Graciela's breasts were drained of their milk.

# CASIMIRO · *1920*

O'Reilly's Curiosity Shop, nestled under a balcony in the Colonial Quarter, did not lure its many customers with ads in *La Información*. A parrot in a bamboo cage by the door shrieked "Buenos días" and "Buenas noches" at the wrong times, an attraction that sold O'Reilly's souvenirs and local trinkets faster than his neighboring competitors could ever hope to.

Casimiro stood at the threshold, afraid his work-stained shirt would brush up against an antique curio. He envisioned it crashing down to break open fancy vials of weak rum, disembowel fat cigars tucked in cedar boxes, free trapped insects from amber jewels, and scatter the postcards of nymphs like a game of American poker gone sour.

"Casimiro! Move it!"

Behind the counter, O'Reilly nodded at Casimiro's spring and quick exit. The burdened donkeys outside snorted, hooves clacking on the cobblestones like castanets.

When Casimiro had hauled the last of the straw hats and gourds and vegetable-dye paintings and tamboras and crates and barrels of fruit liqueurs and had gathered the twine from the boxes and stacked the extra merchandise in the back, he inhaled the smell of fresh apples. He hoped Don O'Reilly would include a taste of those apples in his pay. Apples in May were even more decadent than with December's joyful aguinaldos. Casimiro had to wait by the threshold, hat in hand, as was custom, until O'Reilly finished dusting his goods to the slow tune of a waltz.

"Casimiro . . ."

The few cool coins in his palm came with a handshake. O'Reilly's dismissive hand prevented Casimiro from asking about apples, more coins, a souvenir at least. After all, an empty-handed man sidling up to a woman in the park would be like a peacock without feathers.

Casimiro greeted the young woman sitting on the park bench with a goodbye.

—Aburrrrr . . .

He relished the *r*, which made her pursed lips quiver. He tipped his hat with an exaggerated arc, just as he had the first time they met on the same bench a week ago. The child was not with her this time—a good sign. Casimiro will have her undivided attention.

—Again we meet, he said and sat next to her with his legs crossed.

—Mmm-hmm.

She shrugged as if it did not matter that her hair was freshly hot-combed and that she wore her Sunday dress on a Tuesday.

—Gra-ci-e-la, Casimiro mouthed the syllables around a fresh cigar. —¿Remember *my* name?

—¿Why would I? She crossed her arms.

He spoke slowly.

—Because I have something for you.

—¿How'd you know I'd be here? She looked straight ahead at big-bellied boys rolling wire wheels through the park.

—My spats told me.

Casimiro wiggled his foot without looking away. O'Reilly's spats bit into his ankles, ankles sprained from stealing that heavy crate of merchandise.

—They're nice, if that's what you like, Graciela said, eyeing his fancy feet, his tattered trousers. Then she set her gaze on an idle peanut vendor.

Casimiro noticed the talcum powder dusted near her ears.

—Almost got killed for these spats, just to impress you, he said.

—Impress me, then.

Graciela did not turn away from him this time.

—Bueno, I stole them from the military base in Catarey, see, and escaped the yanquis, who almost killed me. All for you.

He saw her discover the sixth finger on each of his hands, smooth, black lima beans.

—¿Do you want your gift now or later, ¿Gra-ci-e-la? Casimiro asked between puffs of his unlit cigar.

—Doesn't matter. Didn't come for gifts. I'm waiting for my sister.

—¿Oh? ¿Another angel missing from the sky? he teased. His hands emerged from his back, cupping a gleaming apple.

Her brows, which she had filled in with charcoal, rose.

—¡Ay, a yanqui apple!

Graciela slapped her cheeks. Only when Casimiro agreed to share the delicacy with her did she allow herself to crunch into its juicy flesh. With a pocketknife he cut tiny slices to sweeten their banter.

—¿Really, is there a sister? he asked.

—No. And don't chew so loud, you.

—¿Who is there, then? Casimiro gave her more slices.

—Me, a brother, two dead.

When Casimiro spit a seed into his hand for safekeeping, Graciela stared at his mouth.

—¿And the beautiful baby?

His question stopped her from sucking the sweet at her gums. She seemed to remember something, perhaps her child.

—Let's not eat this all now. ¿I can take the rest home?

Her hands plucked the apple-half from his.

—Anything you want, Gra-ci-e-la. Have this park, the sea, the sky, too.

His arms spread wide.

—You don't own any of it.

The half-eaten apple was now wrapped in a handkerchief.

—Have it all anyway, Casimiro said.

—Ah, then, maybe the sky.

They were silent. Both watched a shoeshine boy asleep inside the park's bandstand.

—So. ¿Where is . . . he? Casimiro asked with a deep breath.

—Gone. Dead. Killed. Don't know, she said with a shrug. She spotted a guardia leaning against a tree.

Casimiro put his hand over hers, but she slipped hers away.

—You know, you remind me of someone, he said. He hooked his hands over his crossed knee.

—¿Who? Graciela covered her smile with the back of a hand.

—Ask my spats.

—¿Of who do I remind this crazy Casimiro man? Graciela asked his wiggling foot.

—¡Of La Cigüapa the hag! he teased her gruffly.

—¡Ah no! she said, I don't have chicken feet, ¿do I?

Graciela stretched out her legs, which were wrapped by folds of skirt, for him to see.

Casimiro imagined that the smooth copper legs under her skirt would taste like cuava soap and cilantro; thick oak legs lathered white or oiled to a sheen, that could rub and run and kick and lift.

—Of course you don't have chicken feet, Gra-ci-e-la.

They laughed, then were silent, both watching the guardia beat the shoeshine boy who had fallen asleep inside the park's bandstand.

Graciela smoothed down her skirt and sighed. She refused Casimiro's offer to walk her home, but agreed to meet him at the same time and place the following week. He tipped his hat and said "Buenos días," though night was already leaking through the sky. Casimiro watched Graciela walk out of the park. He ducked behind open portals and johnnycake stands, behind water pumps and carriages, until Graciela abandoned her careful strut to remove her shoes along the road home. When she entered the thatched cabin he assumed was her home, Casimiro squeezed the apple seeds in his pockets and headed off whistling to the cockfights.

· · · · ·

After having given birth to Mercedes, Graciela could not properly grieve for Silvio, so occupied was she for two years with nursing and washing diapers and trying to adjust her feet to the shoes of motherhood, in addition to the regular daily chores. There would be no more waiting for Silvio, Graciela decided, refusing to believe the rumors that he was dead. Her life had to continue: she could no longer let the field mice pepper the hearth with droppings or allow the water jug to teem with larvae. With Mercedita tied to her back, she also tended the plot with Fausto, who had developed into a strapping fourteen-year-old. And in order to provide for other little luxuries, such as sugar, coal, shoes, fabric for blouses, Graciela circulated the word that she had strong washerwoman fists that could miraculously bleach fabric with just a couple of squish-squishes.

It was during this time that Graciela and Celeste grew closer. Putting past remarks behind them, they visited each other and exchanged ideas about childrearing. If one had to go to the market, the other baby-sat. Theirs was a speckled friendship, however, and folks were always warning one to keep away from the other.

—It's high time you find yourself a real man, Celeste said to Graciela when she dropped off Mercedita. —Mercedita can't grow up thinking her uncle is her father.

—Ay, ¿what I need a man for? Fausto takes care of everything I need, Graciela said with a toss of her hand.

—¿Everything? Celeste raised an eyebrow.

Graciela lowered her gaze.

—Celeste, you spend all your time killing men with your tongue and then you want one for me.

But Celeste did rattle Graciela's mind. There were rainy nights when Graciela would wake up with Fausto huddled in bed next to her and Mercedita, claiming the roof's leaks had dampened his cot.

—Well, fix the leaks, then, she would say each time.

And once when he was soaping himself up in the bath shed, her eyes met his between the slabs of wood.

Weekly market trips were Graciela's escapes from the toils of the household. She would go much later in the day than the rest of the women did, even if it meant choosing from the worst pickings, if there was anything left at all. By then, Celeste was home and could watch Mercedita.

—¡Ey, One-Eyed Luis, gimme a bag of bulgur wheat! and

Graciela would wink at him when his wife looked down to get change from her apron.

—¿And how's my other little chichí today? Graciela would ask the Haitian woman, who sold spices and had a son Mercedita's age.

Sometimes on the way home from the market, Graciela dawdled in the town's park to sit and watch people go about their business. On the bench, she lamented that some people were born being able to buy such exquisite clothing.

—I know I waited on a long line to get born, God, ¿so when will my turn come to sip the juice from this life?

She would crunch on her weekly treat of popcorn. ¿What would it feel like to ride on one of those cars, to go up the little step and sit in the little moving box? ¿How could she get her hair to curl and shine like that under her hat when the day's sweat made even her tight braids coil? ¿How much washing would she have to do to be able to buy such brilliant patent-leather shoes? ¿And where could she meet a fancy man, different from the land-roughened ones who took their hats off to her as they rode their horses past her on the long walk home?

· · · · ·

Months after meeting Graciela on the park bench, Casimiro moved into the thatched home built by Silvio. Fausto had at first refused to leave, claiming in his baritone that he had put too much hard work into the plot for some cricket to come and take it from him. But when he heard the gasps of lovemaking coming from the bed across from him at all hours of the night, he left his cot and tearfully walked in pitch darkness to his parents' house. While neighbors stuffed themselves with gossip about men who were too lazy to make their own beds, Casimiro lay his own head on Graciela's pillows basking in new love. He was not impressed with how

Graciela kept house, the baby Mercedita uncombed and roaming under chairs. But he knew he could at least count on coffee and a couple of pieces of plantain and saltfish a day. And he took pride in how easily he could brighten Mercedita's smile with toys fashioned out of seeds, wires, jars, buttons, and twigs.

Graciela would squeal in delight as she pulled out ingrown hairs from Casimiro's chin. And although Casimiro's cocks kept losing battles, Graciela would minister to their wounds and sing to them. After a good day's rain, she would take a stick to the yard, and scratch out for him detailed plans of the palmwood house she wanted up north in Santiago, once they had enough money to build it right. Unlike any woman Casimiro had ever been with, Graciela would let their dinner burn in the hearth to join him in making toys.

One Saturday evening, Celeste showed up at Graciela's door with her grandfather, El Viejo Cuco, and a few other people in tow. They were all returning from a bullfight in the town square and were eager for a place to sit and forget the carnage they had paid to see.

With Mercedita already in bed, Graciela had been mending the hem of an old skirt while Casimiro put on his spats for a night of drunken laughs at Yunco's. When Graciela saw all the people gathered on her porch, she sent out Fausto, who had been visiting then, to borrow bread, some cheese, rum, and sweet wine from neighbors. Casimiro took off his spats and built a bonfire in the front yard. To everyone's delight, Fausto returned shortly with bottles of rum from Yunco's, a couple of leftover loaves of bread from Tun-Tun the baker's, a block of goat cheese, an old guitar, and several more people eager to be in the company of El Viejo Cuco, who could tell you a story for days:

—Once was a li'l gal who'd go to everyone's house in the village, sayin' she hadn't eaten dinner. End of each day, she'd waddle home to her mai an' pai to eat their daily three grains of rice. ¿How could our gal be so fat when we're so poor? Grace o' God, they thought. One day, a hunter set a piece of that goat cheese over there under a box an' waited in the bushes. Li'l greedy gal, on her way to many dinners, saw the cheese an' dove under the box. Soon found herself inside the hunter's shack. Saw a cake on his table, like the baker Tun-Tun's. Li'l gal of indomitable greed reached for it, but the hunter grabbed her wrists. —¡Eat it all if you want! His eyes were tiny, like Casimiro's over there, an' he had large yanqui hands that could tear apart animal skin an' bone. Li'l gal ate an' ate an' ate, till all that remained of the cake was a burp. So fast she'd wolfed it down that she hadn't noticed the string attached. An' the hunter held the part of the string she hadn't swallowed. Li'l greedy gal was trapped forever in the house of the hunter as his slave. Her mai an' pai never saw her again, nor did the generous people of the village.

—With each year your stories get worse, Viejo Cuco, Casimiro said, the sweet wine blushing his nose.

—¡Ah, you're just mad that you got eyes like the hunter man! Celeste defended her grandfather. Everyone roared with laughter, including Casimiro.

When the laughter died down to a few sighs, El Viejo Cuco spoke of a real train that ran from La Vega to Santiago.

—It's like an iron serpent, they say. Swallows people, animals, cane, an' shits 'em out all over the north. Sounds like thunder an' stinks like demons. What I'd do to get on one of those beasts, he said.

Graciela stared at El Viejo Cuco as he stopped to light up a cigar. His slanted eyes caught hers through the smoke and he sat back to meet her gaze.

—Well, Viejo, ¿what more do you know about this train?

Graciela asked. She had stopped helping Celeste clear the empty cups from the ledge of the porch. For a while, El Viejo Cuco did not answer. Graciela stepped delicately over the people sitting on the floor of the porch.

—Viejo, the train, Graciela said. Her voice wavered with impatience.

—In my day, I woulda taken me a fine red one like you, he said. —You're what I call ugly-fine. A gal who can be ugly or fine dependin' on the man she's with.

There was a brief silence as everyone turned to gauge Graciela's expression. Her lip was drawn tight as she chewed at its corners.

—So tell me, Viejo, ¿am I fine or ugly now? Graciela said, looking directly at Casimiro, who had just tipped back his head with a shot of rum.

Viejo Cuco leaned forward and cleared his throat. He rubbed his palms together, the cigar still dangling between his fingers.

—Casimiro, lemme tell you one about your gal.

—Ah no, Viejo, finish about the train in La Vega. Don't tell stories about me, Graciela said. Her head was cocked and she was toying with a braid.

—Your pai always said it, gal, that you were born with the hot leg, like that maroon grandpai o' yours. Walked before you crawled. An' listen up, Casimiro, one time the gal, 'bout as tall as that li'l boy over there, waited till the pai got up at dawn. He'd packed up his donkey for a week in the bush an' woke up his boy, who he said was no good with land, pardon me, Fausto over there. So they walked those dark roads up to the hill, where the Devil likes to show himself. Hours later, as they set up camp by the plot, who should appear, but the gal herself, beggin' for water. She'd been followin' them all along. Left her mai to all the chores, went through all that mess, just 'cause she was curious. The pai didn't snap her neck 'cause she was always his heart, he said . . .

Casimiro's snores cut through El Viejo's voice. The fire had died, only a few embers still crackling. The sliver of moon had receded behind some clouds. El Viejo Cuco stood up and beckoned for Celeste to get his cane. Everyone else also began to stand and dust themselves, some already making their way toward the road. This surprised Graciela. Usually, El Viejo Cuco told stories until dawn or until the host sent him on his way.

—Casi's faking sleep, clown that he is. ¡It's still early! Graciela said. —¡And you didn't finish the train story, Viejo!

El Viejo Cuco took Graciela's face in his hands and planted a smoky kiss on her lips.

—With that man, you sure are ugly, he whispered in her ear before shuffling away.

All the shaking Graciela did could not rouse Casimiro from the stairs of the porch. Before leaving with everyone else, Fausto heaved Casimiro on his shoulders and hauled him inside the house.

—Don't you worry, Graciela. Tie him to the coconut tree and douse him with your dirty bathwater. He'll be as brand-new as when you met him, Celeste said when she hugged Graciela goodbye.

. . . . .

Graciela and Casimiro fought.

From watching his cocks Casimiro learned that in order to wear down his opponent's strength, he should remain calm and passively wait for Graciela to exhaust herself with accusations:

—Yunco's barstools stink of your ass already.

—You squander my hard-earned wash money on your cocks.

—Lazier than a pig in mud.

—Should be building us a house instead of useless toys.

—You never bring me yanqui apples from O'Reilly's anymore.

—On top of that, you take me nowhere.

When Graciela had purged herself of anger, Casimiro would put his hands on her back and massage the remaining knots away.

—Take me away somewhere, anywhere, Graciela said to him when her spirits lifted. Every day for two weeks she insisted, until one morning Casimiro wrinkled his face and told her to pack for an overnight stay. From a friend he had managed to borrow a small boat and then sent word to the Falú family living a few miles south.

—He says we're going to another island, Puerto Rico, you know, Graciela said to Celeste and whoever else would listen. —My man makes his own bed, ¿you see?

The day they departed, Graciela donned the same Sunday dress she had worn during their park-bench courtship. After lending her the dress so many times, Celeste had finally told her to keep it—she could no longer wear it herself without being mistaken for Graciela.—Secondhand Pancha, she snickered behind Graciela's back.


Casimiro steered the boat down the Ozama. Their trip would take a day, after which they would stay overnight at the house of the Falús, friends he knew from his days as a dockworker in Puerto Rico. A quick visit to assuage Graciela's need for adventure. He prayed they would not run into restless Marines along the way. Few people ventured out on leisure trips these days for fear of winding up casualties. The friend who lent him the boat said he was crazy to cater to a woman's silly whims.

—Can't live my life in fear of yanks. If farmers were afraid of weather, they wouldn't plant any seeds.

As the boat drifted down the river, Graciela wished she had a parasol she could open and twirl against the stubborn sun. She watched canoes loaded with goods headed for market. At the riverbank, blissful children sat under canopies, enjoying coconut paste and orange preserves.

—Here, Cielo, buy yourself some guava paste, milk candy, pork rinds, anything you like, Casimiro said and waved to one of the canoes ahead.

He pointed out the different birds that circled above them. He yelled out greetings to folks along the riverbank.

—¿And how is it you know so many washerwomen? Graciela asked.

He named trees they saw along the way. Some curled into wild shapes, snaked around other trees, hung over the water like royal curtains; one hermit grew in the middle of the river.

And as they drifted past a hill on their right, the white columns of an oak house rose heavenly above them. Casimiro told Graciela about how once while delivering furniture made in a place they call Italy, he had been offered a glass of ginger beer inside its majestic parlor.

Graciela followed his six-fingered hand as he pointed to various marvels.

—I gotta beg and borrow just to see what you see, she said.

She unlaced her shoes so she could dangle her feet in the water. Sparse clouds drifted above her.

A warm breeze fluttered her skirts. Graciela blew air through her lips to match the breeze.

—I used to think clouds showed me stuff. Big ships, dresses, even Mercedita in my belly. And Silvio.

Casimiro rowed at a steady pace. He nodded for her to continue, knew not to fight Silvio's ghost.

—But wishes just go with the wind.

Graciela sat up and adjusted her hat to shade her eyes.

Casimiro pointed to hairlike lines woven through the sky. He then shook his head.

—¡Ah, I didn't bring us out here to talk about clouds!

He reached into the river and splashed a handful of water at her.

—¡You scum of the earth! she giggled.

Then Graciela saw some hills in the distance and asked Casimiro how much bigger Puerto Rico was than their country, to which he replied that it all depended on where they were coming from. He stopped rowing and let the Ozama drift them miles downstream to where the Falús lived. Just as they passed a cluster of houses, he swung the boat in toward the riverbank.

—Here we are, Cielo, the beautiful land of Puerto Rico, Casimiro said as they disembarked. He spread his arms and inhaled the wild chamomile air.


It was true that the Falús had once lived in Puerto Rico, but they left in 1902, after Don Bebo Falú's coffee crop lost value due to American interest in sugar. In desperation, Don Bebo had accepted money to stuff ballots at his district elections, and was caught. He and his wife had managed to secure a humble home on the outskirts of Santo Domingo, where they started a tailoring business. When they learned that Casimiro and a woman would be paying them a visit, they were pleased to meet up again with the man who used to go out of his way to deliver hard-to-find fabrics and colorful threads. The messenger boy had given them strange instructions not to mention their homeland or discuss politics during Casimiro's visit. But friends assured them that bizarre requests always preceded Casimiro: not to tell anyone that he had found them yards of gold lamé; to be sure to return to him the boxes in which the red threads arrived; not to announce when he would be in town; not to send for him; not to mention his name on moonlit nights.

—Puerto Rico's a lot like home, Graciela said as she and Casimiro walked through the heavy flora to the Falús', and a frog from a nearby brook jumped in their way.

She was even more delighted with Puerto Rico when Doña Falú moved aside a dressform mannequin to welcome them into their home. Graciela took in Doña Falú's staccato speech. When coffee was served, she plucked a peppermint stick from the tray and, as she had seen Don Bebo do, stirred her coffee with it. Graciela could not wait to tell Celeste how the Puerto Ricans spoke and took their coffee.

During midday meal, Don Bebo and Casimiro spoke about weather and caught each other up on the gossip of world events. The women ate quietly. Whenever Don Bebo began to make references to the yanquis, or to the unfortunate state of the country's economy, Casimiro coughed and asked Doña Falú for more coffee, though a servant hovered about.

After lunch, Doña Falú invited Graciela into the sewing room to show her the dresses she and Don Bebo had been working on. It was a small room piled high with rolls of fabric in all colors, spools of thread, scraps of cloth, with a modest sewing machine sitting in the corner. Graciela approached a dressform mannequin.

—¡They take up so much fabric! she said, fingering the long layered skirt that ballooned out from the mannequin's tightly tapered waist.

—It's the style, Doña Falú said. Graciela peered at the catalogue and newspaper pictures pasted on the wall.

—I wish I'd been taught letters, so I could read the papers of Puerto Rico and know the fashions.

Doña Falú held up a finger, blotchy from countless prickles.

—No, no, I cut these pictures from newspapers Bebo gets from the U.S.

—¿Yanqui papers? Be glad Puerto Rico's not in their clutches like us. You just don't know . . .

Graciela crossed her arms and jutted out her bottom lip.

—Agh, let the men talk about those things, Doña Falú said. —That's part of why I made my Bebo leave Puerto Rico in the first place. They get too passionate about the state of the world, when they can't even handle the state of their own homes.

Graciela wanted to continue talking about how the state of the world had left a scar on her nose and had permanently altered the pitch of her mother's voice, but held her tongue for fear that Doña Falú would think she was unrefined.

—¿Where are your children, Doña Falú?

Doña Falú smiled and pulled Graciela close.

—Why, here in your country. Our children have grown into proud Dominicans. Don't you believe that shady man for a minute, señorita. Casimiro has taken you for quite a ride.

Graciela bit the inside of her cheek until she drew blood. Doña Falú put her arm around her.

—Take it from this old lady, the smartest you do in a life is play dumb. She held up a wagging finger, its tip encased in a porcelain thimble. —Here, a little gift from me. Let nothing ever draw your blood. Now straighten up that brow before he sees you.

Sure enough, they heard melodious whistling close by. Casimiro appeared at the room's entrance, then put his arm around the mannequin. He cupped its bosom.

—Don't be jealous of my other woman, he said when he saw Graciela's face.

—¿What's that you got there, Cielo? he asked. Graciela held out her finger and he plucked off the thimble. His eyes crinkled at the edges.

—A tiny cup for mice to drink their coffee, he said and put the thimble on Graciela's head.

—Or it could be a tiny hat for big fools like me to wear, she said. Her teeth sawed away at the softness in her mouth.

—It's siesta, Casimiro said. —Let's go for a stroll.

The boat ride back the following morning was harder on Casimiro. The river's current now worked against him as he rowed upstream. Graciela had lost her wonder of Casimiro. Her anger toward him had turned to pity when she realized that he could offer her only what little he had. Tattered clothing and empty pockets obscured his real riches, which Graciela knew lay in his imagination like hidden deposits of gold.

—Beautiful country, Puerto Rico, she said as if she had traveled the world. Her speech had more s's than usual—overblown consonants she had picked up from the Falús.

—¿Did you enjoy the plaza? Casimiro asked. Despite her protests, he had taken her there during siesta, when the plaza was quiet.

—Yes, yes, beautiful, that plaza.

—¿Did you like the Falús? he asked, enjoying the rhythm of their conversation. The heavy rowing had left a triangle of sweat on his shirt.

—Oh, beautiful people, those Falús, Graciela answered with a smile.

—¿And, Cielo, did you enjoy our trip to Puerto Rico?

—Mm-hm, we should do this again, Graciela said, her speech returning to its normal looseness as Casimiro docked the boat to shore.

. . . . .

Casimiro was an innovator. In addition to his love of mischief, Graciela thought, part of his appeal was in the casual way he gave meaning to the trivial and stripped importance from the respectable. Innovative ideas came to her, too, but with more deliberation, for greater purposes, she believed. She began to suspect that he leeched his ideas from her dreams at night. Casimiro insisted he got them by closing his own eyes and arranging the colored dots of his mind.

The business with the mirrors had been his idea, of course. Soon everyone in town was asking him to affix reflectors to the sides of their donkeys' heads.

—You're just too lazy to turn your own head, Graciela had said when she first saw him mounting wires on the donkey's ears.

—But it's the damnest good idea, he said and spat on the mirrors for glare.

—Piece of precious mirror wasted on that donkey. ¿When ever did I get a mirror from you?

The mirror in their narrow bedroom was mottled with black stains through which she guessed at her appearance. What she could make out of herself was elongated in several places. Graciela wanted to take Casimiro's pieces of glass for herself and glue them to the bottom of her bed pot to be able to see what all the fuss was about down there. Or she could cut it into small pieces to wear around her neck so people would see themselves as they spoke to her, and act as they would toward their own reflection. Now those were ideas, she believed.

Another innovation, to apply her crochet skills to the manes of society ladies, was considered stylish at first. She offered her new hairstyle, going house to house in the slightly nicer parts of town. Trendsetters wanting to turn heads at Mass would sit still for hours at a time as Graciela crocheted their locks into an impressive lace like church veils. After a good night's sleep or two, however, the hair became extremely matted. Graciela was forced to follow up her services with unpaid hours of detangling.

—No one wants to end up with hair like a maroon's, Casimiro said to Graciela after hearing complaints from one of her customer's gardeners. The hair-weaving venture died quickly.

Casimiro himself could not see why Graciela worked herself up into such a frenzy over ideas, and most especially over where to get her next penny.

—No need to work so hard, Cielo. Santana sent the slaves back to Haiti in the last century.

With his charm, Casimiro dipped into others' crops. Folks thanked him as he walked away with their hard-earned work. Always with a smile he stole. Always with a tipping of his hat. Yunco, for one, poured him free drink after drink after drink in pursuit of entertaining jokes that would keep his customers from leaving. And still, it was not beneath Casimiro to return from Yunco's, way past city curfew, with a shotglass in his pocket. No article was too precious or too cheap to fold into his hands. He brought home random gifts for Graciela. From pewter spoons and saltshakers to lemons and hairpins, Casimiro's kleptomania clung to him like a persistent cough. Graciela would promptly return the article to whomever she thought it belonged the next day. Never did she explain. So that Yunco could not understand how his shotglass got to El Gordo's, and Flavia the johnnycake woman accused Desiderio of taking her best frying fork.

. . . . .

When they first met, Graciela had made Casimiro promise to take her places. She refused to be confined to the market, the river, and neighboring households, but she knew that to wander further by herself would get her branded "a woman with loose skins." She and Casimiro did go to an occasional dance at the bandshell in the park. Before O'Reilly fired him for stealing from the shop, he had given Graciela and Casimiro a ride on his Model T. Casimiro could show her no more than what he knew: other people's belongings, tall tales, and sparkling eyes. Winks, jokes, and many apples later, Graciela's feet began to itch again.

Each time Graciela took the long walk to the market, thoughts of deserting Casimiro and Mercedita perched on her shoulders. It was during these solitary walks that her courage would bubble up. Yes, she could leave in a month. Maybe. Prepare everything ahead of time. She could take the back road that Fausto had told her about, one that left you a bit beyond the market, toward the beginning of the Ozama. And just at the turn of the road, when she saw Tun-Tun the baker's wife—who greeted her profusely, asked about Mercedita and Casimiro and Pai and Mai and especially that strapping Fausto, who should come and unload some flour sacks for them sometime—Graciela would lose her nerve.

Mercedita had taken to throwing rabid tantrums. At Celeste's, Mercedita would stay behind in a fit of tears, though she knew her mother would be back from the market in a few hours.

—She's too little to control me, Graciela said when Celeste

tried to convince her to take the child along for once. —A few hours out of my week is all I ask for.

—Don't give yourself so many luxuries, Celeste said, and did nothing to stop Mercedita from tangling herself in her mother's skirt.

—¡I'm not running from you, just going to the market! Graciela said, unclawing Mercedita from her skirt. Only when she was able to turn her mother's voice into pieces of broken china would Mercedita let her body go limp on the floor.

At three years old, Mercedita could already recognize the faraway stare that stole Graciela's gaze from hers. When Graciela sat at the table to eat, Mercedita crawled under her skirt and stayed there until Graciela nudged her away with a foot.

—¡Go away, little runt, and let me live!

Graciela's toes would press into soft ribs. Then, overcome with remorse, she would pick up her crying child and plant a kiss on her forehead.

—Something's amiss with that girl, Casimiro said while hacking on a sheet of beef he had managed to get hold of. He and Graciela were in the kitchen shed, and Mercedita sobbed at its threshold.

—She's being sour because she can get away with it, Graciela said. —Casi, make sure to cut that beef with plenty lime juice and salt.

Casimiro shook his head and complained.

—Something's wrong with you, too. ¿Do you know how hard it was to get my hands on this beef and those couple inches of sausage links for you not to want them?

That afternoon Graciela had made Casimiro prepare the treat himself because of her sudden and strange aversion to meat outside of the season of Lent. Breaking the neck of a rare hen, then boiling it, plucking it, chopping it, seasoning it, cooking it, made her shudder with nausea. To tear through the flesh felt like biting the live flesh inside her own cheek. Graciela knew this was not pregnancy. Her menses were coming faithfully, and she took precautions when she wrapped herself around Casimiro. (The thought of trails of clinging children worried her; at the risk of fueling rumors that she had become barren, she snuck off to a trusted woman outside of town who made her a tincture.)

—With all this hunger about, my woman has gone mad, Casimiro exclaimed.

. . . . .

The six women squatted with their baskets by the river, naked to the waist. Their voices gurgled along with the water, and clean clothes lay out on the rocks, some already baked stiff. The women had all arrived together, and Graciela's basket was nearly empty. She was the best washerwoman, with the squish-squish of her scrubbing faster and louder than the rest; her clothes always ended up mostly dry when she wrung them out. Now, she tempered the vigor of her washing.

—¿What did you want me to do if the boy comes back with a silver dollar he says he found? Santa explained in self-defense. She had nearly killed her six-year-old son with a horse whip two days ago. And it was not the first time.

—¿How does a boy just find a silver dollar in these times, unless he's out there like a ragamuffin', pickin' the pockets of good Christians? An' I'll do it again, even if he brings me La Virgen's turd.

The river's slow current rinsed the lather from Santa's hands. Her huge basket was piled with clothing belonging to her husband, her four sons, and an ill daughter who could never accompany her. She splashed water on her face, and Graciela knew she was washing away more than sweat.

—Santa, in truth I still think the punishment was worse than the crime, said Celeste. Graciela and the other three women were quiet. All had received and doled out their share of beatings.

—¿Ah what do you know? Your children were raised by their grandmother, Santa said. The bottom lids of her eyes always twitched when she wanted to be nasty. And they mostly twitched when the flask at her waistband was empty, too. This is what Celeste said in response while hanging some linens on a tree branch. As usual, everyone but Santa burst out laughing.

—Your hand always gets the better of you with that boy, Celeste continued.

—I'm an upstandin' woman and I do what I've got to do to keep my family in line.

Her bottom lip curled as she threw back her hands and her breasts jiggled. Ursula reached over and rubbed her friend's back.

—¿But what if he did find the silver dollar? Graciela spoke up. —Never reject luck sent your way.

—¿Luck? ¿Luck? My luck's a donkey for a husband, four bumblin' sons, an' a useless daughter. Santa sucked her teeth. —An' somehow I'm still an upstandin' woman.

—Well, sometimes trying to prove we're so upstanding, we do bad things . . .

Though Graciela did her best to emphasize we, Santa's lower lids twitched.

—Oh, you speak for yourself, Doña Cover-Up-for-Her-Thief-of-a-Man. Don't think I forgot about the day you came to my house to return my ashtray. An' what of the time you poisoned me with your armpits.

—Then, Doña Hairy Tongue, you shouldn't have waited till

after I helped you grind your coffee, shuck your garlic, and wash the pigshit from your tripe to tell me off, Graciela said. She twisted two of Casimiro's shirts until the water bubbles disappeared.

Santa stared at Graciela, then reached for her flask. She took a swig and held it up for the others. Ursula reached for it first.

—An' don't you say nothin' about this, too. Santa continued staring at Graciela. —I saw what the punch did to you at last year's patron saint festival.

—¡For the love of God, Santa! ¿Can't you for once live up to your name? Celeste said.

—Lemme get a drink, Graciela said suddenly. She balled up her wet skirt and stepped over the rocks toward Ursula. After taking a swig, Graciela flung the flask into the river.

—Let the fish get drunk and stupid, too, she said. Her cheeks felt flushed already and she nearly slipped on a bar of soap.

—¡You loose good-for-nothin' twat! Santa said. She stood up on the tallest rock, eyes ablaze. The rest of the women waited to see how much damage Graciela had done.

—Listen to such upstanding speech, Graciela said. —And now she's diving like a fool for her liquor.

Santa's skirt bobbed about her bare torso as she splashed her way toward the glittering in an eddie.

—¡Those rocks are slippery, Santa! Ursula yelled. Santa dipped into the water, arms flailing, panic wrinkling her face. Without hesitation Graciela took off her skirt, not caring that there were always extra eyes amidst the foliage. She splashed her way to Santa, who had regained her balance and swung at Graciela.

—¡Get away from me! ¿Who told you I needed your savin'?

—Well, here's your saving, Graciela said as she dunked Santa's head into the water. Graciela swam back to the bank and emerged from the river gleaming.

—Now she's had her drink and been baptized all at the same time, Graciela said. She squeezed the excess water from her braids.

Santa had reached the riverbank, flask in hand. With no further words, she wrung out her skirt, and put on her dry blouse. Then she gathered the rest of her laundry, mixing the wet with the dry, the clean with the dirty. Ursula helped Santa balance the entire load on her head. Both left the other four women to their tasks.

—Graciela, put on your clothes already. You're gonna be seen, one of the women said once Santa and Ursula were out of earshot. Graciela lay on a rock, her breasts like two gray eyes staring at the sun. Water dripped off her thighs.

—You like trouble with that woman, Celeste said as she rearranged the clean clothing that had been resoaked by all the splashing.

—Look, I don't care anymore. Graciela sat up and threw a pebble far into the river so that it skipped.

—But you always go overboard, Graciela. You know that the drink keeps her troubles at bay, one of the women said.

—Well, then we should all take to the drink to keep from going mad, Graciela said and put on her skirt.

. . . . .

—¿What is it you want that you whine so? Celeste asked Graciela on their way to help Santa husk garlic, grind coffee, and wash pig intestines for the upcoming patron saint festivals. Graciela chewed on a stalk of grass for a few paces. In the valley below them she could see the marketplace's remaining tents coming down.

—It's just that every year the same lunatics come out to the festivals.

Graciela sucked her teeth. She had made her sour mood so apparent that Mercedita held Celeste's hand instead.

—There's a pissy spirit on you that doesn't let you eat meat and scrambles your brains.

Celeste picked up a stone and tossed it at a stray dog.

—I told you who can get it out, Graciela, but you ignore me.

—Celeste, ¡I'm tired of all this!

Graciela stopped and stamped her feet. Her hands were splayed open.

—¿Tired of what, crazy woman?

—¡This! ¡This! Graciela shouted.

—The market, the river, helping that ungrateful drunkard Santa winnow beans every year for the same goddamned festivals. . . . ¡It's not enough!

She shook her hands about her head as if they were on fire.

Celeste and Mercedita glanced at each other and walked ahead of the madwoman.

. . . . .

Graciela left Casimiro and three-year-old Mercedita in the time of drought, when sour mango proliferated with the absence of rain. A time of empty sacks contributed to the World War effort, so that the rich went hungry and the hungry went mad.

The idea of escaping was eating away at Graciela every night since the Puerto Rico trip earlier that year, when the chirping of crickets competed with Casimiro's snores. On one particular night, the idea had itched so much, she rubbed camphor into the reddened soles of her feet.

Her latest gift from Casimiro, a hatbox, waited to be returned to its wrongful owner the following day. The following day. She ran it through her head. Bathe. Prepare breakfast. Tend to Mechi.

Visit Mai. Clean home. Send an errand boy for foodstuff. Tend to Mechi. Make the midday meal. Wash the tub of clothes. Go to holy hour for Celeste's deceased mother. Tend to Meehi. Refill the coal drum. Mend Casi's pants. Prepare supper. Ah, and return hatbox to rightful owner.

The camphor seeped into her skin. And Graciela decided to forget tomorrow, to take a leap. Wake at dawn. Make the sign of the cross. Skip bathing. She would borrow Casi's stash of bills, fill that hatbox, and follow the back road. Find a way to get to La Vega.

# SANTIAGO · *1921*

POSTMARK: May 5, 1920
PLACE STAMP HERE:

THIS SPACE FOR ADDRESS ONLY:
    Eli Cavalier
    Hamburg, Germany

THIS SPACE FOR WRITING MESSAGES:
    Dear Friend,

    As per your request, this is to acquaint you with the
advantage being afforded by the Collector's Club for view
postcard enthusiasts. We specialize in the *exotique erotique*
beauty of racial types. Join us.

    Members receive a monthly catalogue during the term
of their enrollment. Extra Special Offer—I will send you

10 dainty exotic erotic views, excerpts from Carl Heinrich Stratz's stunning "The Racial Beauty of Women," plus a dictionary containing 30,000 words if you will send 25 cents for a year's trial membership in this popular club. Please do so before expiration date stamped hereon.
Peter West, President
New York, N.Y.

. . . . .

Touting vegetarianism had become Eli Cavalier's lifelong goal. Vegetarianism was the key to one's soul. Clean body, clean mind, clean soul. A better world.

Eli saw the people around him sludging about in abundance and rampage. All of Europe had imploded in the greatest war the world had ever seen, until then. Nations squabbled over territories and allegiances. Civilians slaved to produce enormous quantities of guns, munitions, and other war supplies. Millions were being mobilized for the armies and navies.

"This bizarre hunger for blood has its roots in carnivorous culture."

Early on, long before the ferrous odor of blood and the rumble of tanks shook his country, Eli had begun to attack global problems through leaves of lettuce. He peddled his humble message of peace and vegetarianism from house to house, lectured at clubs, addressed public meetings—wherever he could get a hearing.

"Meat, difficult to digest, robs blood from the brain, the seat of human reasoning."

Critics called him naïve, fanatical, illogical. After all, that very meat protein had nurtured his brain throughout childhood, allowing him to formulate his turniped notions. Abstaining from meat itself was the novelty of Eli's message, the very thing that earned him his living. And how dare he spend his time on carrots when there were wars to be fought, nations to defend, enemies to be killed.

The number of Eli's speaking engagements dwindled, as did the subscriptions to his monthly pamphlets. His message thinned out like an anemic broth. His was a whisper in a cacophony of broken people hunting rats for an extra day's breath. Many of Eli's colleagues had disappeared into the smoke of war. Some had fled to live with relatives in other countries. Others donned uniforms and learned to eat from cans of questionable meat. One committed suicide. When soldiers ransacked his house, Eli knew it was time to take his message elsewhere. He packed what was of most value: his pamphlets and collection of erotica. He was headed to new territory, to the peaceful Caribbean, where his advocacy for vegetables might be heard.

. . . . .

The heat made it difficult for Eli to catch up on the sleep that had been escaping him since the train first pulled out of Sánchez, heading west toward La Vega. The palm trees and wooden shacks dotting the landscape had become monotonous, and his game of counting the pineapple stands as the train whizzed by left bile brimming at the back of his tongue. He loosened his bow tie.

Eli preferred traveling in the least expensive coach. He enjoyed the musk of Sunday wear wilted by sweat.

"Life here rots as fast as it is conceived," he had scribbled in his journal.

— ¡Noticias, noticias, noticias!

A newspaper boy wove his way down the aisle. Leafing through *El Monitor* gave Eli a headache, so he read his own pamphlets instead, then tried to strike up a conversation with a fellow passenger. He bought a cob of corn from a vendor in the aisle, only to spend the next half-hour picking kernels from his teeth.

Other passengers gawked at him, in his bow tie and silk-banded straw hat, which he should have removed. Eli imagined their thoughts with a grin. How a man in such formal dress could have such a poor demeanor was beyond them . . . cheap he must be to sit in coach . . . foreigners, with their mustaches too coifed for the tropics . . .

In La Vega, Eli stepped out of the train for fresh air. At this major stop there was a considerable shift in passengers. The station was abuzz with peddlers, idlers, soldiers, urchins, and shoeshine boys. Men herded cattle up a ramp onto stock cars toward the rear of the train, their voices coarse. The air was heavy with coal dust. Eli helped a woman with her bags. He ate a johnnycake. One beggar accepted his coins but refused a pamphlet. Then a bell rang in the station and Eli boarded the train.

When he returned to his seat, he was surprised to find it occupied by a small, humbly dressed girl. Pleased, he took the seat next to her, hoping no one would come and claim it. The girl's face was partially concealed by a straw hat. She looked down at the station crowd through the window. Her hands clutched the hatbox on her lap.

He could tell from the cuticles on her small brown fingers that she was a girl of dark meats. Purplish nipples, perhaps. He closed his eyes and saw the gray creases where ass meets thighs. Eli could feel himself growing hard in the heat. Wanted to dive his hardness into velvet blackness.

The train lurched forward as the girl continued to look out the window. There was no sign that she would turn toward him; her face was flat up against the glass.

Eli inhaled.

"After much experimenting I have invented a means for improving and intensifying the exotic exhalations of the Negress," he had written in his journal in more pleasurable times before the war. By rubbing her flesh with dry lavender or fresh thyme or a concentrate of the two after a salt bath, he believed the black woman acquired an extremely erotic perfume, quite apart from the insipidness of the white woman. This was the basis of a pamphlet he had been putting together prior to his exile, and he hoped to finish it here, where indulging his study was easier, far more opportune.

Graciela drummed her fingers on the hatbox while Eli's disappeared under his pamphlets and into his trousers. He stared at the dark half-moons of her nails, felt a drop of sweat travel from his forehead to his upper lip—meaty ass in his hands, the secret smell of want around him, the one he last fucked large, black, and willing.

Passengers on the train looked out the window, others read or dozed. Some spoke in monotones. Too early for anyone to notice the well-dressed man masturbating under pamphlets.

—¿What is it you doing there?

The voice softened his urge. Eli opened his eyes to find that the girl's face was stronger than he had expected from her small brown hands.

—¿You sick? Graciela asked, looking from his face to his lap.

The pamphlets crumbled under the man's hands. Graciela was trying to convince herself that she was mistaken by what she thought she saw in the window's reflection. He was well dressed, she could see that.

—Yes, yes, my stomach. Always, eh, feel sick on these trains.

Liar, she thought; his Spanish rang strange but confident in her ears. His obvious discomfort put her at ease—after all, he could have continued ruffling his pamphlets had he been sleazier.

—It is the meat I ate that sickens me, he added.

Her charcoal eyebrows rose. His breath was foul to her, like curdled milk, and she, too, had begun to feel nausea whirling in her stomach from all the traveling she had done since leaving home. Though she had been able to lodge and bathe temporarily wherever a washerwoman was needed, Graciela still carried the stench of the vegetable carts and cattle wagons she had hitched on from the southern towns all the way up to La Vega.

—¿What meat was it that sickened you, Señó? Graciela asked.

—All meat. Meat is not good. Not good for the spirit.

He tapped his chest with his index and middle fingers. Graciela covered her mouth and swallowed—the curdled-milk smell again.

—Yes, yes, Señó. You are very sick, she said and covered her nose with a handkerchief.


—You go sing that no-meat song to the rich, Señó. Then they'll leave enough for us to eat fine, Graciela said to Eli between mouthfuls of lard bread.

In her hunger, Graciela happily craved meat again. What a luxury, it seemed to her, for someone to deny meat when hunger distended bellies everywhere. She should have listened when Celeste warned her not to give in to such fetishes; she should not have humbled Casimiro in their own kitchen.

Graciela's pride was too weak and her hunger too pressing to refuse the other half of Eli's loaf, as well as the salted meat he had bought for her at one of the train stops.

—Eh, but think. This is why the poor are nobler. Christ said it, too. He simply ate fish and bread, Eli told her.

Eli held out another piece of bread for Graciela. Breadcrumbs stuck to his mustache. He winked.

—¿You from where, Señó, with those ideas?

—Germany, France. My father, the French one. But things are, eh, ugly there, because my father's country and my mother's country are at war. Everywhere things are ugly.

Graciela could not conjure up a picture of such a place, Germanyfrance.

—¿What kind of animal does Germanyfrance look like? ¿Sheep, goat?

Eli cocked his head, then finally removed his hat.

—Eh, right now, I say they are vultures. People breaking into your house, taking everything that means anything to you. Think of the bridge we cross now exploding with your friends on it.

The train lurched as it made a noisy turn and passengers gasped. Graciela let out a peal of laughter.

—¿For that you stop eating meat? she said above the din.

Graciela covered her mouth with her handkerchief, this time to hide her missing front teeth.

Eli was quiet. Ridicule from the not-yet-converted was nothing new. Since leaving Europe, he had not spoken to anyone about the bridge bombing.

—¿Where do you plan to go? he asked her. We are near Santiago already.

—Don't know, she said and sighed.

—¿How does a woman travel alone at times like these?

Eli injected sting into his voice.

—That's of no concern to you, Graciela said with a shrug.

Eli sat back in his seat. He stroked the ends of his mustache.

—Tell me, please, about the ugly in this country, he asked.

—I wasn't taught letters, and who gives a damn what a girl like me thinks about things . . .

She tugged on a braid sticking out from under her hat.

—This country belongs to robbers. Yanquis, Haitians, Dominicans, everyone's got sticky hands.

Her whisper wavered, as she was not used to having her opinions heard.

—Can't raise their own bastard children and want to run a country. Let me take over, she said. Her thumb dug into her bosom.

—But you yourself seem to be running. You would be first in exile when the pan got too hot, Eli countered.

—¿What do you know of my problems, Señó? Graciela sucked her teeth.

Eli gauged his questions. He gave her his full attention as she told him her dream of a turquoise house and her ideas as to why the yanquis should let the country be. She told him she wanted to learn to read, and to ride a ship someday.

Eli mined the smallness of her world. Like a farmer fattening his cow, he embellished his ride on the ship across the Atlantic, leaving out the numbing seasickness, the howls of widows and orphans. By the time the train pulled into Santiago, Graciela had eaten three more loaves of bread and many strips of salted meat.

—Never stayed at an inn before, she said, answering his bold question in one breath.


Graciela noticed the slower speech, the easier manner of the people as soon as she stepped off the train. Santiago, the City of Gentlemen, the Heart of the Country, pulsated even in its sultriness. For a while Graciela gazed at the women in fitted suits and crepe hats ordering little ragged boys who balanced bags on their heads. A man in a conductor's uniform slurped water from a cup. A chain gang of prisoners repaired a stretch of track in the distance. In the rush of passengers, Eli briefly disappeared.

A rumble from deep in the earth sped up Graciela's heart and blew dust on her skirt. She looked up, expecting the train to roll away from the station. There was a rush of wind and the roar grew louder. Crepe hats tumbled in the dust and little ragged boys stumbled into split ground. The conductor drinking water sputtered and knelt with his arms to the heavens. Doomed, the chain gang huddled around an almond tree. Graciela looked about for Eli, then ran toward the almond tree, the earth belching underneath her. Behind her, the train rolled over like a poisoned serpent. ¿Could Santiago be sinking like the old La Vega? Terror pushed Graciela into the group of men, who were praying away their sins.

—¡Ilumíname Señor! Graciela cried out with them. The rumble swallowed their wails.

In its twenty-year existence La Pola's inn had been three-times robbed, twice burned down, and once reduced to woodpile by a hurricane. With each disaster, La Pola began afresh. Colors and furniture changed. The women changed. And of course, so did the prices. A tinny squeaking, the only constant. The inn had previously been called Mai Pola, and Pola Traz, and Ama Pola, and Pola Quí, and Pola Allá, and by the time Eli and Graciela arrived it was simply La Pola's.

The earthquake of 1921 shook all of Santiago. By the time Graciela and Eli reached the inn, rumors had spread that some people had been swallowed whole by the earth and that crops and cattle had been lost.

Not a shutter rattled at La Pola's. As the city mourned its losses, men headed to the inn to sap themselves, to prove themselves, to drink, to cry.

—Nothing will ever shake this house built on solid rock, La Pola rapped her knuckles on the bar counter as she addressed Eli, who was there to lose himself.

To Graciela, the glass rosary around La Pola's neck was droplets of water. She wished La Pola would offer them to her in a goblet, maybe, where they would be transformed into bits of ice. And a curious relentless squeaking from somewhere was pounding away at her forehead. It had been a long day full of too many surprises, and though she was glad to have found Eli again amidst the chaos, her thirst for water was overcome by homesickness. What she would do for a long, cold gulp of Casimiro and Mercedita, Mai and Pai, to quench the sandy guilt that had been grating her throat since she had left.

La Pola twitched her nose toward Graciela.

—¿And who is this one here?

—Eh . . . this is Graciela. My woman for today, you know. Eli winked at La Pola and wrapped his arm around Graciela. With his thumb and forefinger he squeezed the flesh of her upper arms hard to keep her from speaking.

—She cannot stay. ¿What do people think I am here, ah? La Pola's voice was scratchy from forty years of running a business, and more recently from pipe smoke.

—But I'll pay for her stay. You still make your money.

—The Haitian said only you were coming. And tell me, ¿do you buy food from one canteen to eat it at another?

—Watch your talk, old bag. You don't know of me, Graciela said to La Pola, prying Eli's fingers off her arm.

La Pola smiled wide teeth of gold. In Graciela she saw the same rawness and appetite that had plunged so many of her girls into the sewer of the trade, that had put so much shine in her teeth. No,

Graciela would not command as high a price as the fairer girls. But the naps under that scarf appealed to foreigners like this one. And that skirt's hem could be hitched up higher in the back. Potential. This cow, she thought, needed to be fattened.

La Pola removed her glass beads and put them around Graciela's neck. Such a sudden peace offering wet Graciela's lips.

Eli paid for two rooms. The price was higher for overnight stays, and that day in particular there was more traffic at La Pola's than usual. The earthquake had not only displaced many men, but had convinced them that the world was ending and it was time to either repent or to sin.


La Pola left Eli and Graciela sitting at the bar. The bottle of herb-steeped rum Eli had purchased stood between them.

—Best in-house drink I ever had, he said and slid a shotglass to Graciela. Though she had drunk many times with Casimiro during the festivals, this rum tore through her throat like a sword then ran prickles up her arms.

Between shots, Eli told Graciela what he had learned from his Haitian friend: that La Pola had always been more businesswoman than prostitute, closer to her great-great-great-grandfather than the women before her.

—Eh . . . that craft's stained deep in her blood. Mother, grandmother, great-grandmother, great-great-grandmother, they all sinned for the pay. Legend goes that the family business started with the rape of La Pola's enslaved great-great-great-grandmother, in the times of the colonies, before your slave rebellions. Quirós, slave-owner sent by the Devil himself, had naked slaves serving him meals, cutting cane on his plantation. Shrewd as an elbow, as you people say, he made money from his three obsessions: money, sex, and mixed-bloods. Said blood-mixing spit out better fruit than the original. Eh, son of a bitch sired his own babes for sale, making deals while these girls were still on the tit. ¿La Pola's great-great-great-grandmother? Was the first of his slaves to supply his stock. But whoredom ran in the Quirós blood long before he came along. His own grandfather was said to be one of the original leeches seeking fortunes since the days of the Tainos. Horny bastards even humped table legs for lack of women then. Had to import whores from our Europe, who didn't mind seasickness, then yellow fever, and only God's eyes know what else . . .

Eli howled and beat the countertop, knocking over the bottle of rum with his fist. He lifted his shotglass. Graciela had not expected this of him.

—¡Salud! ¡God bless this beloved country!

He leaned in closer to Graciela, took her chin in his hands, and planted an open kiss on her nose.

Graciela's room was furnished with a bed and a nightstand. In addition to a washbasin and bar of soap, there was a small statue of La Virgen de la Altagracia on top of the nightstand. The face, once delicately detailed, was chipped. She was a faceless woman with her arms spread.

—Your room is a holy place that keeps men from disgracing animals, virtuous women, and, high heaven forbid, each other, La Pola had told Graciela, handing her the key.

Along with the glass beads, Graciela tossed the statue and bar of soap inside her hatbox. Then she slumped on the bed and watched the beams above it spin. She rarely spent the night on any bed other than her own, had never drunk so much rum as to let a handlebar mustache and lurid stories of whores and slaves speed up her pulse.

Her nose twitched. Inebriation had dulled her sense of smell and Graciela felt disoriented. ¿But was this not what she had wanted, to experience the unknown?

Casimiro and Mercedita, however, rubbed her conscience again, like two shifting pebbles inside a shoe. ¿What if the earthquake had reached them, too? La Pola had said it only shook up the north, ¿but how much can a toothless old whore know, anyway? Graciela's headache pounded; she could not block out the tinny squeaking outside.

—¡Mercedita! Ay, ay, ay, she sang. She could not stay on the bed, which rose and fell like a ship on the high seas in a storm. She got up and leaned against the wall. So this is seasickness, Graciela sang, this is seasickness, and she jumped on the ship again. Now the bed felt as if it were sinking. And Graciela remembered the day before she had left home, when Mercedita had thrown one of her tantrums. She had been under Graciela's skirt during breakfast, arms gripping her calves, until Graciela sent her scrambling away with a sharp kick. No remorse then—until now.

—¡Pick up the child and put a kiss on her forehead, stupid! she said out loud and sat up on the bed to try to stop the sinking.

—¿And what are you doing at this moment, Casimiro? she muttered with a shake of her head. Probably the same routine: having his afternoon drink at Yunco's, earthquake and all. —Salud to you, too, Casimiro, she whispered, toasting with an imaginary glass.

Graciela came to with the strums of a guitar. They seemed to come from the bar at the far end of the courtyard, where the night was starting to brew. In the adjoining room a man coughed. Then Graciela heard a knock at the door, and a thickset woman entered without waiting for response. Quietly she waddled in with a tub the size of which Graciela had never seen before, and set it at the foot of the bed. Just as quietly, she disappeared, leaving the door open behind her.

Graciela leaned out over the threshold to survey the courtyard, onto which the twenty rooms at La Pola's opened. In the center, like the hub of a wheel, a votive statue of La Virgen de la Altagracia looked down upon the surrounding flowers and offerings. The source of the round-the-clock squeaking: off to the side was a water pump, which the thickset woman had been pumping. The woman returned to Graciela's room with two buckets of water that had been left out in the afternoon sun to warm.

—¿And this? ¿Who is it for? Graciela asked as the woman sprinkled into the empty tub clumps of salt, which she had produced from her apron.

—The man you came with, he sent it for you. Get in before it gets cold, she said, avoiding Graciela's bloodshot eyes. In her speech, Graciela could hear the same Haiti she would hear in the vendors' talk in the market.

—Before you let him, make him wash, too, over there. The woman jutted her bottom lip toward the washbasin.

—Those yanquis, they're the ones who come bad with the syphilis, she added.

—No, he's from Germanyfrance, Graciela snapped to let the woman know her place.

When the woman left, Graciela began to gnaw the inside of her cheek. ¿Was it proper for Eli to send her bathwater? She had a flash of her own hands scrubbing a guinea hen with lemon for cooking.

—Devil's always toying with my peas, she said and rubbed her brow.

The tub. Graciela jumped up and did a jig around it. She had never washed herself in one. Usually she squatted in a shack behind the outhouse splashing water from a cup, or she dove head-first from the highest rocks into the Ozama. Grime from the long train ride, earthquake dust, and the walk to La Pola's soon stuck to the edges of the tub. The tub's circumference prevented Graciela from sitting comfortably, so she knelt. Salt grit at the bottom of the tub cut into her knees, where rice had dug its marks many times before.

Afterwards, on the bed, the lantern light from outside flickered a band across her belly. She could still hear muffled guitar notes. Water had dried on her skin, leaving behind a faint marbling of salt. One of Graciela's legs swung off the bed. The possibility of the door swinging open tickled the back of her mind. Her arms were outstretched and she yawned.

Not much later, Eli entered without knocking.

—You look like the cat that ate the rat, he said.

He was out of his jacket and wore only pants. A new authority rang in his voice, as if he were lounging in his own home.

—Sit up, he said.

From a small pouch he produced some leaves. He opened Graciela's legs and rubbed the dried leaves into her pubic hair.

—Lift your arms.

He did the same to her armpits.

—¿What is it for? Graciela asked. She was disappointed at his brisk indifference toward her nudity.

—Seasoning for my meal, Eli said.

—You know, the other whores are already jealous of you, he continued as he squeezed thyme and lavender under her thighs.

—¿What whores? Graciela asked, cringing from the rubbing. She could tell she was being watched from the moment she and Eli had walked into La Pola's. But she had never expected her bedraggled state to elicit envy.

—Yes, yes. Everything they envy. A bath. Warm water. My money. That servant woman talks.

Eli snorted.

—One had her face cut up for putting on airs.

—I have no airs, and I can cut up faces, too, Graciela whispered.

—Some things are made by nature for pure enjoyment. . . . Stand up. Let me see you.

He made Graciela walk around the tub of dirty water. Had her bend over from behind. Had her raise her arms. Had her untie all of her hair.

She did. And more.

He could easily replace her with a smaller waist and a rounder ass, she knew, so she shimmied harder. This second time around, no one had to slap her to warm himself with the fire in her face.

—Stop now, he said.

In bed Eli sniffed her. A beast on a hunt. As she lay on her stomach, Eli's sour-milk smell stung Graciela's nostrils when he pushed himself inside of her. Holding her thighs closer together buffered the burn. She tried grinding herself against the bed to own some of the pleasure. With the heel of his hand, Eli pressed the small of her back until Graciela felt a place deep inside her yield and she could not move.


—Go on after men, if you think that's freedom. End up worse than where you started, Mai had shouted after Graciela the day she followed Silvio. And then Mai hissed the same warning in her ear when Graciela opened her doors to Casimiro.

And now Mai's voice echoed in Graciela's mind again as Eli sat up next to her on the bed and scribbled in a small notebook. Graciela was propped up on an elbow, studying him while she tried rubbing the soreness from her labia. Mai always spoke in Graciela's mind, but Graciela tried to pulverize the words just as quickly as they came. Otherwise, the words would tie her hands and feet together.

The rapid movement of the writing tool in Eli's hand drew Graciela's attention.

—¿What you doing there? Graciela asked.

—Shhh. Prescriptions and meditations, he said without looking up.

¡What absurdity! she thought. ¿How could a man think of letters at such a time? Graciela watched him put the pencil to his mouth, then continue scratching it across the book. She was tempted to ask him to teach her of letters, but Eli seemed lost in a secret, privileged world.

—You people are crazies, she said.

Graciela rolled away from Eli and up against the wooden planks of the wall. Perhaps Mai had been right. Men were no more free, for all their mobility. How ridiculous to have expected Silvio, Casimiro, or even the fool beside her to hand her a world that was not theirs to give.


Eli was gone from her room in the morning. In the tub, scum floated over the bathwater. Bits of lavender and thyme lingered in the crevices of Graciela's body. Dawn was sticky and breezeless. Graciela stuck her head out of the door to check that the pump in the courtyard was clear.

An entire week had passed since she had packed the hatbox with a Sunday dress and her few belongings: a brush and comb, charcoal for her brows, a head scarf, coconut oil, Falú's porcelain thimble. With the stillness of morning came homesickness. She was not used to hearing the silence of night-living drunks who awoke past noon.

Graciela missed Mercedita's morning gurgles and Casimiro's puttering in the yard. Perhaps she should have succumbed to the pang of guilt she had felt the day before, when she hitched a ride to the train station in La Vega on a horse and buggy. It was a guilt that sparked upon arriving in La Vega, when the talkative driver pointed to a gigantic protrusion in the distance. —¿You see that crucifix sticking out of the ground? They say it was the steeple of a church in the old La Vega—before God sunk that Sodom and Gomorrah. The driver had turned back to the horses and let the whip snap, leaving Graciela to wonder how a whole city could be buried underneath her. God and His ways, she thought, all of a sudden wanting to see the crimson dust of the road back home. Hatbox under her arm, Graciela had ventured out not daring to look back, lest she turn to salt, lose her nerve, and wait for Casimiro to go out onto the road and steal himself back his salty woman.

Now at La Pola's, Graciela used buckets to empty the water, then dragged the tub to the pump. The clatter roused visitors and workers. One woman emerged from her room, eyes swollen from sleep, and leaned against the doorjamb with her arms crossed.

—¿Who said you could use our water supply? she shouted. Graciela turned around and took in the woman's bony frame.

—You go to hell, Graciela said and continued to fill a bucket with water. The woman they called Sopa de Hueso disappeared inside her room, then reemerged.

—Say that again, so I can hear you, the woman said with more nerve.

—You. Go. To Hell.

Graciela hit the floor. Water from the pump gushed up her

nose. She swatted at the hands around her neck. Hoarse barking. A numbness cut into her cheek. She realized the barking was coming from her own throat. When she sat up and touched her face, her hand ran red. Graciela thought her hand was cut and felt for a wound. The bone-soup woman was quickly surrounded by a crowd of people in all states of dress and undress who had gathered by La Virgen de la Altagracia. La Pola shuffled through the crowd. Her hair sprang about her face, and a breast threatened to flop out of her nightclothes.

—Get up, good-for-nothing rat. Whole shantytowns have tumbled like cards into this valley and I'm kind enough to let you stay when my own people are on the street. How dare you bring me trouble.

La Pola dispersed the crowd without saying a word to the bone-soup woman, her best moneymaker.

Graciela washed her face in the room, unable to stop the flow of blood from her cheek. Heavy tears burst from a well deeper than her eyes. Then, a knock at the door was followed by the woman who had originally brought in the tub. She dabbed a rum-soaked cloth on Graciela's cheek without meeting her gape. Her hands were careful to avoid contact with blood.

—Sopa de Hueso's quite a something, ¿eh? the woman said. She shook her head.

—Had you waited for me to come with fresh water . . .

Graciela grit her teeth against the sting. The woman refused her a swig of rum from the bottle.

—Don't want your yanqui syphilis on my bottle, she said, still tenderly touching the wound.

—¿And this? ¿What is it for?

Graciela recoiled from the needle and thread in the woman's hand.

—Your cut, I'll sew it for you. Lie back now, she said.

When Graciela resisted, the woman pulled back and said,

—Ugly now, pretty later, ¿or ugly now, ugly later?

They were tight stitches that made Graciela gnash her teeth on the balled-up sash of the woman's frock.

—I'll tell you this. Leave here if you love your life. That yanqui and La Pola only have nastiness after you, the woman whispered after she had made a neat knot and bitten off the excess thread. Graciela stroked the stitches.

—Trust me. Tears won't save you. I help you only because I have an account to settle with La Altagracia.

A few hours later, as instructed, Graciela waited for the servant woman to kneel before La Virgen de la Altagracia in the courtyard. Then, hatbox under arm, she snuck across to one of the alleyways surrounding the entrance of the bar. There, she squatted over the moat of sewage that trickled out to join a bigger stream on the street.

When the woman made the sign of the cross, Graciela hurried around the wall to the entrance of the bar, where she and Eli had first entered. The previous night's ballyhooing lingered in the dark and damp air like stale vapor. At the other end of the bar, the door to the street was a rectangular sun.


The earthquake had chewed up the train tracks at the station. Fissures across the Santiago soil steamed as if releasing the city's life force. People believed spirits from the cemeteries emerged at night to reveal directions to treasures buried in the days of the colony. One disappointed man looking to find fortune came across a Taino vase intact, which he used as a spittle cup. Churches filled with the repentant. Everywhere there were funerals. Processions sometimes carried empty caskets (the bodies of the missing, perhaps still struggling to breathe under a tumble of rocks). Those eager to return to life as usual busied themselves with the repair of their homes and shops.

After hours of walking through rubble, and balancing the hatbox on her head, Graciela stopped to sit at an abandoned fruit stand. Thirst welded her tongue to the roof of her mouth; the river she crossed miles back had been muddied. A spoiled orange lay on the ground and Graciela was forced to peel away the mushy matter. She managed to press out enough drops to wet her throat, then continued walking in search of water.

Her wound throbbing like a heartbeat, Graciela began to think about how the straw mattress she and Casimiro slept on sagged beautifully in the middle. And she replayed the melody of Mercedita's wails in her head. She closed her eyes to remember the fragrance of the outhouse, as well as the music of the leaky roof and the field mice celebrating in the kitchen cabin. What she would give at this moment to hear a scolding from Celeste.

Ahead was a cluster of trees, some of which had fallen and blocked the road. A fence of bushes partially concealed a cement house, with an automobile and a horse and carriage parked in front. Faint music played from the house. With trepidation, Graciela opened the wooden gate to the property.

As she approached the house, the growing music sounded strange; it crackled as if being cooked in hot oil. Going closer, Graciela discovered that the door to the house was open. She stood on the porch steps, chewing her lips. ¿Should she sneak about the property in her desperate search for water?

—¿Hola? Graciela shouted.

The music sounded as if a live band were playing, yet the house seemed deserted.

—¿Who goes? answered a childlike voice.

In a few moments a young woman appeared, fleshy cheeks and sunny eyes. The mouth slashed a thin and harsh line into her face.

—¿Yes? she said, sizing up Graciela with a quick sweep of her eyes.

—Good afternoon, Señá, I've been walking all day. ¿Is it possible for a drink of water, maybe medicine for pain?

Graciela's hand touched her throbbing cheek.

The woman invited her inside. Graciela was pleased to find that the kitchen was not a separate thatched cabin like hers back home but a part of the rest of the house. A vine of flowers snaked along the wall of the kitchen. And Graciela was delighted when water poured from a silver pipe in the wall—the best water she had ever guzzled.

—Thank you for the drink and the pills, she said. —Your house is so very beautiful.

The woman's eyes stayed sunny, and she asked Graciela what the rest of the town looked like in the aftermath of the quake. Graciela described what she could, while noting the woman's ruffled blouse and feeling ashamed of her own tattered Sunday dress.

—You are not Santiaguera. ¿Where are you from?

Her fine hands were like Mercedita's.

—Me, I was seeing to my family here. But the earthquake took 'em, Graciela said, then pointed to the oozing stitches on her cheek.

The woman's eyes clouded over, then brightened again. Her hired help had left for the funerals, she said, and she was not to humiliate herself anymore with daily household tasks.

A man burst into the kitchen. He stopped short when he saw Graciela.

—So you got a new girl. Good, this house was turning into a nest of dogs, he said as he washed his hands in the sink.

—Humberto, this woman says town is horrible. Look at her face. And I had thought the errand boy was lying when he said he couldn't find kerosene.

From her saccharine voice, Graciela could tell the man was her husband.

—Don't you concern yourself with those matters. I have things taken care of, he said. His forearms boomed out of his shirtsleeves.

Graciela had only wanted water. Now she had to plan her next move. The only other ways she could travel south to the capital were on foot, donkey, horse and carriage, or, if the heavens opened up, by automobile. She wondered if Mercedita and Casimiro could do without her for a few days more. Honestly, it bothered her that they might be perfectly fine. In the midst of running water and heavy silverware and the young woman's ruffled blouse, Graciela convinced herself that Mercedita was surely in the good care of Mai or Celeste, and that Casimiro had most likely found Graciela's replacement at Yunco's.

Here she was with a glass of limeade and a sliver of ¡ice! floating in the pulp, when water was all she had asked for. Whenever the pain of the stitches became unbearable, Ana offered Graciela more medication. And hunks of almond biscuits were banishing her vicious appetite. She felt a surge of accomplishment. Just hours before, she was being stitched up like the rag doll she had once sewn for Mercedita. Despite momentary pangs of homesickness, Graciela preferred the uncertainty of wanderlust to the dreariness of routine. Too much passion and curiosity for her own good, Mai and Pai always told her. But Graciela believed that neither Celeste, nor Casimiro, nor Mai, nor Pai could ever understand the pleasure to be had in letting risk wake every one of their senses from the stupor of routine. People back home were simply too content being the spectators of their own lives. Graciela sat up straighter in her chair.

—¿How much is it you pay, Señó? Graciela asked Humberto, who raised his eyebrows.

—Ana, tell the girl that she will have the servants' quarters out back, board, and a modest allowance, and that I have had girls thrown in jail for theft. And tell her I am much more than Señó.

—¿But how much is it you pay, Señor? Graciela corrected herself. Humberto studied her as if there were a familiarity in her heart-shaped face. Graciela covered the fresh scar on her cheek— she knew it made her look brazen.

—We will talk about it more, you and me, Ana whispered to Graciela. Humberto backed out of the kitchen to take care of what he insisted were more important matters.

In return for the room and board and a modest allowance, Graciela broke dishes and stained precious upholstery. Burned dinners and sewed crooked stitches. Mai would have been ashamed. Still, Ana Álvaro treated her well, while Humberto hovered about, issuing orders.

The Álvaros had only recently acquired their wealth. The end of World War I had turned the world's appetites away from blood to sugar, cocoa, coffee, and tobacco—a sudden dance to earn millions in cities like Santiago that had produced these delicacies. Parks, roads, theaters, social clubs, businesses, and concrete homes sprouted like weeds. Humberto and his father-in-law had their hands deep in the tobacco and sugar industries when the boom began. *La Voz de Santiago* regularly covered the Álvaros' socials, which the couple held to show off their newest imports. Ana's marriage to Humberto had brought together two families not far apart in the local gene pool. It was a question of keeping not only the fresh, new money within the families, but also the Spanish blood of cousins.

By 1921, when strains of ragtime from their new Victrola coaxed Graciela to their doorstep, sugar beet was once again thriving in France, and the world's war-torn pockets were being re-stitched by hand. The Álvaros' tobacco and sugar did not command so high a price these days. Their dance was coming to a halt.

During her short tenure, Graciela helped Ana discard stacks of Sears catalogues (some of which she snuck into her hatbox). Ana's naïveté surprised her. They were the same age—eighteen— and Ana knew of letters, had already been to most of the country's provinces, and had possessions Graciela could only conjure in the skies. Yet Ana reminded Graciela of a little girl with no one to show her toys to—knickknacks and dresses and furniture and music boxes and porcelain dolls and even the very parasol Graciela had seen in the clouds.

—Come here, Ana summoned Graciela when Humberto was in town on yet another round of "important matters." —Let me show you something.

They went to the master bedroom (where Humberto and Ana had been trying, without success, to conceive all year). From the belly of a cedar wardrobe Ana retrieved a book.

—I don't know how to read, Señá Ana, Graciela said.

—I am not showing you any writing. This is my album. And you are to call me Señora, silly girl.

Ana sat on the floor next to Graciela and opened the book.

Pasted on its pages were panels of various scenes. A man pushed a cart of sugarcane. A woman with voluminous curls tumbling from under a hat held the parasol that so haunted Graciela. There was an enormous house with many stairs and a blue, red, and white flag fluttering from a pole. A man and woman smiled, their teeth unnaturally white.

—¿And these people? Graciela asked, passing her hands over the panel to feel beyond the flatness of its scene.

—Don't. You will ruin my wedding picture.

Ana pulled Graciela's hands away, picking them up by the wrists.

—¿Those are you? Graciela said as she moved her head closer to the photograph. Then she sat back and laughed.

—Yes. Yes. That is us.

Ana smiled, amused by Graciela's amusement.

—Your teeth. Your teeth are so white, like horses'.

Graciela continued to laugh from behind her covered mouth. She could not understand why Ana was so proud of being inside that panel with such white teeth.

—We went to the studio in town after the wedding, and, ay, what a glorious day, but I had to ask them to touch up the flowers, ¿see?, and to lighten up Humberto a bit, and then they did the teeth . . .

Ana ran a finger over the whiter parts of the picture, her brows drawn close. Then she stood up to show Graciela some sample poses. Graciela watched in silence. She felt a pull in her belly at the thought of herself inside such a panel. With Silvio. She and Silvio—his eyes open, no less—were probably being watched somewhere, too. A burn crept into Graciela's eyes.

—One year, already, Ana said. She stroked the white, hand-embroidered bedspread. A teardrop dangled from her chin.

—¿Why the tears, Señá—Señora? Graciela said, trying to contain her own. She could not feel sorry for Ana, who looked toward the molded ceiling of the bedroom, where the cherubs in the wallpaper ended their romp and the chandelier sparkled in the morning light.

—Mai used to say, Go on after men, if you think that's freedom. You only end up worse than where you started, Graciela said.

Ana looked down again at the wedding picture. As Graciela, too, stared at the couple, she remembered Silvio as he had been just four years ago. Maybe she would visit the warehouse when she returned home. She ached to see Silvio again to erase the image of a corpse bobbing at sea.

—I hope to Jesus his teeth aren't so white, Graciela said aloud and brought her fingers to the gaps in her own teeth.

Ana snapped the book shut and flung it into the closet.

—You are so vulgar. I try with you, but you are just so vulgar, she said, shaking her head.

Graciela was instantly sorry. She had squandered another opportunity to see more of Ana's possessions and perhaps receive some toss-away gift. Laughter always seized her at the worst times.

—Go finish scrubbing the porch before Humberto gets home for siesta, Ana said.


Graciela lived in the servants' quarters, but Ana, out of loneliness, allowed her access to the rest of the house when Humberto was away. Graciela was no longer taken aback by the intricate mosaics in the bathroom. Crystalline water and warm daily baths lost their novelty. And she easily satisfied her incessant craving for scarce meat in such starving times—ham and blood puddings, guinea hen, beef, goat, turkey, rabbit—and did not care to distinguish between hunger and gluttony. Now Graciela felt a dread when she imagined returning home to a hearth, dirt floors, and water jugs filled with larvae.

Graciela also saw that comfort alone (or the privilege of white skin) did not guarantee eternal gaiety. At night she could hear china breaking under the wails of opera coming from the phonograph; string instruments and Humberto's baritone muffled Ana's voice. Fear of discovery kept Graciela from climbing out of bed in the servants' quarters and approaching the house to make out the murmurs.

Ana knew about the money problems and about Humberto's important matters. The day she pulled out the album for Graciela to see, she had wanted so desperately to share her anguish with a friend. After the lavish, well-publicized wedding, she did not dare complain to her family and bridesmaids about her rotting marriage.

As Ana napped on the hammock in the porch one morning, Graciela cleaned the master bedroom. Puffy eyes and childish irritability were the price Ana was paying for lost sleep. That morning Graciela had swept up the pieces of broken china without being told, then snuck a teacup and saucer into her hatbox while Humberto prepared the horse and carriage for town. Earlier, Graciela and Humberto had been alone in the kitchen, and he had complained, to no one in particular, that the scarcity of gasoline in the damned country kept him from using his car and forced him to use the horse and carriage like a common peasant. He eyed her strangely between forkfuls of eggs.

—¿Has Ana told you that our room needs a good dusting? We pay you to clean and cook here, he said, avoiding her eyes.

—Yes, Señó—I mean Señor.

—¿Where exactly did you say you were from again?

He added more salt to his eggs.

—Thereabouts the capital, but my family is from Santiago, she said.

She could tell her dark skin and rapid speech filled him with doubt. He seemed to recognize her from somewhere in the past. With a huff, he cleared his throat.

—When Ana wakes, tell her I went to town to see about steamship schedules. Be sure to keep the house locked. Looters are slithering about like river snakes.

Ana woke at noon. Without asking for Humberto, she complained about needing a bath and breakfast, and once satisfied, rocked herself to sleep again on the porch. Graciela rolled open the shutters in their bedroom, letting sunlight and breeze dissipate the staleness of troubled sleep. As she dusted the bottles of perfume on Ana's vanity table, she pretended the room was hers. She dug her nose into silk dresses hanging in the cedar wardrobe. Her feet were too wide to fit into Ana's square-toed patent-leather shoes, her hair too spongy to tuck under the lacy wide-brimmed hat. Then, with a sudden rush, Graciela remembered the photo album.

As she flipped through the pictures again, she realized that the photograph of Ana and Humberto was less impressive then she remembered it. Orange-tree blossoms, roses and white lilies trailed from Ana's left arm, while Humberto clutched her right bicep. Graciela ran her thumb over his wavy hair. He looked defiantly at Graciela, half his face covered in shadow; Ana directed her gaze downward.

A cock crowed outside. Graciela closed the book, then opened it again. She had forgotten to take note of the couple's shoes. Ana's footsteps dragged across the porch, and Graciela plucked the photograph from its metal slots. She slipped it inside her blouse and it slid down to her waist.

Ana strolled into the bedroom.

—Remember to rub oil on the vanity's wood.

Ana rubbed her eyes and threw herself on the freshly made bed and pummeled the cushions. Graciela wanted to pummel Ana the same way.

—I hate him. ¡Hate him with all my guts more each day! Ana moaned into a cushion. She turned over on her back to study Graciela.

—¿Has he put his hands on you yet? she asked.

—¿On me? Graciela adjusted her skirt.

—Yes, you, stupid girl. ¿Has he bought you anything yet to keep your mouth shut?

—Ana, Humberto has never touched me, ever. And don't call stupid the girl who washes your bloomers, Graciela said.

Ana looked down as she had in the wedding picture. Her bloomers from the previous day had been stained with the monthly reminder that, again, she had not conceived.

—¡Get out! I am just so sick of everybody, she sobbed and dove into the cushions.


Soon she would have to leave, Graciela knew. Her hatbox already contained a Sears catalogue, a teacup and saucer, and a photograph. And that very night after Ana's outburst Graciela heard Humberto creeping among the plantain trees around the servants' quarters behind the house.

It was late. Graciela had waited for the music to subside and the house lights to go out before opening the hatbox to re-examine her newest loot. Humberto's careful footsteps crunched through the blaring of crickets. She shoved the box under the bed, blew out the lantern, and locked the door. Minutes later his knock was brief, but firm.

—¿Who's there?

—Open the door, woman.

Once inside, he had Graciela light the lantern. He looked around the small room without regarding her.

—Your family is not from Santiago, he said.

Humberto sat on the bed and Graciela moved toward the door. He picked at his nails.

—No need to be afraid of me. You're too ugly for funnin' with, he said. Graciela glanced at the hatbox near his boot heels.

—More important matters bring me back here. He lay back on the bed with his hands hooked behind his neck. His eyes focused on a moth making shadows on the ceiling.

—I have been missing my gold watch from Switzerland for the last few days. I say to Ana, 'Ana, my love, ¿have you seen my gold watch from Switzerland?' And she says, 'Humberto, my darling, ¿what would I do with your gold watch from Switzerland?'

Humberto's words flew like little moths inside Graciela's head.

—The only other person who could know where my gold watch from Switzerland is would be the one who cleans our room. So I ask you, ¿where is my gold watch from Switzerland?

—I don't know where your gold watch is or where is Swezerlin, Señor Humberto, if you're calling me thief, Graciela said.

—If it does not appear in the house by tomorrow, you'll know where the local jail is, lying bitch. They cut off fingers there.

Humberto sat up. He looked around the room again.

—Señor Humberto, I'm not a thief, she said as he shoved her aside to open the door. He focused on her for the first time since he entered the room.

—But you lie. And, Señorita, the next time you see your friend La Pola, you tell her I send my regards.


Graciela lay in the dark long after she heard Humberto trudge his way through the plantain grove to the house. Like a spark, it seemed, she ignited fires wherever she set foot. After being at the Álvaros' for five weeks, the prospect of jail—and severed fingers—made her feet itch again.

Now full of self-pity, Graciela again ached for her life with Mercedita and Casimiro. ¿Did Casimiro writhe in his sleep with the thought of her? Mercedita must be throwing tantrums and running Celeste or Mai into the ground. By now Casimiro must have found a girl to tend the house, clear the cobwebs from under their bed, light the hearth, feed their few hens, fill the water jugs. Mercedita takes her milk with a dollop of honey, if possible, he should tell the new girl. When it rains, ¿would that girl know to move the mattress over to the left so that the leak in the roof will not make Casimiro dream the Devil? ¿And speaking of rain, had Casimiro discovered Pai's pistol underneath the rainwater barrel? Somehow Graciela had to make it home.

In the dark she hurried through the plantain grove, past the house, and through the wood gates of the Álvaros' grounds. Ahead, the sun was beginning to bleach the sky morning. Graciela hoped to hitch a ride south toward the capital before sunrise. The thoughts of La Cigüapa's apparition, or looters, or worse, yanqui soldiers lurking in the bushes Graciela kept at bay with a mantra of child-hood rhymes. ¿How could she have forgotten to bring along Pai's pistol in her hatbox?

After an hour of walking and singing to herself, she heard the steady clop of hooves behind her. Her skin prickled with the thought of Humberto at her heels. The sky had lightened to a royal blue, and behind her, Graciela could make out the silhouette of a boy on a donkey.

—Buen día, the boy said when he was closer. The donkey was loaded with empty water containers. ¿Could she ride as far south as he was going? And in this order—on foot, overburdened donkey, vegetable cart, truck, horse and carriage, foot, canoe, horseback, and grace of God—Graciela returned home.

# HOMEBOUND · *1921*

Graciela sauntered into her house as if she had never left. The sun still lay deep in the east while she felt her way around the chairs and table to the partition where she and Casimiro slept. In the moonlight her fingers came across the delicate limbs of her daughter, then the massive ones of Casimiro. Their light snores were even, as if her absence had pacified their sleep. Satisfied to find Casimiro and Mercedita sound, Graciela felt her way through the rest of her home.

There was order she had not expected. As always, she relied on smell and feel. In the kitchen there were no dirty pots at the hearth. The yard had been swept clean of leaves and debris. Lime had been thrown down the hole in the outhouse, the wood scrubbed clean with vinegar. Fresh rainwater filled the barrels. She envied the invisible hand's efficiency.

Graciela lay in the hammock to stare at the moon, whose largeness kept her from sleep. An owl hooted close by. Wisps of clouds encircled the gigantic moon, which hovered above the trace of hills. With her husband and daughter and neighbors all retreated to their subconscious worlds Graciela felt she owned her household again. She extended her hand, so that by shutting one eye, she could see the moon perch on her palm. Dull pain ran up her forearms.

For days she had been suffering from feverish headaches, and her bones and joints ached. It had been a long journey home. As she lay in her yard, the six-week adventure behind her faded. Eli, La Pola, Ana, Humberto were like the people of a dream that in the waking hours dissipated. ¿How was it that what had been so palpable to her in one instance became so vaporous the next? While Graciela was gone, she had sensed pieces of Casimiro and Mercedita—a lingering smell, an image, a feeling. And then, only a few minutes ago, she had touched their pulsing flesh in the dark. ¿Would it be the same with Silvio someday, even though for now she could conjure up just a narrow back, a scent of sweat, a shiver near her neck? The desire to see him trembled in her throat, as if a hand had wrapped its fingers there.

From her hatbox Graciela removed the photograph of Humberto and Ana. The silver moonlight exposed two sets of glinting teeth. Graciela closed her eyes to better see the couple in her memory. Nothing about their teeth was funny now. This photograph, a voracious craving for meat, and a scar were all the vestiges of the people she had encountered. ¿What had she left in them?

In the symphony of crickets, Graciela heard the ocean.

—Silvio, don't you spook me now, she whispered.

To think that a part of herself was floating about without her. ¿Could that be why her feet itched so, why Silvio still roamed around her? In a few weeks, after the dust of her return settled, she decided she would call on Irene, the woman who—with a pumice stone, a razor blade, and coconut fat—could carve out silky baby's feet from Graciela's swollen and calloused ones.

A cloud paused before the moon. Soon Graciela's toes and fingers slackened, her breathing stretched her belly.

—¿Satisfy your whim? Casimiro asked between sips of morning coffee.

He was calm, his legs crossed as usual. Graciela did not answer him. She rearranged the new pewter dishes on the shelves. In the weeks she had been away, her kitchen had become unfamiliar territory.

—I put the oil in a bigger canister. Covered the mouse holes, too, he said.

Graciela was more disoriented by his casual tone of voice than by the changes in the kitchen. Casimiro put aside his coffee to carefully braid Mercedita's hair into four knots. With the sleeve of his shirt he wiped her nose. Mercedita refused to go near Graciela, huddling close to her stepfather. It pained Graciela that Mercedita had wailed when she awoke that morning and saw her mother for the first time in over a month.

—Give Papá a wink-wink, Casimiro said. —Go kiss-kiss Mamá, he added, to no avail.

For a week after her arrival, Graciela dared not venture out of the house. People visited with the excuse of borrowing sugar, milk, smokes, in order to get a glimpse of Graciela's purported scar, and some, to give her a solid scolding. Contrary to Graciela's suspicion, no one else had entered her home while she was away. Casimiro had not employed anyone to take care of household duties—

including those in their bed. To the consternation of their neighbors, he had done all the cooking and looked after his stepdaugh-
ter's needs, despite the protests of Mai and Celeste.

¿So what is my place here? Graciela asked herself. Then ¡ha!
she laughed with the realization that Casimiro had been one step
ahead of her all along: he had overcompensated, knowing she
would be back. All his work had been temporary, and he came out
looking splendid.

¿Think I won't leave for good, you? she said to Casimiro one
night, when the baby talk between him and Mercedita drilled on
her nerves. Weeks had passed, and he still had not asked ¿why had
she left, where had she been, why the scar? Graciela wanted to see
him break, was eager to see him show relief that she was back.
Instead, he spent his days joking about town, collecting junk, and
fashioning crafts with cans and wire.

—Leave if you want. I only own myself, Casimiro said in the
dark a few weeks after Graciela's return. He lay on his side, his back
turned to hers. They had not been intimate. She wanted to see him
on fire so she could desire him again.

—I had a man while I was away, she said. Casimiro lay very
still, and Graciela could tell that at least his ego was hurt.

—The things you say have no names . . .

—¿And the things you do, ah? Graciela shouted. His faults
were his eternal humor and foolish ideas. His was a frivolity she envied. She herself felt sewn shut, lost in her own anguish. Life was a
lake for him, whereas she would drift out to turbulent waters. His
wild creativity coupled with the work he recently did about the
house had earned him pity, praise and, well, accusations of queer-
ness.

—Graciela, keep talking like you do. Remember that the fish
dies by her mouth, he said and got up to retrieve his clothing from

a chair. Before she could think of anything else to say, he was at the door.

—I try with you, woman, he said.

And he was gone to Yunco's.

· · · · ·

Each day Mercedita tested Graciela. Whenever Graciela called her, she turned a deaf ear, until Graciela gently took her in her arms. Or Mercedita would gather worms in the yard, and throw them in the rice sack in full view of Graciela.

—¡Worms and rice for lunch! Mercedita told the neighbors. And each time, Graciela followed her, explaining—to bewildered neighbors and to a delighted Mercedita—that the new dish was from a place called Germanyfrance. In time, and after having passed many such tests, it was Graciela rather than Casimiro who combed Mercedita's hair into four knots every morning. Although Graciela worked hard to earn Mercedita's favor, Casimiro's pleasant demeanor only made her angry.

—¿Nothing to say to me, you? she asked him at odd moments.

—Just say what you want me to say, he shot back and Graciela would feel the rumblings of another battle of words.

· · · · ·

The month of Carnaval culminated with the townspeople gathered at the river to celebrate the republic's independence from Haiti almost eighty years prior. Hordes of iridescent children dressed as devils and painted in traditional blackface romped by the water. They playfully beat the "chaste and sinful" alike with inflated dried cow stomachs. Beads, ribbons, whistles, cowbells, and tiny dolls that had been ripped from their costumes during the horseplay littered the riverbank.

A few feet upstream, Graciela kept an eye on Mercedes' blue horns as she herself sat with a group of women, Mai, Celeste, and Santa among them. Everyone had shown up to celebrate. And though Graciela knew she had been a target for gossip in the previous weeks, the smoky aroma of pig roasts and the hollow sound of skins alongside the children's laughter had inevitably lightened her spirits. Some of the men were already lost to rum- and drum-induced dance. This year, Graciela preferred to simply watch the dancing. Her increasingly achy joints might keep her shoulders from rolling in their sockets, might sour the sugar in her hipbones.

Graciela closed her eyes. Mai had removed her handkerchief and was braiding her hair. Sure, Mai's face always looked as if she were chewing steel, but the tenderness in Mai's fingers made Graciela feel like a child again.

—Graciela, you got more naps than a plantation, Celeste said, tucking a yellow flower into the puffs of hair yet to be braided.

—I'm tired of your hair-talk, Celeste, Graciela said. She tried to throw a patch of grass at Celeste, but Mai's grip kept her head steady.

The conversation strolled to hair oils, to men, to ailments, to food, to clothing, to memories.

—Carnaval's been so nice this year—no stupid yanquis trying to paw us up, Santa's teenaged daughter piped up.

—I'm tired of yanqui-talk, Graciela said with a drawn-out sigh and a stretch; the Mai-tight braids made her forehead glow. —There's not much to those sons of bitches . . .

—. . . as well she should know, ¿right, Ma? the girl replied quickly and turned to Santa.

Graciela pretended not to hear the "little bitch's" under-handed remark, and decided not to lash out because the poor girl had shocking skin—bad-liver skin, sacred brown skin disrupted by splotches of pink. Instead, Graciela busied herself brushing some fallen hairs from her shoulders.

—Now, now . . . Santa said to her daughter.

Graciela was surprised that Santa had not drunk at all that day. Perhaps the fact that Santa had managed to get her "donkey for a husband, four bumblin' sons, an' useless daughter" to the river was enough drink for her, Graciela thought. She chuckled. The drumming in the background had grown fierce, and many people were starting to gather around the drummers. Celeste announced that she wanted to dance, and soon everyone began to climb the hill toward the pulsing by the mango grove. Graciela wanted to turn back down toward the riverbank. A commotion where the children played made her search for her beloved pair of blue horns. From her vantage point, all she could make out was a crowd of red and blue capes. An eerie chanting coming from the children made her abandon the group of women.

—¡Mercedita! Graciela called out when she came across her daughter's discarded horns on the way down to the river's edge. With the village eating, talking, dancing and drinking, the children always ended up on their wicked own. Graciela remembered her own pranks as a child. Energies pent up by ever-vigilant adults exploded with the February festivities. Somebody should be on alert, thought Graciela, especially after that drowning years ago . . .

Graciela took in a breath as she reached the gathering of children by the water's edge. No, it could not be her Mercedita. Not her little girl . . . But there she was, at the cipher's center, pounding away at a girl who had come in traditional blackface. Never had Graciela seen her quiet child so ferocious: her baby kicked and punched the other girl in tune with the chanting.

—¡Beat the Haitian, beat the Haitian!

Coal and blood streaked Mercedita's hands, the "awfully big" hands Ñá Nurca had noted after the storm in Graciela's womb. The eyes behind Mercedita's papier-mâché mask blinked wildly as Graciela pulled her off the child by one of her hair knots and shook her.

—¿What are you doing, you little shit? Graciela repeated until her voice grew hoarse. The surrounding children laughed, then began to beat Graciela with their cow stomachs, tentatively at first, but then with more boldness, until Graciela could not distinguish the sound of drumming from their blows, until she could not tell which child she herself was beating. And she made sure to keep her grip on Mercedes, while trying to hold back from really hurting the other children, but the chanting around her gained momentum. She did not know what to do but to shake the monster in her grip, shake it, slap it, so that everyone knew she was not an idle parent. ¡The embarrassment!

—¡If anything, I should be the one beating your black ass! Graciela heard a woman yell.

Suddenly Graciela felt her wrists immobilized. Somehow Casimiro had broken up the throng and embraced Graciela from behind. The rest of the children had been disbanded by efficient mothers who dragged them away by their ears. The voice threatening to beat Graciela belonged to a honey-colored woman nursing the bruised child with a rag to her bloody nose.

—¡Your daughter sure as hell knows we ain't no Haitians! the woman continued, as Casimiro stood between her and Graciela. He made Graciela take a shot of rum to stop the chatter in her teeth. Already Mai, in a barrage of hisses, had taken off Mercedita's mask and nudged her into the group of women ready to clean her up.

—I tried to discipline her . . . Graciela sobbed. She dug her face into Casimiro's shoulder, away from the oglers who had rushed down from the drumming hill.

—¡So many other kids in blackface and she attacks mine! the woman continued with a voice that pierced through the group working to calm her down.

Graciela clung to Casimiro. Her joints ached as the woman's voice ebbed.

—Just when Mercedita and me were getting along. ¿Did you see how she was hitting that girl? And those little animals . . .

Casimiro was quiet as he held her. His chest was warm, comforting after the chaos. Graciela felt a shaking in his chest and looked up at him.

—¡Casimiro, don't you laugh at me! Graciela pulled away, eyes watery, mouth pulled taut. He continued his shaking.

—Those little demons were feasting on my poor Cielo, he said and smoothed back the hair that had sprung around Graciela's temples.

—Be easy. Don't forget that you still have accounts to settle with us.

Mustafá the shopkeeper had always been very good to Graciela; he never complained about the length of the list of items she had purchased on credit. And Graciela knew she could send Mercedita the few houses down the road to Mustafá's without worries that she would be shortchanged.

He was a lanky Syrian man with violet skin and a nose thin as the edge of paper. His wife, Adara, who was said to be many times shrewder than Mustafá, helped him with the kiosk. For years they had supplied the surrounding homes with odds and ends: blades, rum, tobacco, snuff, flour, tonics, suckers, gumdrops, needles, and thread. Mustafá took pride in the fact that, unlike other merchants, he never snuck in extra weight on his scale, nor did he ever deceive even the most illiterate of his customers. A stupid businessman he was, Adara said when he extended credit to people like Graciela, whose payback list was also gobbling up their supply of ink and paper. Yet somehow, at the end of every month when Mustafá and Adara settled accounts, the books always showed a profit. Yunco maintained that it was because they must be related to those sugar-mill-owning Turks and therefore were not to be trusted.

But just like Graciela, Mercedita grew to trust Mustafá. She was proud of being allowed to go by her four-year-old self to purchase important staples for her mother, like candles and lard and sticks of cinnamon. Mustafá taught her how to ask politely for an item instead of pointing. Under Adara's incredulous gaze, he went on to teach Mercedita how to examine the merchandise to make sure she was getting her money's worth before plopping down her coins—even when there were no coins. Before Mercedita was old enough to go to the school run by the nuns, Mustafá showed her how to count, so that she would know how many coins to offer and whether to wait for change or not. Sometimes, when Adara was not at the counter, he would slide Mercedita a free packet of tamarind balls.

There was a Haitian boy from a nearby batey who loitered about the kiosk, begging for food in Kreyol and picking up any scraps. He was about Mercedita's age but already had the darting eyes of an old man. Mercedita wondered why he reeked so strongly of rotting cane, and why he always had cuts on his arms and legs.

—Tell that boy we don't give handouts, Adara said to Mustafá, looking right into the boy's face. But the boy would not leave, even after Adara tossed him a strip of jerky, even after she chased him away with stones.

A few weeks before the pre-Lenten Carnaval festivities, Mercedita had found the boy at the kiosk again. She was terrified of going inside that time, because she noticed the dried mucus in the corners of his eyes. And then, just as Mercedita was about to turn and retrace her steps back home, the boy sprinted into the kiosk and emerged with a hunk of macaroon. Just as quickly, Mercedita saw Mustafá catch up to the boy, who had tripped over a tuft of grass. He became a rubber doll in Mustafá's hands; his shoulderblade distorted as Mustafá twisted his arm until the piece of macaroon dropped. She felt an odd delight at seeing the boy in pain—such a weak and skulking boy. Her mouth watered and her fists tightened.

—Do it harder, Mustafá, so he learns, she blurted.

Later, after Mustafá had sent him away sobbing with a packet of macaroons, he explained to Mercedita that Haitians could not be trusted. Animals, he said they were, who had, in their twenty-year rule, destroyed the fabric of the country by expelling its best white families; and as the beasts came, with their savage religion and their savage tongue, they took away the honest work from people like his grandfather, a hardworking Syrian who had hailed from the sultans of Spain, and Mercedita was never to behave or compare herself to people like that little boy, never to act so hungry, so slave-minded, so indolent, so black . . .

—Well, ¿what do you expect from the girl? Mai responded to Graciela's complaint, her mouth distended by peanuts. They both looked over at Mercedita, who sat on her haunches and poked the ground in Mai's yard with a stick. Graciela could tell Mercedita had been listening to their talk by the cock of her head and the listlessness of her poking.

It was a cool Sunday afternoon, and for the first time, Graciela saw her mother take a break from the kitchen and a myriad of other chores to idly sit with her to crunch on peanuts. The platinum light at that time of day embossed Mai's face so that the depth of its wrinkles and pores was sharpened. Mai looked so vulnerable in this light that Graciela dared to share her frustration, to be just as vulnerable. But Mai's frown had quickly disturbed the wrinkles and the pores and splintered the light in other directions. It was best not to pursue the matter of Mercedita's violent behavior with Mai if she wanted to avoid yet another round of accusations. It would be Graciela's fault that Mercedita did not speak much, her fault that Mercedita stabbed lizards with branches, her fault that Mercedita stuck her tongue out at whomever she felt like, that Mercedita had called Mai a "hairy spider" just the other day, her fault that Mercedita had beaten that little girl at Carnaval a few months prior.

Graciela turned to watch Fausto, Pai, and Casimiro work on the thatching for a new bath cabin. Earlier that May, Pai, Fausto, and some men from town—minus Casimiro—had made sure to harvest the fully grown reeds of grass; by then the dry grass had lost its seeds and a wax layer had formed to protect it from the elements. After having worked in the sun all morning, the men who had come to help Pai left an hour ago. Graciela had originally volunteered to help also, but decided she was going to switch roles with Casimiro and play lazy, along with Mai. Fausto and Pai had laughed hard at the comment when she said it aloud; they knew how difficult it had been for Graciela to drag Casimiro to help out at her parents' home on a Sunday. But in his usual calm, Casimiro had responded to the teasing with a solemn nod toward Graciela. –What a lady I have, he said, taking off his hat with a ceremonious bow.

—That Casimiro has not taken a break, Mai said when she saw Casimiro make yet another trip to the water tank. Then he leaned against the trunk of a palm and wiped the side of his face with his forearm. When he noticed Graciela and Mai looking in his direction, he shook his handkerchief at them.

—¿What's all that smoke? Graciela asked Mai.

—Your man's hard work has got the dust stirring up here, Mai said as she gathered the peanut shells in her skirt.

—Behind him. Over there. Graciela pointed to a gray puff that camouflaged the cluster of cabins on the hill facing Mai's yard. At first she had thought it was a blanket of mist.

—That smell, Pai said. He climbed up the ladder to get a better view, with Mercedita at his heels.

—¡Mercedita, get over here! Graciela said. She ran and yanked her child away from the foot of the ladder. Graciela's cabin, which sat on the hill facing Mai's yard, was no longer visible.

—¡I knew I smelled fire! Fausto said and went to untie the donkey from its post.

Mai stayed behind with Mercedita, who was already in the throes of a tantrum. Graciela joined Casimiro, Pai, and Fausto, as well as the rest of the people running out of their own cabins, on the mile-long hike to the bottom of the neighboring hill. They arrived a half-hour later with watery eyes and stinging nostrils to find a sooty and blank-faced Mustafá mumbling in Arabic. Graciela was relieved for a moment to learn that her cabin was intact. But the smoldering kiosk and Adara's blistered corpse, which lay on the ground, its eyes welded open, made Graciela cry. No one could piece together the sequence of events that had left Mustafá peeling Adara's skin from his own and the kiosk a massive pile of embers attracting the fireflies, already circling about. And in such chaos, no one had thought to give Adara a bit of dignity. Graciela draped her own shawl over the body, then scolded herself for also choosing that moment to thank God that the paper containing her list of debts was also mixed in among the ashes.

• • •

—Casi, before November we should change the thatching on all the cabins—the kitchen shed especially, Graciela said months after the fire. She had just bathed herself and Mercedita for the second time that afternoon and already there were half-moon sweat spots under her breasts.

—All the thatching looks fine to me. Casimiro pointed his cup toward the four cabins. The summer's drought had kept him guzzling more water than rum and whittling tiny farm animals out of wood.

—It's been years since . . . Silvio . . . put the thatching up. Graciela whispered "Silvio," making sure that Mercedita was out of earshot and feeling awkward uttering his name in the presence of Casimiro.

—I'm telling you, woman, the roofs are fine, Casimiro said. Curls of wood covered the ground around his hammock.

—With this heat, I'm just scared, Graciela said. The smoky smell of Adara's flesh still pestered her nose, even to the point where, again, she could not stand to eat any meat cooked over a spit.

—There you go running away with things. These roofs last decades. Look how Silvio's handiwork outlasted even him, Casimiro said, then looked away when Graciela's lips tightened.

—You got some nerve talking like that, Casimiro, she said after a few seconds. Casimiro shook his head and got up from the hammock. —The day God frees you from your laziness, I'll probably be gone already, Graciela added. She detested the evenness of Casimiro's expression.

—I cannot spend one peaceful afternoon here without this woman assigning me some task, he said to the little horse he had been trying to coax out of the hunk of wood.

—¡Talk to me, you foolish man! Graciela slapped the wood out of his hands. Her chest was heaving, and she could not understand how his calmness could stoke such flames in her. Casimiro bent down to pick up the wood, and on his way up, brushed his lips against her arm. In one sharp move, Graciela slapped the back of Casimiro's neck and tried to get at his face. His hold, which dug between the tendons in her biceps, surprised her into stillness. Nothing: Graciela found nothing in the eyes that met hers. They did not blink or quiver or tear. Then Casimiro's grip slackened. Her shoulders dropped.

She had lost her temper in a disagreement over thatching. ¡Thatching!

The fetal horse went into Casimiro's pocket, and he began whistling the first few notes of an old merengue.

—I'll be back before nightfall, Cielo, he sang and danced his way to the front gate.

· · · · ·

When Graciela could no longer stand Casimiro's even temper, she arranged for Mercedita's care and told Casimiro she was going to spend the day at the grave of her grandfather on the other side of town.

La Gitana lived a ways from Graciela and Casimiro's house, the house built by Silvio that would have to do until fortune brought them a turquoise palmwood house with zinc roofing.

If one wanted to have her palm read by this Gitana—who everyone knew was not an actual gypsy and was, in fact, a man— one had to face the hills and walk toward the interior. A trail carved out by the curious, the scared, the desperate, the sick, the greedy, led to a stone house surrounded by poppy. Wicker rocking chairs dotted the porch for the waiting customers to watch the hummingbirds before their own fates were revealed.

Women envied La Gitana's long hair, which formed a tent around their palms when he bent over to read them. He smelled of rosewater on holy days and of lavender on regular days. His outmoded corset caused him often to fill the air with husky sighing, which the unfortunate and fortunate alike interpreted as misfortune. Always he chewed on a sprig of parsley.

Born Lorenzo Báez, La Gitana had an air of worldly knowledge, of having consorted with the country's great poets and leaders of the time, though he could not read and crossed his ankles under heavy skirts. He could recite long poems and famous speeches. Fiercely anti-yanqui, his fantasy was to join La Unión Nacional Dominicana and offer his spiritual services to the patriotic cause (the real reason: his fierce attraction to its leader, Don Emiliano Tejera).

When not translating fates or selling sage advice to the very people who snickered behind his back, La Gitana cultivated his home with the same enthusiasm he did his soul. For most of his life La Gitana had lived alone. Because he could see his own future, he took few risks, and settled into complacency. Rarely did he leave his house to buy the delicacies the fates had afforded him. Two orphaned boys ran errands for him, tightened his corset, and rubbed his back with camphor, occasionally sneaking frogs into his bed pot. La Gitana considered himself blessed.

—¿What of my Casimiro?

Graciela closed her eyes as La Gitana's finger traced the etchings on her palm. La Gitana knew that despite his soothing touch, his lavender evoked in Graciela a bad memory. His brow lowered as he felt the hand's texture, rough like the shell of a walnut. He pressed the palm and felt its unusual density, lightly pulled back the resisting fingers. Lesions like copper pennies stained the meat of Graciela's palms. Then La Gitana leaned in to examine the daunting system of lines. These lines were a tangled map of roads; some led to dead ends, others ran into each other, then swirled in opposite directions. One path led away from a road toward one of the mounts. The Venus, Mars, and Moon mounts melded. ¿What was what? La Gitana managed to find the mounts of Mercury, Sun, Saturn, and Jupiter under their corresponding fingers. The major lines on the palm made him question his own gift of seeing beyond, a gift he had always flexed like natural breath. The lines of the Sun and Fate and Affection contended with each other in a way he had never seen in a palm. Other, lesser, lines crosshatched Graciela's palm like an unusual plaid. La Gitana traced and retraced the many lines, refusing to be dizzied by the labyrinth.

—¿You ever listen to your own language with strange ears? she asked.

La Gitana lifted his head at Graciela's voice; the ends of his hair tangled in the fingers of her open palm. He was annoyed by her intrusion, even more by her ability to sense his disorientation.

—Like for a moment you are not of this world . . . Graciela waved her hands around, further entangling La Gitana's hair.

—None of us are anything. We are bigger. We are smaller. We simply choose which we want to be, La Gitana said as he claimed back the last strands of hair from Graciela's fingers. —Now let me finish my spirit work.

*One line on the palm was a dirt road packed with crimson dust. La Gitana walked on this road. In the distance, he made out transparent monkeys running with their hands splayed apart. The monkeys had pulsating hearts inside their skulls, and brain tissue jellied be-*

*hind their ribs. As they ran, the dust they stirred coated the organs crimson. The syphilis.*

La Gitana's curtain of hair hung lower over Graciela's palm.

*La Gitana fled from the road, cutting through bush, only to fall into a rushing river that spit him onto train tracks. A giant serpent approached, shaking the earth, smoke rising out of its head. La Gitana was swallowed up into the serpent's mouth, then felt his spirit float up to the clouds, away from this wicked unfamiliar land.*

The curtain of hair shimmered as it parted to reveal La Gitana's face. Graciela, obviously bewildered by his bulging eyes, stayed silent. La Gitana sat back in his chair. He rubbed the bridge of his nose to fight vertigo. From a sachet in his bosom he drew a sprig of parsley.

*La Virgen de la Altagracia appeared in the clouds, her bloody palms extended. The wounds spoke directly to La Gitana. —Lorenzo, the future can be changed. Be not complacent.*

From a sachet in his bosom La Gitana drew another sprig of parsley.

*Rotten apples. He was in an infinite orchard of trees bearing rotten apples. La Gitana rolled his tongue. He yearned to walk down the*

*aisle of trees, pick one fruit and experience its dry, grainy meat. Then
a flash of blue light.*

—¿What is it you see for me?

La Gitana did not respond; the parsley folded into his tongue.

—¿But how? he whispered. —¿How do you have so many
lives?

The Lifeline was not one, but many, a fountain that splurted
from the base of Graciela's thumb.

—Gata, they call me, and Graciela meowed as if she were gur-
gling honey in her throat.

La Gitana's eyes remained fixed on the palm from which he
had just returned.

—Forbidden fruit, thus a light stole part of your spirit, he said
slowly, his index finger making circles in the air, his finger of
Jupiter. —Apple trees everywhere, but they yield bad fruit, grainy
apples that sand away the future from your palms. Many futures,
but you cannot move forward.

Slashes of weak sunlight fell on La Gitana's eyes when he
looked up at this strange woman whose hands did not seem to be
weighed down by the possibilities—and the disease—they held.

—Stop living between nostalgia and hope. ¿What will be your
next elixir when past is present, then future?

He did not blink the light from his eyes as he fingered the
rosary around his neck. Graciela surely had the syphilis. Whether
or not to tell her was the question.

—Besides, it is a waste to worry about the future. It comes soon
enough, La Gitana said.

The silky hair contrasted with the bluntness of his face. La
Gitana felt Graciela's desire to touch him, to feel his face dig into

her breasts, the silk of his hair enveloping her in awful lavender. Graciela looked down at her palms when La Gitana saw the want on her lips.

He came closer to her once more, and with a rush of perfume, grabbed her hand. He traced a line across her palm with the long nail on his pinkie, his finger of Mercury. There it was, he thought, digging his nail into the Line. It was not a line of Head or a Line of Heart. It was the rare Simian Line. The line of the monkey on both hands, in which Head and Heart lines were one.

—¿Why did you come to me? Such hands follow their own laws. La Gitana backed away from the splayed palm.

—To see where I go. How far away I go. You understand, Graciela said.

Her palms were raw where La Gitana had dug his nails in spite of the lesions. Graciela licked the lines.

—I advise you to be still, Gata, or what it is they call you, he said. He doled out the words.

Graciela was on her feet. Her palms spread.

—¿Be still? There has to be more than just red dust where I walk.

—Not all opportunities are open to you. Not all are appropriate. I can simply tell you that what is yours will come to you.

The reading was done. La Gitana dared not describe to Graciela what he had seen: punctured soul, poisoned blood that flowed thin. In his visions La Gitana could not grasp where or how Graciela's soul had been robbed, how the blood had been tainted with the syphilis. He knew she had no future. He clasped his hands in his lap to let her know not to probe any further.

—*Lorenzo, the future can be changed. Be not complacent,* La Virgen had said to him through the wounds in her palms. Never before had a vision challenged him so directly.

Tomorrow he would take a risk: leave his home and visit the learned woman with the book on chiromancy two towns away. She could tell him if he had failed this case, if his powers were waning, and by what forces.

La Gitana rose from the chair. He stood inches taller than Graciela. The grace had disappeared from his stride as he walked toward the room's entrance. He was transformed into a painfully corseted man with uncut hair. Not waiting for the clink of coins inside the urn, La Gitana gave a husky sigh and parted the drapes.

. . . . .

Graciela left La Gitana, and on a whim, decided to visit the old warehouse. For hours she walked to the Colonial Quarter, traversing shantytowns and hillsides. La Gitana's words had left her with so much confusion, that she was angry at herself for having gone to see him.

Throughout her walk, she entertained herself by pretending to be, in turn, a vendor, a roaming doctor, a beggar, a nun, an orphan. The game kept her feet from aching and gave her different eyes.

As a beggar, she saw profit from the people she encountered and was able to eat along the way (—Please, water, some food, money). As a doctor, she observed children with distended bellies and infected eyes; the copper lesions on her own palms and soles of her feet no longer disturbed her as much. As an orphan, she saw Mai in every woman's face, but she halted the game when Mercedita appeared in a child's forlorn eyes.

Eventually Graciela made her way through the narrow streets of the Colonial Quarter, trying to recall the paths she and Silvio had taken years before. The people she stopped to ask for directions were of no help, as she herself could not translate the idea of her destination into words. Each turn presented her with a maze of identical alleyways, so that she had no choice but to close her eyes and return to her game and pretend to be an adolescent girl with ashy knees and boundless lust pumping through her veins.

The Malecón was longer than she remembered it. She walked along the docks until she spotted the warehouse looming ahead. Men in uniform were posted like gargoyles. Others walked about and some stopped to observe her. Graciela realized how foolish she had been to think that she could find the photograph of herself and Silvio in this mammoth place.

A workingman carrying a box on his shoulders walked by her. He sized her up, and Graciela noticed in his quivering eyes that he thought she was fishing for customers.

—¿What are you doing alone in these parts? he called out to her.

—¡'Scuse yourself! Graciela said.

—No money today, but try me tomorrow, he said with a smack of his lips.

—¿What is it they do there anyways, pervert? she asked, pointing to the building. The man put the box on the ground and as he kneaded his lower back, he told Graciela that the Americans had replaced an old Galician's warehouse with an armory.

—A pity that we sharpen our own enemies' knives, he whispered, then peered at Graciela. —You're too pretty to be a spy . . .

—¿A woman can't ask questions for herself?

Graciela wrapped the shawl tighter around her shoulders.

—If the yanquis keep weapons in the armory, ¿why are there Dominican guards walking about? Why don't they just take the weapons themselves and do what they got to do, as the real men they claim to be when they show off their stupid uniforms?

—Quite a patriot, the man said. —But you women think things are easy. These yanquis have superior firepower, airpower—

what they call the "Curtis Jennies"—and torture methods more brutal than in the days of the Haitians.

Every so often he looked over his shoulders at the sea's horizon or focused on a steamship that bubbled its way to the dock. He was sitting on his box now, and Graciela was not sure whether to stay and listen or to walk away. The irritating sound of metal was everywhere: dock chains were being pulled, a bell clanged somewhere, a man near the dock hammered a rivet into place, the clink of the beggar's tin cup. Suddenly, gunfire.

—¡And that! Graciela jumped.

—Practice. Soldiers practice on a range back there. His thumb jerked in the direction of the armory.

—You seem like a woman of decency, now that I can see you clearer. Sometimes a woman has a job out here, he said with a wink. —Or she comes to bring her man some food. ¿What brings you here? He stood and picked up his box again.

—I don't come here to work. Don't need to work. I have everything I'll ever need, Graciela said.

—You don't look like a woman who can afford luxuries, with all due respect, the man said, eyeing Graciela's sandals.

—And with all due respect, it's none of your business what luxuries I can and can't give myself.

One of these days, Graciela vowed to herself, she would get her hands on a pair of square-toed, patent-leather shoes.


Graciela found her way back to the narrow streets of the Colonial Quarter.

—Silvio, I wish you'd get out of my mind, so I can just go home, she groaned when a callus on the sole of her foot forced her to lean up against an entranceway. What she would do for a few sips of whatever it was the little boy inside the store behind her was drinking. And perhaps a bite of the almond nougat he was biting into, or some of that sesame candy the elderly woman beside him was unwrapping.

To hell with it, she said to herself, and took off her sandals. Cobblestones in the shade of the buildings were cool against her feet. There were places where water had been thrown from the balconies above, and as she walked, Graciela curled her toes into the stones.

Hurry now, she told herself. The day felt long, as she had been up since before dawn. It was already close to siesta, and she had to get home before dark.

Graciela passed the butcher shop, the smoke shop, the news-stand, a new wig shop, the tailor. She could not help but poke her head into a shop displaying piles of books, quills, and, to her delight, a globe of the world.

—¡No beggars! a man perched on a ladder yelled to Graciela as soon as he saw her loitering in the doorway.

—With a nose longer than a donkey's cock . . . she muttered once she was out of the shop.

—¡Pardon me, there are children of Christ!

Graciela was shocked to bump into a nun who was leading a group of schoolchildren out onto the street. Instantly Graciela's hands went to her mouth, more out of recognition than shame.

—¿Sol Luz, that you? she said, voice still muffled by her hands.

—Such a vocabulary. You have some nerve . . .

The nun made a quick sign of the cross. With her hip she held the convent door open for the last of the children. As if Graciela were not there, they brushed past her and the nun slammed the door shut. Graciela felt a sudden draft on her face—it smelled like damp wood—and that is when she plunged her head into her hands. It was as if that cold draft set fire to a piece of wood hanging inside her chest. The smoke of its burning made her cough and heave, its heat welling up her eyes, steaming up her palms.

—¿Don't you recognize me, Sol Luz? she cried. For a moment her own hacking sobs against the door sounded in her ears like Mercedita's. The heat inside Graciela made her forget her own hunger, put a lunacy in her that made her not care if she looked like a common beggar. Graciela cried over the callus on her foot, the lesions on her hands, and La Gitana's conclusion that too many obstacles stood in her path—he had told Graciela nothing about her fate with Casimiro.

Soon she was tired of weeping; her tremors came from a place inside her that was made not of wood but of a stone that would take a stronger fire to burn. Not here, with stray dogs sniffing at her feet. When her surroundings came back into focus, Graciela realized she was slumped at the foot of the convent doors, her kerchief having fallen from her head. Her body was weary. Those that walked around her glanced briefly, as if she were a brick someone dropped in their path. A child from the balcony across the street waved to Graciela, and after running inside for a few moments emerged with a tin cup tied to a string. She dangled it down to street level, where Graciela thankfully gulped down the water inside.

It was better for Graciela to go home to her family than to see Silvio so sad, trapped in a photograph in some corner of that warehouse, just as she had seen herself reflected in the convent window.

# EVACUATION
## (PURE AND SIMPLE) · 1924

It had taken four years of national and international protest to co-
erce the American troops to pull up camp and leave the country.
For eight years they had stationed themselves in the Dominican
Republic, collecting regular payments on the nation's debt to
the United States—and any other Dominican loot that was there
for the taking. During their stay they built roads and improved
sanitation and education, further compounding the national debt.
Anti-yanqui sentiment had grown among the general population.
Censorship, curfews, courts of military justice, and the torture of
dissidents had stirred popular outrage. Intellectuals launched a
campaign for a "pure and simple disoccupation." Even as the
wealthy enjoyed the spoils of the occupation, protests came from
many sides.

In the wake of the Americans' departure remained a corps of

locals well trained in the tactics of repression. The troops left behind a certain appetite for American goods. In some sugar towns, like San Pedro de Macorís, there grew an affinity for baseball, which, with time, would replace cockfighting as the national sport. The troops also left a trail of deaths and births: mourning mothers and mothers with fair-haired children.

When the Americans left the Dominican Republic, the masses danced merengue with more vehemence than ever.

. . . . .

At Yunco's the accordion whined, challenging the bongos, as some spoke from the waist down and others listened with their eyes. *¡Ay mi negra!* 'Round, left, right, around. *¡Ay, ay, mi negra!* The crooner did not like borrowed women. 'Round, left, right, around, swirl the waist, twitch the hip, quiver the shoulder.

Graciela danced, chewing hard, looking straight ahead over Casimiro's soaked collar as if her swirling waist and twitching hip and quivering shoulder could redeem her previous absence. *No borrowed women, I like no borrowed women. Bass! Left, right, left, mi negra.* She let the merengue vibrate to the ends of her bones.

Left, right, around, the dancers ached with the perico ripia'o rhythms ripping from the arms of the three-man band. The music's pulse steamed away the Sunday drizzle. Yunco's wife had prepared a bottomless pot of seven-meat sancocho, and a healthy dose of rum circulated the crowd, making the blood alive and liquid again in the celebration of freedom.

Drunks danced alone, eyes closed, rum in their left hands, right fists over their hearts. Everyone caught the ping-pong rhythms. Children in crinolines chased each other under and between frenzied legs, losing marbles and coins. The music baby-sat.

*¡Ay mi negra! I like no borrowed women.* Casimiro guided Gra-

ciela tightly against the bass riffs, around the güira's lisp, through the crooner's *ay mi negra*. Under his arms, 'round, left, right, around. Expert in moves of the feet and the arms, he pretzeled her.

Graciela was dizzy with music and musk. The raspy lyrics throbbed in her nostrils. Casimiro's spats and her lace-ups courted each other to the speed of the accordion.

*¡Ay mi negra!* Faster, 'round, left, right, around, and stop. Hip to hip, toe to toe. Then everything was still, but hip and toe.

Everyone clapped on the last note. Yunco's patio smoked. The floor under the thatched-roof bower had taken days of foot stamping and layering of limestone, earth, and water to prepare for dancing. Lanterns burned and their smoke joined that of corncob pipes, cigars, and hand-rolled cigarettes. The gray air and patchouli sweat made noses twitch. Pompeye pomade kept hair of all textures from rising with the steam. A table offered cinnamon-egg-coffee punch, meat patties, and, at midnight, Yunco's wife's unforgettable sancocho.

The band, unemployed since talkies had replaced silent flicks, had gladly traveled down from the north to play perico ripia'os and other merengues. When they had the nerve to start up the popular "Mi hombre" fox-trot, they were booed.

— ¡At Yunco's, no yanquis! ¡At Yunco's, no yanquis!

Disagreements, vendettas, envy, and gossip had all been put aside in the zeal of patriotic celebration. Home was home again. Yunco did not care that his place would have to compete with the local bar, now that the troops were gone. Even the teenaged girls' chaperones sacrificed gossip for mouthfuls of milk candy. Flavia the johnnycake woman was not as mad at Celeste for fooling behind her back with El Gordo. Casimiro himself made numerous trips to Flavia's frying pan, consuming over ten free johnnycakes. And Graciela was not sour with his enjoyment.

—Casi, with so many johnnycakes, you'll turn into El Gordo, she said, with a watered-down-whiskey grin.

—Last thing I want is a belly, or, worse, to share a bed with fried dough, Casimiro said.

—¡Let's dance! she sprang up, nearly knocking down the bench.

The next song was a story about a possessive woman who follows her man to his job, to the store, to the bar, to the barber, to the park. By the time the jealous woman got to the outhouse, Graciela's feet were too tired to continue.

. . . . .

Casimiro had the long, conic fingers of an artist. Just as he had a way with anything that came into his hands, he was a natural with Graciela. There were six fingers on each hand, the extra digits sitting like lima beans on the edges of his hands. He had ignored advice to tie them with string until they dried up and fell away. When he cupped the abundant flesh under Graciela's skirt, she felt as if a river flowed between his fingers and her skin. On some mornings, his fingers wiped the crust from her eyes with a tenderness she did not feel for herself. Never had she seen such delicate and gentle hands on a man. Her own hands were small and rough, like the shells of a walnut. Yet when they met with his, Graciela felt her hands lighten. For Mercedita, Casimiro turned his hands into birds that alighted on her shoulders or laid eggs on her head. On evenings when thunder and rain scared Mercedita, they all sat in the kerosene-lit bedroom making stories from the shadows of their hands. It would be Graciela's quick-moving shadows that chased the other hands up and down the hanging bedsheet, Mercedita's screech of delight drowning out the thunder. And later, when the lamp burned out and Mercedita was sound asleep, Casimiro's hands strolled in Graciela's mass of hair, down her nape to the base of her spine and lower, where his middle finger slipped into the smooth cleft. And Graciela's hands caressed the hollow of his back, nails curling onto pimples, digging into the buttery flesh without mercy.

.   .   .   .   .

There was no mercy in her hands when, with seven-year-old Mercedita in tow, Graciela shadowed Casimiro on his junk-collecting trip: to the store, to Yunco's, to the barber, to the cockfights, to Yunco's again, and, finally, to Flavia the johnnycake woman's bed. Graciela had dressed Mercedita as a boy and dragged her along for access to the more difficult places. It was an all-day affair, and Mercedita whined for a break.

The hard work paid off. Graciela attacked Flavia with her very own hands instead of with a meat cleaver. Casimiro motioned for Mercedita to go outside and sent her a good-hearted double-wink to keep her from crying. As the sharp sounds of fists on flesh filled the room, Casimiro put on his pants and patted down his spring of hair with Pompeye pomade. Graciela had managed to pin Flavia against the shutters for a few seconds, but Flavia freed herself with a well-aimed flurry of blows. Casimiro watched the blur of women for a bit, then carefully stepped around them to join Mercedita outside the cabin.

–Ya, Mercedita. Let's go home.

He dried her tears, and hand in hand they took a leisurely walk home.

A crowd eager for excitement had gathered outside the Johnny-cake House. El Gordo knew there was something wrong with his wife when noon came and there was no smell of frying johnnycake coming through Celeste's window. He had jumped out of Celeste's bed as soon as a neighbor shouted in word of the spectacle. El Gordo found his wife wild-eyed and screaming obscenities. She maintained that Casimiro had come to the house to pick up a special dough she had made for one of his strange projects.

—¿Can't you see he's queerer than a duck? she cried, her face marred by Graciela's scratches.

In this manner Eli Cavalier's syphilis ate its way throughout the town.

# MERCEDITA · *1925*

By the age of eight, Mercedita had found ways to hold on to her elusive and distant mother. She made sure not to speak too much around Mamá Graciela, for fear that her words would paint the far-away glaze in her mother's eyes. Dared not hug Mamá Graciela, so that she would not squirm away in discomfort. When Mamá Graciela was cooking, Mercedita liked to sneak into the bedroom cabin to try on her mother's skirts and blouses. If Mamá Graciela expressed a need for a bath, Mercedita made sure there was a clean towel and enough water in the bath shed. Never did Mamá Graciela have to remind her to do her chores, something she had heard her mother brag about to Celeste. And how angry Mercedita became with Papá Casimiro when he made her mother yell. Keeping Mamá Graciela pleased—even trying to be like her—was Mercedita's insurance that she herself would never be abandoned.

. . .

The hatbox was so faded that the Victorian girl on its lid looked ghostly. Graciela had hidden it from Mercedita, only pulling it from under the bed when she thought her daughter was asleep. One time, when Casimiro came home past supper drunk with disappointment over Saca Ojo's scuffled feathers, Mercedita had heard her mother hissing at him about the sparse coins in the hatbox. And still another night, Mercedita had caught Graciela kicking the box under the bed, her eyes sparking in the moonlight.

Mercedita waited until the day Graciela stepped out to borrow sugar from Santa, who always tangled her mother up in conversation for a good while. Under the bed, Mercedita held her breath — there were spiderwebs woven to the bed legs, defiant against palm brooms and nosy little girls. Like a spider herself, Mercedita crawled out, her mission abandoned.


Mercedita looked up from the washtub bubbling with Santa's smocks. The yard behind Santa's rickety house was littered with bedsheets and towels. The old woman, who chewed words like cud, rocked on a wicker chair, puffing a corncob pipe. Mercedita could feel Santa watching how she rolled cuava soap into the clothes.

—Your mai didn't tell me you were such a good washergirl. Wish my daughter could wash like that, but her goddamned rotten liver . . . Use those hands while ya can, my girl. Before you know, you'll be a bag-a-bones like me, Santa said.

Soapsuds burned the cut on Mercedita's hand.

—¿It's true you have a forked tongue, Santa? Mercedita asked.

—¿Who told you that? Santa had chuckled, face fractured with spiderwebs.

Mercedita attacked a yellowed armpit. Santa swung back and laughed at the zigzag gushing of lather.

—Just like your pai, eager to do all things better than every person.

Squish-squish in the lather louder, the way Mercedita had seen Graciela doing whenever they went out to the river. Mercedita wrung a towel thin as gauze over a ditch. She felt older than her eight years.

—Can't imagine Papá putting on airs, she said, a clothespin bobbing at her lips like a cigarette.

—Oh no no, ma girl. I'm not talkin' about Casimiro, Santa drawled. Sucked cheeks made the embers in her pipe glow.

¿And which riddle was this now? Santa spoke with a creepy tongue, if not of spirits and ghosts, of La Cigüapa, and three-headed yanquis. Mercedita clipped towels to the clothesline. Smiled at her own foolishness.

—Oh Santa, Papá the stork. Don't think I don't know about how chichís come.

Santa squinted, as if trying to sharpen a blurry memory.

—No, my girl, not Casimiro. Fool stayed with your mai the way she was after your real pai died dead.

Santa settled back. This time one eye squinted against tobacco smoke and the bright silver clouds.

Lather dripped— spiders crawled— from Mercedita's arms as she glared at Santa.

—Know things, my girl. Know these things.

Rocked some more, puffed on her evil pipe.

—Look how big you are now. Soon a señorita. You hide those little grapes under that dress there, like Graciela tryin' to cover the sun with her finger.

A nail dug in her voice. Made Mercedita's nose burn. Mercedita shuddered at the thought of her own chest bulging like that naked madwoman's, whom she had once witnessed cursing by the roadside.

Mercedita rinsed the last rag, splashed the pail of dirty water at squawking chickens. Santa rocked in silence. Bedsheets fluttered on the clothesline.

—Mmm-hmm. A man named Silvio was your pai, my girl.

Lids like a lizard's shut for a nap.

Mercedita did not claim the bit of money she was due. She ran home holding in the anvil at her chest until she reached the bath shed. Under the hive of wasps, she vomited.

—¡Mercedita! Graciela squinted through the spaces in the planks.

Graciela wondered if her daughter's sobs meant that Mercedita had been afflicted with the bleeding disease at a terribly young age. Mercedita's face was crosshatched with platinum light, and Graciela remembered the coming rainstorm, then undid the wire that held the door closed. There was a sharp smell of bile.

—Come. Graciela put a firm arm around Mercedita and led her across the yard, through to the main cabin, past the partition of their beds.

—¡Crying like a chichí! Graciela said, her hands soft with compassion.

Mercedita was afraid to speak, until Graciela's gentleness broke her moans. —Papa Casimiro's not mine . . . Then the sobs started up all over again.

—And who—

—Santa, she said it. A man named Silvio . . .

The sobs were uncontrollable now and the slap to Mercedita's cheek came razor-quick.

—Stop the crocodile tears, Graciela said, her voice cracking.
—Santa said nothing, you hear?

Before Mercedita could crumble again, Graciela had already gathered her skirt and run out of the house, across the road to Santa's.

It was only a few months later that Mercedita remembered the hatbox when Graciela was off borrowing honey from Celeste. By then she was less afraid of spiders. This time, she emerged from under the bed victorious, her long black braids lightly powdered, the hatbox in her hands.

Since Santa's betrayal and Graciela's long silence, Casimiro had brought Mercedita more suckers than he did Graciela, and even a yanqui apple once. Still, Mercedita had turned fresh-mouthed with Casimiro when he refused to let her go to the river with friends. After Mercedita yelled at Casimiro that he was not her real father, Graciela made her kneel on rice and whipped her up good with a wet branch. No more visits to Santa, nor was Mercedita to entertain real-father-lies with anyone else, Graciela had made that very clear. But just months ago, Santa had fallen ill and, easing her grudge, Graciela made the old woman some guinea soup and bread pudding. And now, Graciela seemed to be back to her most cheerful self.

Inside the hatbox Mercedita found papers that smelled like uncooked rice. She gasped at something black and furry amidst the papers, then saw it was a lock of delicate hair bound with ribbon. There was a palm-leaf crucifix Padre Orestes made for them one Palm Sunday. She also found a porcelain thimble, a photograph of a white-skinned bride and groom, a teacup and saucer, a bar of soap, and a catalogue with pictures of all sorts of things, from chairs to pomade. Wrapped in newspaper was a stiff and flattened cord the color of eggplant that, unbeknownst to Mercedita, once linked her to her mother. She unstuck the cord from the page— wished she could decipher the tightly packed ink underneath, as Mustafá the storekeeper could. A glass rosary dribbled out of some tissue.

¡Squawking at the front of the house! Mercedita threw everything into the box, kicked it under the bed with the same haste as her mother. She strung the glass beads around her neck and tucked them under her blouse.

—¡Mercedita!

After helping Graciela sweep the cabin, feed the chickens, scrub the outhouse, rinse the rice, get water from the pump, change the bedsheets, wash Casimiro's sweaty clothes, mend a skirt, and, finally, pick the peas from their pods, Mercedita sat under the almond tree behind the house. Peppered by the shadow of leaves, she removed the rosary.

—Diaaablo . . . Mercedita whistled. The glass beads lit tiny rainbows on the palms of her hands.

. . . . .

Casimiro studied Mercedita from across the table, then sucked on his cigarette. It was a new habit he had picked up, and Mercedita liked the way his eyes squinted when he puffed out smoke. With Graciela retreated to her bed, wincing with aches, Mercedita felt daring. She knew she did not have to whisper and earlier that evening had begged Casimiro to let her try a puff. He had finally given in; Mercedita always knew how to appeal to his childlike sense of subversion. She had learned how to suck in her cheeks and inhale—not swallow—the smoke. Within minutes she felt dizzy, and the waves of nausea made her realize how incomprehensible adults and their habits were. But Casimiro ordered her to finish the entire cigarette, until Mercedita threatened to wake up Graciela and tell on him.

—Now you know never to indulge in vices, he said and left the cabin to go to the kitchen shed.

—Papá, tell me the truth, Mercedita confronted Casimiro after he had gone through the trouble of starting up the hearth to boil some anise tea for her queasy belly. —¿Are you my real father?

—¿I thought you were trying to finish up the numbers Mustafá gave you? Casimiro said. Mercedita sipped from her cup, then chewed on her pencil. From the wrinkles around Casimiro's eyes she could tell he was proud to see her scratching out addition and subtraction problems on the brown paper.

—You're too dark, Mercedita said and rested her arms beside the pale sheet of cassava bread on the table. Then Mercedita waved her numbers in the air and exclaimed that he was even darker than the piece of paper.

—¿Has Santa been putting this father garbage in your head again? Casimiro said. Mercedita could hear the absence of the usual mirth in his voice. —¿Am I not enough father for you, Mercedita, that you have to go looking elsewhere?

When Mercedita saw Casimiro's jaw harden, she decided not to pursue her questions any further.

The numbers Mustafá had carefully written out for her no longer excited her. She bent down to color inside the fours and the eights, she turned the threes into little fat men, and she scribbled away the addition and subtraction signs.

—Let me never hear you mention fathers again, ¿you hear? Casimiro said in a way that made the wrinkles disappear from around his eyes. He grabbed her pencil and tilted her chin up to make her look at him. Mercedita could smell the tobacco on his fingers. She decided that when she was grown she would never smoke or lie to children.

Often Casimiro came home to find Mercedita waiting for him on the porch.

—I thought the black boogeyman put you in his sack, she liked to say each time. Casimiro would charge like a bull and drape her on his shoulders and threaten to throw her down the latrine. It was a game they had played for years, even when alcohol slurred his growls, even when Graciela complained about the noise.

—¡People must think we're animals! she would shout above Mercedita's yells. They chased each other around the household as if Graciela were not there, in a fit of giggles that grew louder with Graciela's annoyance. The terror funneling through Mercedita was magnificent; her body would flip into the air and fall into Casimiro's solid arms. The surrender to free-fall pumped laughter through her veins, a laughter Mercedita had found so hard to taste otherwise. When Graciela saw her ecstasy with Casimiro, she tried to secure her own favors with her by not scolding Mercedita thereafter.

—Teach me how to fight, Papá, Mercedita asked Casimiro on the day she turned eight. They were both out of breath. She could feel the heat thumping around her head and between her legs in the coolness of the evening. Horseplay was always fun, but now she wanted to try her hand at being the aggressor.

—¿Why would I ruin a charm like you? Casimiro was hunched over and whooping in gulps of air. —I'm getting too old . . .

—I think Mercedita is getting too old for this, Graciela said. She had finished washing the dinner dishes and had gone out to the yard to throw the dirty water right by Mercedita and Casimiro's muddy feet.

—Just isn't right no more for a girl to be playing like that with her father.

—Your mai's right, Casimiro said to Mercedita once Graciela had gone back into the kitchen shed.

—¿But what did I do? Mercedita asked. She was sick of being scolded. It seemed the women around her could not keep from wagging their fingers at her; if it wasn't her mother, it was Mai or Celeste or Santa.

—Everything I do now is wrong, she said and crossed her arms. The immense night sky above her made her feel even smaller.

—You just have to be more mindful. A growing girl like you has to protect herself against all kinds of bad elements, Casimiro said. He reached out to button her blouse to the top and wipe a smudge of mud from her cheek. —Go. Go help her finish cleaning up the kitchen.

· · · · ·

Mercedita could not understand why her mother had suddenly limited her runs to Mustafá's, until she overheard her talking to Celeste.

—. . . and you can see her tiny waist, even with the blouse tucked in . . .

And Mercedita knew Graciela had whiffed the sweet-sour musk that had recently begun emanating from the sleeves of her blouses. Mustafá must have, too.

—¿Where did you get this soap from? Graciela had asked Mercedita, after a scent of lavender sent her shivering out of the bath shed. Graciela claimed to have found the fancy soap on the floor of the shed, though Mercedita always made sure to hide it after every use.

—Mustafá gave it to me, Mercedita said. —Mamá, look at the dress I made for the doll. Wait till I make you one.

She held up the rag doll, whose calico dress Graciela fingered slowly.

—No more give-aways from that man, ¿you hear? Graciela scolded. —Just isn't right to take things on credit after that poor man's fire, she added in a softer voice.

—But he said it was a gift . . .

—¡Bah! No such thing as gifts from men, Graciela said. —I don't know if at Celeste's you've heard the story El Viejo Cuco liked to tell, about the "Li'l Greedy Gal."

—¿Who's she? Mercedita asked. She had already heard the stupid story several times, but wanted to see how Graciela would tell it. And, for the first time, Graciela sat next to Mercedita long enough to tell her a story.

—Once there was a little girl who'd go to everyone's house in the village, saying she hadn't eaten dinner . . .

# CHRIST'S HAREM · *1929*

Casimiro's joy of life stuck to Graciela like misery. In the nine years she had lived with Casimiro, Graciela (and everyone else) had begun to suspect that he was sterile. There had been many times she had forgotten, or could not afford to travel across town to get her herbs. That Graciela did not want more children did not matter; Casimiro's sterility shamed her more than that long-ago johnnycake tryst with Flavia, more than his penchant for moonshine, more than his good-natured laziness. And years ago the late Viejo Cuco had told her how ugly such a useless man made her.

At twenty-six, Graciela knew she was coming well into her years. Already she could see men who used to turn their eyes on her start turning them toward Mercedes. She did not feel like an ugly woman, poor as she was; she knew what the lingering glances meant, from men and women alike, when they were in her presence. And many times she found she could not resist the advances of the occasional cane worker who called out to her on the way to the market. There had been others, too. But she knew better than to shit where she ate, making her regular escapes from Casimiro to "visit her grandfather's grave." Always Casimiro nodded, with the calm acceptance that never ceased to confuse Graciela. Yet since Flavia, she had not known of any other woman.

—That is your other woman, she would tell Casimiro whenever he pulled the flask from his pocket.

· · · · ·

Mercedes was an ever-present eye. She was a girl of few words, like her other father, Silvio. Sometimes Graciela would catch her staring from a distance. When their eyes met, Graciela would glance away quickly, finding it hard to focus her gaze on those penetrating eyes. Mercedes would walk away. Must be that affliction, Graciela thought, since Mercedes, already twelve years old, had started her menses. No longer could Graciela write her daughter off as a child. It scared her to see Mercedes' poise, no matter what went on around her—scared Graciela, because she could already see in her own daughter the maturity she herself lacked.

—This one's haughty. Too good for talk 'cause she got it in her head that her blood is milk, Graciela told Celeste.

—In the end, Graciela, you pay for everything.

Not everything from the kiosk was paid for, Graciela was to find out. On the rare occasions she did send her daughter to buy goods from Mustafá, Mercedita would return much later than expected, with coins still jingling in her apron pockets.

—I only asked for a pound of sugar, ¿why'd you get two, Mercedita? Graciela demanded.

—Be happy your order was doubled, Mamá. And I told you to call me Mercedes.

It was the kind of reply that made Graciela want to crush the cartilage of Mercedita's ears between her fingers. She tried to hold herself back, remembering her own battles with Mai at that age. But the day Graciela saw Mercedita tying her hair in bright-colored ribbons and announcing that she was off to get cinnamon to make some sweet beans, it was too much.

—¿Since when do we make sweet beans on a weekday, Mercedita? Graciela yelled.

—I said . . . Mercedita began, and before Graciela knew it, she was pulling at her daughter's hair, until the colored ribbons fanned out like a rainbow on the ground. Mercedita held her temples. Graciela then walked her inside the house by the corner of an ear.

—¡Papá! ¡Papá! Mercedita screeched while curled up in a ball on the bed. Graciela was glad that Casimiro was not at home. The last thing she needed was for him to be telling her how to keep her own daughter—not his—out of trouble, because oh, how she herself knew all about trouble.

—You stay put, she said to Mercedita before running over to Mustafá's.

Mustafá the Widower, as he was now called, folded his arms when Graciela stormed into the kiosk and banged on his counter. She was surprised to also find Casimiro there, stuffing Mustafá with jokes and drinking chilled maví. Her anger was big enough for the two of them.

—I know you're in search of another woman, she said, —but you put those eyes elsewhere, ¿you hear?

Casimiro's familiar chuckle made her fists curl.

—Casimiro, your woman is out of control, Mustafá said. Casimiro put his hand on Graciela's arm and she shoved it away.

—Keep it up, Mustafá, and I'll tell everyone that the Turks put this kiosk up for you, she said, not knowing how else to threaten him—there were few weapons in her armory.

—Too bad you don't know how good that girl is with numbers, Mustafá replied. He turned around to arrange some items on the shelves, leaving Graciela fuming over the nature of his comment.— *Your woman is out of control,* she repeated under her breath. A foolish man like Casimiro was supposed to control her when she herself felt that her core was unhinging and becoming a gooey, runny mass.

·  ·  ·  ·  ·

Graciela's feverish headaches and achy bones and joints had subsided, but the red lesions on her hands had slowly spread to her face. And when she washed, she felt a difference between her legs. She knew she had been sick since returning from the north years ago. No matter what anyone said, Graciela believed that her illness had grown in the hole Silvio's departure had left inside her. Celeste had pulled her aside and asked her about the syphilis, saying that one of the floozies from Yunco's knew it when she saw it, that they could get her the mercury treatments. But Graciela could not explain to anyone that a yanqui-man had put a different curse on her and Silvio long ago; he had put roots of light on them more potent than anyone in town ever could.

One morning, Graciela had the idea of taking one of Casimiro's mirror pieces to the bath shed. The shaky mirror revealed folds of flesh she never before thought existed where so much pain and pleasure had passed. All her life she knew the place by feel and smell, never equating it with the rubbery layers of gray-brown and pink. She could not distinguish healthy tissue from the sickly tissue she suspected, and with alarm concluded that the gray-brown areas were dying.

In a dream she saw the statue of La Virgen de la Altagracia beckoning to her from La Pola's. La Altagracia's hands were spread apart in welcome. They had stigmata, open wounds like the ones Graciela had seen in the wedge of mirror. Each wound opened and closed, its lips producing harmonizing arias that softened the bitterness in Graciela's spirit. Then the warmth turned cold. A finger in the sky had blocked the sun. The lips on La Altagracia's hands closed and became slugs that crawled up to her wrists. Whiteness spread across the paint on La Altagracia, and she turned to a pillar of salt. Graciela woke with the image of slugs fizzling into raisins.

. . . . .

This time Graciela packed nothing.

—I am going away, she told Casimiro, numbness slackening her mouth.

He had been sanding the side of a small canoe in the yard.

—Do as you please, woman. Your demons stink already.

For a while there was silence between them, except for the sha-sha of the sanding belt.

—Casimiro, it is that I—

—¿Who took your spirit, woman? To leave me, and that girl almost grown . . .

Graciela's voice rose. —I'm just tired. I'm sick of you, she said with a stamp of a foot.

The canoe shook in Casimiro's hands as his tears wet its surface. That he did not bother to dry them struck Graciela.

—No, Graciela, you're sick of yourself.

She chewed on a tender spot behind her lips. She could not understand what ravenous hole in her spirit made her want to jump out of her skin. A hole that, with time, had left her cold toward Casimiro and Mercedes and that now kept her own tears at bay. Cold that turned her heart to wood, just like the heart Casimiro had carved for Graciela when he was still wooing her. ¿Would he have strung that oak heart around her neck had he known what was to come? The very thought of herself like this, so unfeeling toward a man and child she was supposed to love, made her hate herself.

For a moment, Graciela considered confiding in Casimiro of the other part of her that La Gitana had said was roaming, about that warehouse and Silvio, the yanqui-man, Eli, La Pola, Ana, Humberto. But now was not a good time for divulging. Too much was already broken between her and Casimiro.

—I've decided to go to the mercy nuns in the Colonial Quarter, she said, hoping to ease Casimiro's judgment.

—To a harem of Christ. ¿And for what, Graciela? His eyes were dry again.

—La Altagracia came to me in a dream . . .

And suddenly her dream, however powerful it had been the night before, seemed silly.

—¿And did La Altagracia also happen to tell you what to do with Mercedes? Casimiro put down the sanding belt and folded his hands.

Graciela tightened her belly in an even greater effort not to laugh at the thought of La Altagracia doling out such specific instructions.

—Celeste and Mai agreed to mind her until my return.

Casimiro's face remained so expressionless that Graciela could not stand it.

—So now you can go on kneading Flavia's dough and empty-
ing Yunco's kegs and making junk outta junk and tending to your
cocks, she said with a shiver from the sudden chill that spiraled up
her spine.

Then without further words, Casimiro began to sand away the
wet spot his tears had left on the canoe.


Telling her daughter goodbye was more difficult. Graciela took her
to the riverbank, where she bought her a caramel sucker. ¿Why the
trip to the riverbank? asked Mercedes, more vocal than she had
ever been. Then she asked why they were going to Celeste's if
Graciela was not going to the market. Graciela said it would only
be for a bit, until she came back from church, and no, Mercedes
could not go with her. But Mercedes asked again why they were
going to Celeste's. ¿Why did Papá cry? ¿Why are your eyes so
funny? ¿Why do I still need to stay at Celeste's when I'm already a
señorita? ¿And why don't you ever tell me about Silvio?

A girl spreads her arms toward her and calls out Graciela's
name. This is Graciela's lasting image of her daughter.

.　.　.　.　.

Graciela arrived on foot at the Colonial Quarter. The quadrangle
towers of the church of Nuestra Señora de la Mercedes had faithfully guided her like a constellation. Her knees had swollen tight,
as had her hands and ankles. It had been a long walk from home,
the sun bearing down on her, the hillside winds blowing dust into
her ears . . .

*I call you, Graciela, but you just let my voice echo. Too drunk on
the silly path, too high on the weeds along the way. But know that
you always walk toward the light, even when you sit along the road*

*for a sip of water or to pick at the calluses on your feet. You will al-*
*ways walk.*

The church's coolness this time was welcoming. Noon sun and a
growing fever had flushed Graciela's skin. She removed her straw
hat and made the sign of the cross, hoping the abrupt shift in tem-
perature would not shock her face into paralysis. Colored blocks of
sunlight burned into the darkness, illuminating pews, statues, and
slices of floor. Graciela remembered that as a child she had ached
to stand inside a block of light. Now she slipped toward the blue.
Then the yellow. The red.

The statue of Christ bleeding was washed in a block of white
light. On his head, the crown of thorns looked like diamonds.
Fuchsia blood on his hands and feet, the only sign of his agony.

Across the church stood La Altagracia in a diorama, Joseph
looking over her shoulder at their child. She was fair. Her open
hands were pure, but her heart was aflame and entangled in a web
of thorns. Graciela rubbed the statue's plaster heart, wondering
whether Casimiro had finished the canoe she had left him building. A pain in her chest forced her to sit on the nearest pew. She
closed her eyes, not knowing what to say in prayer; whether to beg
forgiveness, or ask for help, or give thanks, or simply curse her
pains. In the block of sunlight she fell fast asleep . . .

. . . *always toward the light.*

When she woke, the sunlight had shifted to the eastern side
of the church. Graciela was bathed in cold sweat. Preparations
were under way for evening Mass. A priest and a choirboy spoke in
hushed tones by the altar as they put fresh flowers in vases. Occasionally, they looked over their shoulders at Graciela. Rising from
the pew was difficult on account of her swollen joints.

—'Scuse me, Padre, ¿where is it I can find the nuns?

Her voice cracked the stillness of the church. Scratchy and loud, it was not the church voice of pious nuns who could dissolve holy toast neatly on their tongues and who could address a priest only when spoken to. Yet the priest conceded with a buenas tardes and exit here and turn there and you will find the convent and may the Lord guard you from all sins.

A nun opened the door to the convent of Nuestra Señora de la Mercedes. She peered past Graciela out to the street before addressing her.

—¿Buenas tardes? she said, more question than greeting.

—Buenas y tardes, Graciela said. —I am sick and have nowhere to go. ¿Is it possible for me to stay?

Wrinkles gathered on the nun's forehead. From her grasp on the doorknob, Graciela knew her concern was more about following rules than helping an ailing person at the door. The nun peeked down the street again, then ushered Graciela inside.

—Wait here, please. I must consult with the Superior. This is not a public inn, her voice clicked in the darkness. She motioned for Graciela to sit in the small lobby and disappeared down a hall.

Somber portraits of harsh-looking women in wimples and habits hung in the lobby. Books behind protective glass lined an entire wall. A small table displaying a collection of miniature crucifix sculptures made Graciela wish she had brought her hatbox along. Occasionally, other nuns walked by, and with a simple nod, acknowledged Graciela. Their black habits brushed the floor as they walked. ¿How would she stand the heat had she to wear so much cloth on her head and around her neck and chin? Graciela came to the convent not to give her life to the Lord, but because it was the only safe place she thought she could go to be free from the cage of her day-to-day. She hoped to recover from her mysterious ailment, eat better, perhaps even learn the letters. Those veils must be part of the torture of getting closer to God, she thought, and hoped that her stay would not require her to surrender to such a demanding relationship.

The convent was ancient. High ceilings reminded those who entered that they were mere insects of God. Each floor had a balcony facing the street, a secret treat for holy women who had to be chaperoned outside of the convent and were forbidden to mention any man's name but Christ's. Adobe walls bounced the daily sound of bells around the patio, which the nuns kept perpetually in bloom and fragrant. Such charm—a product of creativity and fastidious cleanliness—did not betray the paltry amount of money the church allocated to the convent. Because the church had temporarily stopped funding the small school for children, the nuns had turned their disappointment and extra time to study, prayer, household duties, and other labors.

The first nun returned just as Graciela was tenuously approaching the world globe on a shelf by the books.

—The Superior will see you. She is very busy, so do not waste her time with foolishness, she whispered.

Graciela followed her down the hall. After a sudden turn, she saw again a life-size Jesus; this time he grimaced in all his bloody agony. In the corner of the adjacent room an emaciated woman sat behind a desk.

—¿What ails you, creature? the Superior asked Graciela. Her

vestments were of a lighter hue than the other nuns'. She was far tinier than Graciela had expected, yet she seemed a force not to be fooled with.

—I don't know, Señora —

—You are to call me Madre. I am no one's señora, except the Lord's, the Superior's voice cut in.

—I'm feverish, and these rashes . . . Graciela held out her palms like La Virgen de la Altagracia.

—. . . and you've asked to stay here, I am told. Understand that though we are Ladies of Mercy, this is neither a clinic nor an inn, the Superior answered.

—We have not the funds to open our doors to so many of the suffering—and I am sure you come without dowry. Our school has recently been suspended at the expense of the Jesuits. ¿Where is your family, may I ask?

—I don't have a family, Madre. Graciela massaged the meat of her palms. She hoped telling lies in a convent would not further jeopardize her health, but she had already come too far to be turned away.

—I've come here alone and sick, as you see. If I am a cause of trouble here then I'll leave. God squeezes but he doesn't choke, Graciela said.

The Superior smiled slightly.

—Words of wisdom to keep this place alive, she addressed the other nun. With a deep breath she summoned the nun closer and whispered a few words into her ear. Then she turned to Graciela.

—Many women come here to give their lives to the Lord. It is not an easy life, they find. We have many rules here. Saying yes to the way of the cross is harder than anyone imagines. And we live simply.

· · ·

Graciela was not to appear in public. She was not to start a conversation and would demonstrate her virtue with silence and humility. If she felt she must engage in conversation, she was not to prolong it. She would confine any discussion to work and nothing else. She should never be idle. She would bear her cross like all the other nuns, though she was neither a novice nor a postulant, but a guest who must ask permission for everything. Convent life was built on three legs: poverty, chastity, and obedience. Graciela must put her flesh to death, so that her love becomes solely focused on God's will. Through prayer and the rosary she could overcome the demands of the body, kill its urges. She must accept the constant presence of only three persons in her life: God, Christ, and the Blessed Virgin Mary. If ever she should feel the onset of loneliness or despair, it could only be because she is no longer expressing love the way that she must. Therefore, she must not make friends.

It was Sol Elisa who had first opened the door for her. She guided Graciela to a small room under a flight of stairs in the back of the house. The room was furnished with only a bed and a nightstand. In addition to a washbasin and bar of soap, a small statue of La Virgen de la Altagracia sat on top of the nightstand. Her face, once delicately detailed, was chipped. She was a faceless woman with her arms spread.

—Sol Candida's old room, Sol Elisa said, without elaborating. The change in her normal routine and a lingering connection to the outside had straightened out her brow.

—¿Where is Sol Candida now? Graciela asked.

—Gone. She was not an appropriate servant of the Lord.

. . .

Graciela awoke always in darkness, when the first nun up for dawn vigil initiated the creaking of the stairs above. How she wished to shake the feeling of being walked on by moving the bed from under the slanted ceiling, but there was no other way to situate the bed in the tiny, claustrophobic room.

Within a few days Graciela was shaken into the rigid routines of the convent. Though only a guest, she still had to adhere to the life of the nuns. Every night she removed the drab dress she had been given in the same manner, folded it on her chair, also making sure that her sandals lay in the form of a cross at the foot of her bed. It was a hard and cold bed, made colder by the little bit of hair left on her head. On her first day, Graciela's thick mass of braids had been shorn and offered to La Virgen de la Altagracia. The Mother Superior had made Graciela discard her kerchief, as there were no combs or mirrors for grooming. Caught glancing at her reflection on a polished brass surface, the Superior had scolded her.
—This is no place for vanities. You must destroy your ego and prepare yourself for eternal life.

Graciela's day was divided between the chapel, the kitchen, the workroom, and the garden. At four A.M., a bell, and then the creaking just inches from her face woke her for early vigil. Already she knew which cracks in her door eased in the first thin strips of candlelight from the seven candles of the hallway altar. Upon strict orders of the Superior, she had less than five minutes to wash her face in the basin, dress, and head to the kitchen, where she was to bake the breakfast breads and brew the coffee. The nuns would come in after vigil with contained hunger. All were polite, acknowledging her presence without a word. Then she had to begin peeling and chopping the vegetables for the noontime and evening soups, which she was not allowed to season. By the third day, hunger had begun to twist inside of her, especially at night. ¿How could she live without sugar, without salt, without conversation or laughter? And then, between her kitchen duties, she had more work: helping the nuns make church vestments for the priests, as well as washing piles of laundry for both the convent and the priests. Salvation through prayer, seclusion, and mortification. But Sol Elisa, in an effort to defend her own life, told Graciela that through this suffering, the loved ones who are already in Purgatory will be sooner delivered to heaven.

Despite the Superior's disapproval, Sol Elisa found that Graciela frequently possessed her to break the Grand Silence. Whether out weeding in the garden or washing down the floors of the chapel, Sol Elisa found ways to whisper. She herself had been delivered to the convent as a child in the time of the Occupation. At seven years old, soldiers had come into her home asking for her grand-father, a known gavillero who had organized major anti-yanqui bat-tles in the hills. When Elisa's grandmother denied having seen him all day, the child innocently piped up that she had run into him earlier that afternoon at the home of So-and-so. For Elisa, the ten years she had spent at the convent were less a sentence than a gift to her murdered grandfather.

—I waited on a long line to get born. Pushed the weaker souls aside, Graciela whispered back. —Mai had four little devils, one after another. All of them died after she laid them. Then I came. I had to be big in this life. That's what the elders said. Mai never said nothin' like that. Wished I was a boy to make Pai happy. You're uglier than a running monkey, she used to say if she thought I was too happy. My younger brother could burn down a village if he wanted. The elders warned Mai, Try to make something of that girl. Send her to the nuns to learn to read the Bible.

. . .

At night, Graciela often broke out in cold a sweat. Mercedes' open arms haunted her and Graciela would pinch her eyes shut to slowly play out the fantasy of the moment her arms embraced her daughter. Other times, in her ache to wrap her legs around Casimiro, she would grind herself against her balled-up dress. So much hunger in her body; hunger so unbearable that on a couple of occasions she dared to scavenge in the garbage barrels in the courtyard for carrot and potato peelings. But just when she sated some of the gnawing in her stomach, the pains in her bones and muscles would start up. What kept her from leaving the convent was her hope that her fervent prayers during vigil would stop what felt like the slow disintegration of her body. She held on to the Superior's words:

—Put the flesh to death so that your love becomes focused on God's will.

But in moments of agonizing pain and unbearable hunger, words were merely symbolic.

—¿What is your will, what the hell is your will with me? she cried, biting hard on the head of the statue.

When sleep finally did come, Graciela's dreams seemed to drag her through other bodies. In those worlds, beastly interrogators grew long prongs from their shoulders. A guardia bashed her teeth in with textbooks. She even wore a dress made of rotten fish. And a few times Mai sat on her bed and picked lice from her head.

—Something in me is leaking, was the only way Graciela knew to explain her nightly battles to Sol Elisa.

—It is that you lose your way in prayer, Graciela. Your mind is poisoned with the garbage that lies outside the convent doors.

The dreams continued. In one, rats chewed at the calluses of Graciela's heels. She tore through dense forest, her heels further ripping on thorns and exposed tree roots. Fear of rats, then of running guardias, then of slave-hunters with dogs. Above her the sky was India ink, punctured by a bright white crack of light. Graciela came upon a mammoth coral reef flanked by coconut trees. The cluster of coral came together to form a pair of lips, from which came a heartbeat. She climbed the coral and slid deep into the cave's center. The smell was of old sea barges and Graciela found a pan of frying fish. Instinctively she stuffed some crispy pieces in her mouth.

*Be leery of free things; they fatten their piglets before the feast.*

—Any port in a storm, Graciela responded, and she licked her cuticles.


—Don't think no one knows about your nightly raids into the courtyard, Sol Elisa said the next time Graciela complained about her dreams.

—I'm ailing. ¿What can milk three times a week do for me? Graciela said, feeling as if her bones would crack.

—You are poisoning your prayers, I tell you, Sol Elisa insisted.

Graciela watched Sol Elisa savor the rare porridge they had been allowed to break their three-day fast with. How she wanted to smash Sol Elisa's mouth with the wooden bowl.

—People like you turn off the moon, Graciela said, so loud that the rest of the nuns at the table stopped eating.

—I believe, Sol Elisa whispered slowly, referring to Graciela's illness for the first time, —that the syphilis has taken you far, far away.

Song Two

# MERCEDES · *1930*

Mercedes held Fufa, the hen she had raised for five years on bits of other hens, flapping beneath her grip. With a swift and accurate blow she brought the machete down on its neck, let the headless body make crimson circles on the dirt before taking it to the kitchen for boiling. With efficient strokes she swept up the feathers and nudged the blood into the dirt.

—You kill with such gusto for a lovely soldier of God. The voice was nasal.

Andrés leaned against a tree, watching the sauciness of Mercedes' walk. His short arms crossed in front of him, bright green eyes glimmered. At eighteen years of age and four feet ten inches tall, Andrés was officially a dwarf.

What nerve of Bow-Legged Dog, to stand there comfortable as a tree. No wonder people called him by the Devil's nickname. A quick prayer urged the thought out of Mercedes' mind.

—Go away, Andrés. You know I don't buy your stinking lottery tickets.

Her friendship with his sister, Odepia, was not going to make Andrés' babbling any juicier to her ears. Nor was Graciela's departure a year ago, or Casimiro's recent death from male matters, which in a short time had toughened Mercedes.

Mercedes preferred a friendship with Odepia, who carried girth like a precious liquid, and had been able to slacken the lines of grief already hardening around Mercedes' mouth. Odepia's parents and seven siblings had made it their duty to pass by the house daily, with food, greetings, and surrogate warmth.

Also thirteen, Odepia found Mercedes' empty house a haven. Mercedes already outraged neighbors with her cool refusal to live with her sour grandparents, Mai and Pai. Refused, too, Odepia's family's offer, as well as Celeste's suggestion that her eldest son take over the house with his new wife. Mercedes stood her ground, despite harsh comparison with that "mare-assed runaway mother of hers." Neighbors, then, made sure to keep sharp eyes on the comings and goings about the house. By washing and ironing clothes from her home, and sometimes helping Mustafá in the kiosk, Mercedes was able to eat decent meals with no other orders but from God Himself.

Mercedes and Odepia outtalked each other about the Almighty Lord Their God Padre Santo Omnipotente as the weekends would exhaust themselves across the sky. They showed up tightly combed at every Mass, ready to belt out prayers and show off their fire.

Each Sunday, Mercedes held her shaking hands together, howled on the steps of the altar. Sundays stilled the fear that had lodged inside her, deadly as a razor blade. Prayer eased rage. With prayers louder than the mumbling around her, Mercedes could fade Graciela's face from her mind.

*Señor ten piedad.*

Mercedes asked for mercy on the Sunday of her thirteenth birthday for having paid a long-faced woman to ignite candles. Make my runaway mother miserable, she had told the woman, who with Mercedes' wash money could bribe the cluster of saints. Bigger, Mercedes had told the woman to open the sores in Graciela's flesh, let them bleed raw, ravage her face with roads.

—Don't you worry, dear. I'll make sure your mai never returns, the long-faced woman assured Mercedes with a sign of the cross.

But for two nights thereafter, Mercedes had sweat-drenched nightmares in which fish rotted in her own mouth, while rats chewed at the calluses of her mother's heels. Mercedes knew that her simple prayers thereafter would not be able to close the sores on Graciela's skin. And the long-faced woman refused to undo her handiwork the next day, afraid of backpedaling from the higher forces.

At Mass a week later, many hands held Mercedes when she collapsed at the altar. She could hear the older women weeping for this innocent orphan. Mercedes' own sobs were hollow, and though she convulsed her body, she could not get her eyes to tear. But she knew she had convinced the congregation that an unfortunate girl like herself, abandoned by her evil mother and orphaned by her benevolent stepfather, had every right to be greedy with the Holy Spirit.

. . . . .

After the withdrawal of American troops from the Dominican Republic, the government of Horacio Vásquez created the illusion of a pacific and democratic environment between 1924 and 1930. Citizens were relieved from having to trade more stories of atrocities at the hands of the yanquis. Everyone was eager to hear, instead, stories of progress and peace, such as the one of the West Indian Aerial Express Company that flew passengers and mail between the Dominican Republic, Cuba, Haiti, and Puerto Rico. People rejoiced at the news that telephones were being installed; that schools previously unable to pay yanqui taxes were being re-opened; that reinforced concrete was being used to build modern, two-story buildings; that aqueducts would replace wells. Sumptuous Mediterranean-style houses lined the more affluent streets. There was work, money, abundance, peace, well-being.

Amid this belle epoque of travel, luxury, and social clubs for a minority of the population, Horatio Vásquez turned a blind eye to the true self-cannibalization of the nation, as the personal fortunes of government officials mushroomed on empty promises of public—often unnecessary—works. So unwilling was Vásquez to curtail such rampant corruption, that protests by non-Horacistas were called "mermaid's songs."

. . . . .

*. . . that they should be with Him, and that He may send them forth to preach, and to have power to heal sicknesses, and to cast out devils.*

—It's not worth all that, the question of God, Andrés said when he saw the purple prayer calluses on Mercedes' knees. He liked to make his daily appearance in the kitchen shed around the time Mercedes coated her steel pots with clay.

Andrés shared news from the newspaper reader he frequented.

—Life goes on as usual: President Vásquez is out of the country, and the wolves in the palace are licking their chops.

—The Lord better keep an eye on the Head of the Army. I just don't trust that Trujillo and all his guns . . . with our president so sickly, Mercedes said while she rotated a clay-smeared pot over the hearth to dry.

—You talk as if that Vásquez puts bread on your table, Meche.
Andrés watched Mercedes poke at the coals in the fire.

—Well, there's much more progress all around. Why, Yunco's
even talking about installing one of those telephones at the bar,
Mercedes said.

—Progress is never for the needy, Andrés said.

—Ah, needy is all in the head. Christ was a carpenter. What
we all need to do is work. Look, with all this Horacista progress,
there're now plenty of construction jobs in the city. Go see about it.

Mercedes' hands flew about the kitchen.

—Let me go to the store whenever you need anything, Meche.
I don't like that Mustafá and his ways with you, Andrés said.

—I read that in the newspaper myself, I'll have you know. Don't
you come to my house trying to control me, little man.

Andrés smiled whenever Mercedes tried to insult him.

—Oh no, God's anointed foot soldier has drawn her bayonet,
he said.

—In the end, Andrés, justice will be served and the pillaging
everywhere will stop, she said. Mercedes herself doled out justice
whenever a vendor cheated her or a lewd comment came her way.
She did not merely pray to the Omnipotent Lord Her Savior, as
Andrés liked to tease her; many times Judgment Day came from
her own hands.


Mercedes tried her best to love Graciela—wherever she might be.
She prayed hard that the Lord stop the gnashing of her own teeth
at night, keep her from the razor-rage of the memory of her mother
walking away, leaving her with Celeste. Celeste, who measured
how much soup she drank, pulled her ears to check for dirt, whose
son told on her the time she ate an extra piece of yam.

She must forget the past. Live normal, in the shadow of the Lord Almighty, King of Heaven and Earth, of all that is seen and unseen. Bitterness would get her nowhere, except into the cauldron of hell, where she was pretty sure her mother stewed.

Calluses on her knees were a small price to pay to be a warrior of God. Andrés told Mercedes there were plenty of other things she could do if she really wanted to suffer as Christ Himself had. And young as she was, she suffered plenty for Him. Suppressed her natural urges, like bathing in the rain, in a thunderstorm, where she was born. Kept her hair from flying loose about her face the way she wanted. Tried not to let the new attention from men put a tremble on her lips. But those simple desires required hard bargaining with Him. After all, many men had already attempted to court Mercedes. Now that neither Casimiro nor Graciela was around to act as a buffer, Pai and Uncle Fausto stepped in to make sure Mercedes would not become an easy catch. They frequented the kiosk to remind Mustafá that Mercedes was no lone finger but part of a bigger hand. Celeste's ever-watchful eye, as well as the rest of the congregation's, also worked to filter out most advances; men and boys alike had begun to place bets as to who would win Mercedes over. After feeling so unwanted by Graciela, Mercedes did her best to find her own worth: an ability with numbers and the reputation of a God-fearing hardworking girl were strongholds she herself had erected, and then there was her royal white blood.

. . . . .

—¡You abandoned me yesterday! Mercedes said, her fingers raw from rubbing the glass beads of her mother's rosary.

Andrés was puzzled by her anger. His sister, Odepia, had spent the previous day with Mercedes, and their mother had even sent

Mercedes some bread pudding. He had gone off in the morning to try to secure one of the Horacista construction jobs everyone was talking about, then spent the rest of the day selling lottery tickets.

—¿Who wants a dwarf on a construction site? Andrés said to Mercedes, without the slightest hint of self-pity in his voice.

—I don't care what your reasons were for not coming this morning. You could have sent word . . .

It was the first time Mercedes had expressed pleasure at seeing him, and it made her look away from his green eyes. Lately, she had been asking Odepia a lot of questions. ¿Which foods did everyone (Andrés) in the family like?, so that Mercedes could prepare them a meal. ¿Why don't any of your brothers come to Mass? And Mercedes found herself trying harder to solidify her friendship with Odepia.

—Promise you won't tell, Odi.

—¿What, Meche?

—I have a rich father that no one knows about.

—You're crazy.

But when Mercedes showed her the sliver of the handsome groom from her mother's hatbox, Odepia made the sign of the cross and swore not to repeat the story that Graciela had indeed abandoned Mercedes in order to find this Silvio-man of wealth.

—¿See how our brows are alike? And if you pull my hair tight, it makes waves like his.

—Wow, Meche, we sure could use that kind of blood in our family, Odepia said in jest. —But the bride, she looks *nothing* like Graciela, Odepia continued, despite Mercedes' frown. —Maybe Silvio left your mai for this princess, the daughter of a king in . . .

Odepia paused. She could not think of a place. Then Mercedes' frown smoothed away and she finished the sentence for her: Germanyfrance.

. . .

Word began to circulate that, all along, it was not the kiosk Arab but the green-eyed lottery dwarf who had been sticking it to the haughty Bible-thumping daughter of the runaway mare.

Celeste paid a visit to Mercedes, demanding to know exactly what was going on.

—Don't you be stupid enough to throw yourself away on that crumb of a man, she said. —Pray that word hasn't yet gotten to your grandparents. I would as soon marry you to my married son than have you running around with that thing.

Mercedes cried because "that thing" was on her mind all the time. She imagined bending down to meet the lips of "that thing" whenever he came for a visit. Aside from old Mustafá, only Andrés had the patience to talk with her about presidents and the way the numbers in the lottery worked and how President Vásquez's construction projects in the Colonial Quarter were all a hoax. At the same time, she was embarrassed by her feelings for Andrés. When he climbed on the chair for a cup of coffee she would focus on his too-ample bottom in order to tame the warmth she felt. And when he chided her for her constant prayer, she would notice the stubbiness of his arms. Then, a blink of those turquoise eyes would make her feel like God.

On the advice of Celeste, Mercedes had begun to reconsider her other suitors. Mustafá, who had been her constant teacher, always spoke to her with care, made sure to keep his eyes from roaming below her neck. But when they locked up the kiosk for siesta and Mercedes prepared to walk the few yards home to a basket of wash, she noticed the odd tilt of his head. She pitied him, this man who had not taken a wife years after Adara's death, whose face had further pruned when last year's hurricane yanked off the roof of the kiosk. —You are like my daughter, he said with pride when he saw how fast she could pile up numbers in her mind and belt them out—added, subtracted, multiplied, divided. He patted Mercedes on the back and the warmth of his hand made her shudder at the thought of being a wife to a man who had seen her as a child.

¿Other suitors? There was Luis from the mill and Elio with the controlling mother, Vicente who worked at the gold mines and Pablo the cattle rancher, Alberto the guitarist and Godoy the Horacista. In all these men Mercedes noticed the same quality: eyes that could never stay fixed on hers when she gave them the change for their beers. She saw how such men would take up with a virgin, then when they had had their share, go looking for the next one. Andrés had always looked at her square in the face—even in the days Mercedes had called him Bow-Legged Dog—and spoke to her with unwavering frankness. He openly proclaimed his disbelief in religion—though not in God. Mercedes found the purity of his honesty godly, especially since daily hunger had made liars out of the best of them.

—¿Why do I love you, Meche? Andrés had scratched his head at the question she had flung at him.

—For one, you are a woman, and ¿what man doesn't love him some woman? You work hard. Smartest woman I know. You make the best sweet beans, call me Bow-Legged Dog. Oh, woman, just feel it. No one ever really knows why they love anyone . . .

# PRODIGAL
# DAUGHTERS · *1930*

Sick and ready for death, Graciela returned home after only a year.

Mercedes and Graciela did not recognize the other.

At fourteen, Mercedes, more voluptuous than her mother had ever been, still wore four braids rolled into knots. With adolescence, Silvio's face had cut its way through the roundness of Mercedes' youth. Brows feathered over her eyes in one long arc, and her mouth was dark, as if she had feasted on concord grapes.

At twenty-seven, Graciela was now a small copper woman with a map of her world on her face. A tiny keloid where the smooth skin of her cheekbone had been torn by the bone-soup woman wriggled when she smiled. Her eyes had lost their luster, but gained depth in the bargain. Faint splotches spread like continents on her skin.

The neighbors knew to back away from the house, to let the air thin out between mother and daughter. They hovered about the outside gate like buzzards waiting for signs of death.

To Graciela's puzzlement, Mercedes had filled the house with stray animals. The massive hurricane earlier that year had nearly destroyed all the cabins in the household, and, Mercedes explained with a shrug, animals began to appear everywhere. Graciela did remember how the raging San Zenón had destroyed the convent's precious garden and crumbled the crucifix on the roof. And now in her home, a goat chewed its way through the kitchen. Two piglets played under what used to be Graciela and Casimiro's bed. Five cocks chased each other in and out of the bath shed. Still, Graciela found the house more sterile than ever. She felt Casimiro's absence; a sullen look in her daughter's eyes betrayed bad news.

—¿And this? Graciela asked, pointing to a frayed poster nailed to the wall of the kitchen cabin. Six da Vincian disciples looked about. Graciela's eyes were drawn to John, who was leaning almost amicably toward a leering Judas Iscariot.

Mercedes shrugged.

—*The Last Supper*. Odepia gave it to me. ¿Remember her?

Mercedes followed her mother about the house. Graciela ran her hands over ceramic vases and other new additions to the household as a hen pecked about her feet.

—¿That smell?

As always, her nose was sharp.

—¿Who's here? ¿Where is he? she said.

Mercedes lowered her head. She had been waiting for the proper moment.

—Papá is gone. Last year, she mumbled.

He died, she said, of male matters, blood in the urine, alcohol, maybe, no one was sure. The grass on his grave was tall, long grass she had not the strength to clear. Graciela looked harder at the creature she had birthed in a thunderstorm. Then she walked over to Casimiro's favorite chair and sat down. On the chair's back dangled his miniature horse carving. Graciela fingered the horse's little hoof.

—¿Where is he? she said with a sharp sniff.

—Papá's at the plot, over by Alfredo's. Mercedes pointed in the general direction.

In Casimiro's absence, Graciela found that the shadows in the household seemed to gobble up any hint of light. Perhaps Mercedes' animals, who romped around the place like children, had come to restore his playfulness. The gloom in the cabin came more from the closed shutters Mercedes insisted on so she would be able to concentrate on prayer at any time of the day. Somehow Casimiro's mirth found a way to poke through the darkness: a tin "government official" mechanical bank that could open its mouth and swallow pennies, a mobile of dog teeth, and the miniature horse twirling in Graciela's hand.

—I wouldn't be surprised if you've let a real horse trample my bed, she sighed and hung the carving on the chair again. It was easier for Graciela to feign anger at Mercedes over the animals, the different house. This way, guilt for her own absence—and thoughts of Casimiro—would not cave her in. Graciela bent over until her face nearly touched her lap and soaked her skirt with squeals. Mercedes stared at her mother, opened her mouth to speak, then shut it again when, a few moments later, Graciela rose from the chair and wiped her face with her skirt.

A deep breath.

—So, ¿what else is new here?

—Mamá . . . someone else lives here.

—Please, no more animals, Mercedes.

—¡Andrés! Mercedes called out.

Graciela turned to see a small man with the clearest green eyes she had ever seen emerge from behind the sheet that divided the bedroom from the sitting room.

—¿And this? she said, the breath blown out of her again.

—Enchanted to meet you, Señá Graciela, he said in a voice taller than she was. He offered a chunky hand.

—You, whoever you are, call me Señora, she said, afraid to join her fingers with his stubby ones. Mercedes walked over to Andrés and took his hand in hers.

—Mamá, this is my husband. And this is ours, here. You are welcome to stay if you want.

Quite an eloquent insult to hear inside her own home, Graciela thought. But when she saw the way the lines around Mercedes' mouth disappeared when Andrés emerged, Graciela turned slowly to him.

—¿Couldn't you have waited till you were a bit older, Mercedes? she said, her eyes blazing into Andrés'.

—You didn't, Mercedes answered.

Graciela, already worn from crying, from the convent, from life, closed her eyes. When she opened them, she faced Andrés.

—If it's you who butters my daughter's bread, then do the job better than I have.

# A SAGE · *1930*

—Bury me naked. No rags. No flowers. No prayers. No tears.


Graciela's aortic valve had been weakened by the wear and tear of syphilis. By then, everyone knew. The town had seen the same monster ravage El Gordo and Flavia the johnnycake woman, sailors, entire brothels, and even those people of good repute who "had their little music inside."

    Mercedes and Andrés slept in the sitting room so that Graciela could live comfortably for what they all knew were her last days. With Graciela's return and the animals running about, the house seemed a circus to the visitors who arrived more out of wonder than concern. Day and night, Graciela's murmur filled the house. Her litany: a yanqui-man put roots on her using lavender, thyme, and a box with light that now had made her blind. When the sores on her feet did not bother her too much, she shuffled about, knocking over Mercedes' biscuit figurines with the spasms of her hands. The blinder she became, she believed, the easier it was for her to see.

—Not afraid of death, she said, a placid grin making her more beautiful than anyone had ever seen her. Then she would gasp at the pain in her belly that came with dry heaves.

—If you could see what I see you'd want to come with me.

And she would speak continuously of a military man who was rising to power, a demon among them who would claim the cloak of God and feed the nation to the wolves. Visitors listened to this prodigal daughter, not knowing whether her words were dementia or those of a sage.

Early one morning, a few months after her arrival, an aneurysm propelled Graciela to the clouds with which she had always communed.


The crack of morning through the zinc and wood ceiling was bright. Graciela tugged at her nightgown, wriggling like a worm until her skin was cool against the bedsheets. Her nightgown slid into the bed pot on the floor.

Running. The pillow was cool against her copper hands—copper turned green from the sea, the evil sea. Pillow, cotton softness smelling of the cane field where her forgotten grandfather held her hand as a child. Long stalks that hid him once from torches running in the night. Graciela's leg cramped under the sheets.

—Graciela, her marooned grandfather's words returned to her.

—Goat that breaks drum pays with his skin.

Her skin. Bay rum skin that once gleamed like waxed fruit under lamps.

Graciela saw Mercedes inside of a bird flying backwards through the clouds.

Tasted apple tartness from a kiss on a park bench. Casimiro's teeth on her lips daring her each time to leave Mercedita in the care of comadre Celeste.

Celeste of the borrowed shoes and the borrowed dress and the borrowed motherhood.

Graciela's cough banged the headboard across the wall, where a groove had formed. She wiped the phlegm with a towel.

His towel, Casimiro's. Once Casimiro. Casimiro under long grass. Her Casimiro in the twitches of her nerves. Graciela sat up to touch the emptiness of the pillow next to hers.

"Like this, you idiots."

Man in a warehouse. Graciela had wanted to rip the box from the man's hands. She held the towel against the light. Find that man, the yanqui-man again. Let the yanqui-man hold her dress this time. Let Silvio leave them alone in the smoky warehouse with the cracked land and sky. Just her and the yanqui-man who might have taken her away to the clouds, to the ships, to where she could have worn long lace dresses and carried a parasol and talked garbled but pretty.

Pretty. Up to the light she held her crucifix. Pretty amber of honey-honey Jesus. From Sol Elisa. Goodbye, Elisa.

She had a premonition of her granddaughter unraveling hummingbirds on a curtain, feet on a bed. Graciela wondered why Mercedes would give this crucifix away to such an ungrateful child. Child who would bid no blessings in the morning. A girl who would not wash her bloomers after each bath, who would go to school but not know how to write a simple letter.

Graciela lay back on her pillow. It was warm and, even in sickness, she could smell the sweet sebum from her own scalp. Bed-sheets tangled around her until her head lay on the other pillow. His pillow, Casimiro's, the mysterious crab in his prostate exhausted of its duty, having snip-snapped away at his life, and the rum drilling holes in his liver. Many times she had left his pillow cold and dry, too.

Graciela had always run away in times of drought.

Her coughs deepened the groove in the wall. Thirst again. Always thirst. The glass on her nightstand was empty.

In the kitchen Mercedes made the drink of dreams for her mother after Andrés had gotten up to make his early rounds selling lottery tickets. She ground the oats good for the bowels, poured the milk good for the bones, squeezed the oranges good for the colds, pinched vanilla good for the tongue. One almond good for wisdom and energy. A stick of cinnamon bad enough for the pressure, and one, two, three, four tablespoons of sugar bad for the blood.

Mercedes took the drink to the bedroom where Graciela lay buried in bedsheets. The room's brightness made her squint. She drew the drapes across the window, let the kerosene lamp cast a softer glow.

—Mamá.

Graciela's mouth was agape when Mercedes pulled back the sheets.

—Whipped it up sweet-sweet the way you like it, she said as she set the drink on the nightstand. Graciela's hands rested there, the empty glass shattered on the floor. When Mercedes bent down to gather the shards, she noticed the nightgown soaked in urine.

—You'll take me to an early grave with you one of these days, Mercedes said. Her head shook as if she were older than fourteen.

She sat by the bed and lightly shook Graciela. After rubbing her billows of hair, tapping the sunken cheeks, Mercedes made a sign of the cross.

With no desire to cry, Mercedes covered the naked body with sheets. Insatiable thirst made her drink from the glass. She also fed the corpse some of the beverage, letting froth dribble down the side of its mouth. Mercedes then swept the shards, emptied the bedpot, and wrung the nightgown dry. Good washergirl hands, Santa once said. After running a soapy cloth over the body, Mercedes dressed it in a fresh nightgown and gathered the hair into haircombs.

Then there was nothing left to do but spread the news.

That evening, the town's first and only doctor closed his bag. Having heard for the last few months about the curious case of the prodigal sage woman who had predicted Head of Army Rafael Trujillo's recent ascent to power, Dr. Juan Ibiza had risked Trujillo's roaming band of terrorists and traveled miles to see Graciela's corpse. With the air of a frustrated poet, he confirmed to the crowd that had gathered in the house that Graciela's soul had been robbed by *Treponema pallidum*, great impersonator of human diseases, grand murderer of savages and noblemen alike. In the tight bedroom, Dr. Ibiza wiped his neck as Andrés paid him with several lottery tickets.

. . . . .

The chorus of mourners began the first round of the rosary in the crowded home:

*Díos te salve María, llena eres de gracia.*

Mercedes' fingers swallowed up the glass rosary beads. Mamá Graciela's pancaked corpse lay cushioned in the casket, surrounded by lilies and carnations, gardenias and baby's breath, very much like the ruffles of her turquoise dress. Inside the casket's lid, Mercedes had wedged a tattered copy of the Shroud of Turin given to her by Padre Orestes, as if this primitive reproduction of Jesús Cristo could ensure Graciela's ascent to the clouds.

The monotonous call and response of the Hail Mary fluttered the candle flames and flickered the lanterns:

*El Señor es contigo.*

—If you don't bare it, nothing'll fit in life, Graciela once told Mercedes . . .

*Bendita tú eres entre todas las mujeres.*

. . . about risk . . .

*Bendito es el fruto de tu vientre, Jesús.*

. . . with a wave of those copper hands . . .

*Santa María, madre de Díos, ruega por nosotros los pecadores.*

. . . that curled around the ear of a teacup each morning.

*Ahora y en la hora de nuestra muerte.*

Amen. On the second round of the prayer, and at the sight of her mother's hands, Mercedes paused to take a sip of water. Now water instead of air caught in her throat. She let the prayers continue without her, so that finally Mercedes could succumb to the tears she had fought throughout her uncle's grandiose speech before the rosary litanies. She could not help but doubt Fausto's impassioned message of Graciela's eternal happiness after death, about Graciela's passage into the Kingdom of God, despite the tribulations of her life, honorable brothers and sisters in the Lord.

The once-bumbling Fausto had moved to another town and matured into a stylish man who occasionally spoke at funerals, birthday parties, weddings, or wherever else the gift of gab would open pockets. It had been a long time since anyone in the family had seen him, so Mercedes was relieved when he showed up for the first day of the wake. But she saw nothing of the old Fausto in the man who spoke to those gathered as if he were butchering his way through secret dungeons of the Spanish language. Mercedes saw Mai sit up higher in her chair every time Fausto conquered a cluster of complicated consonants. And she held back a giggle when Pai's harsh snores yanked even himself awake. At one point Fausto broke out of his verbal reverie and his glazed stare fell on Mercedes. Immediately she summoned tears.

Next to her, Andrés reached up to hold her. Sobs came like sudden rain, then stopped.

—Don't cry if you don't want to, Meche, he whispered.

What remained was calm acceptance, unlike her reaction to Casimiro's death the year before. Casimiro's death had been simpler, had belonged to her. Mercedes' cries for him had flooded her body for weeks and eventually drove her to the lap of Christ. But now, there were so many more details to take care of with her mother. The wig had to be returned to Celeste, as did the shoes. And she worried there would not be enough oatmeal drink and dumplings for everyone, including the stragglers expecting a free meal.

Mercedes pulled away from Andrés to wipe her eyes. Quickly her fingers counted through the beads she had missed. When she found her way back into the prayer, her voice soon rose above the rest.

After the multitude of oglers, the random whoops and theatrical faintings, after the refreshments had been devoured, Mercedes slowly approached the casket. There were flakes of foundation on her mother's face, the dress sunken where there used to be love and milk, so long ago. Mercedes felt like wiping Graciela's face with a cloth, perhaps re-creating the haggard face of Jesus. Sweet oranges and milk and cinnamon and vanilla suddenly on her tongue, Mercedes remembered Graciela clasping her hands above her chest and pulling in her shoulders when a problem in her head could find no exit. —¡Ilumíname, Señor! she would cry. ¿Had God finally illuminated her at her hour of death?

Mercedes claimed the amber crucifix from Graciela's chest. She touched Graciela's straight-hair wig: a donkey's tail, a puppet's curls instead of comforting coarseness. Mercedes pulled off the wig. Then the shoes.

—Thought you were going to forget about those, my child, Celeste's voice rang behind Mercedes.

There were still crumbs of bread on Celeste's cheeks. Celeste bent her head in brief prayer over the body of her friend, then plucked the wigs and shoes from Mercedes.

Mercedes howled, releasing the white-hot rage she had suppressed. She arched out her arm in an overdue fist on the corpse's chest, and pounded. Celeste clawed at Mercedes' arms, then Andrés and Odepia managed to pull the tangled women away from the casket. Mai and Pai, who had sat silently throughout the wake, busied themselves with arranging the kinky hair and shaping the sunken chest back to life.

# MERCEDES Y
# ANDRÉS · *1987*

With time, Andrés accepted Mercedes' working with Mustafá. He told Mercedes that he had never liked how Mustafá's prune-face softened when she arrived at the kiosk in the morning. Mercedes knew that Andrés did not like that she could talk of numbers with Mustafá, too. And, of course, greater was his dislike of her interaction with the many men who loitered by the kiosk. Mercedes' connection to the kiosk, however, provided their home with much more in the way of staples than the average household had. Mustafá let her keep any damaged merchandise, any surplus, whatever she needed; so much, in fact, that many neighbors preferred to "borrow" a few ounces of flour here and a bottle of tonic there from Mercedes rather than buy them from Mustafá. In addition, as Mercedes pointed out to Andrés, her connection to the kiosk had allowed him to sell the extra lottery tickets that put some gold in his fillings, gold that gave him the awful habit of throwing back his head and opening wide when he laughed in public.

—Allah willing, Mercedes, this will be yours when I die, Mustafá said whenever he was overcome with the grief. On those days, he would confuse his customers' names; Mercedes would have to recount change for him or clean up wherever his hand faltered; Mustafá would sit on the stool behind the counter, his eyes lost in ridges of skin.

—¡I am going to Monte Cristi! He jumped up from his stool on a day he had cut his thumb on a blade while opening a package of freshly delivered guava paste; after he had called Celeste Santa and Santa Celeste; and to Mercedes' horror, had called her Adara. Yes, she agreed with him, a trip was what he needed, a break from the store to refresh his scorched spirit. In fact, Mercedes said, Andrés' sister, Odepia, had moved to her husband's family out there. Mustafá, after all, never came out to the festivals, never left the kiosk, not even when he closed for the day; and the cabin behind the kiosk was but a place for him to rest his head. In Monte Cristi, Mustafá said, he had a prosperous older brother who every year sent him a postcard with greetings. This time, he would take his brother up on his longtime invitation to visit the ranch. Mustafá decided to entrust the kiosk to Mercedes for two weeks, and without telling her he "wet the hands" of a few trusted friends from the local police to keep an extra set of eyes on the place while he was gone.

It was during late September and early October of 1937 that Mercedes felt the power of her authority. She was twenty years old, a young woman with thin lips that darkened when her temper flared. With Mustafá away, customers tested Mercedes' will. On the first day, she wrestled down a teen who tried to jump over the counter after the local police had made their daily rounds. And on the second day, she found the series of padlocks filed down partially. Mercedes' terror was that she would find herself one day as Mai had long ago, in the time of the yanquis, with a pistol barrel scratching in her hair. Neighbors had promised to keep their ears alert for any strange "movements" around the kiosk, but Mercedes could not help suspect that trouble was waiting for her, that heists were being planned, even within the so-called police. Andrés accompanied her every morning, visited in the afternoon, and was there in the evening, when she locked up. Before dying, Graciela had told him about the pistol under the water tank, and since then it was the lottery-ticket vendor's loyal companion.

—I cannot live in constant fear like this, Mercedes said to Andrés after weeks had passed without word from Mustafá. Andrés maintained that Mustafá had to have some kind of connection that kept the little kiosk protected in the midst of so much hunger. Perhaps the Turks, as Yunco had suggested years back, provided protection from thieves, or crooked policemen, or leeches from the surrounding towns.

El Generalisimo Doctor Rafael Leónidas Trujillo Molina, Benefactor de la Patria y Padre de la Patria Nueva began his thirty-year rule on the heels of the Americans' departure in 1930; he had won the election with more votes than there were eligible voters. For the last seven years, many—Mercedes included—feigned devotion toward the man-god, whose portrait was required to be hung in every household. The capital city of Santo Domingo became Ciudad Trujillo.

Mercedes' fear during Mustafá's absence was magnified 18,000 times with news of the genocide of Haitians living on the border between Dominican Republic and Haiti. The month of October opened with thirty-six hours of carnage in which drunken Dominican soldiers, on orders from Trujillo, took their machetes and built a damn of human bodies in the western Dajabón River. Reports filtered into the kiosk by word of mouth; the news arrived all the quicker with the many terrified Haitians seeking refuge from the horror in a yanqui-owned sugarmill a town away.

The army had used machetes so that the Dominican peasantry could spontaneously participate in the massacre. Decapitations were commonplace. And in the Haitian-Dominican border towns, the stench of human blood did battle with the air. Killings happened within Dominican families with Haitian, part-Haitian, or dark-skinned relatives.

Old Man Desiderio, in his usual morbidness, had stumbled into the kiosk after his audience at Yunco's to contribute to the pool of information.

—But the Haitians have been polluting us with their language, their superstitions, their sweat, for too long, Mercedes said, as Desiderio's pornographic descriptions attracted an audience.

She did not care what anyone thought about her views. God had His ways of exterminating heathens and their evil ways, and they were not always pretty, she said to the crowd that had gathered at the kiosk. As a soldier of God, she accepted the ugliness and necessity of war.

Old Man Desiderio said that no God-talk and nothing—nothing—those poor creatures did could justify the atrocities that had come to pass in the last few days: that the Dajabón ran so red with blood that wild dogs came from miles away to partake in the feast; that pregnant women were raped, then disemboweled like cattle; that hundreds of survivors were still huddled in the homes of many a benevolent Dominican as he spoke.

—To think that *parsley* could determine the worth of your life,

Desiderio said with a shake of his head. He rubbed his chin and there was some foam at the edge of his lips. Mercedes regarded Old Man Desiderio's dark skin and broad features with disgust. She remembered the Haitian boy who used to beg at the kiosk when Adara was alive and wondered if he or any of his relatives were clogging up the Dajabón.

—How lucky for you that your tongue can taste the "r" in *parsley*, she said to Old Man Desiderio. –Otherwise, your blood would have blended with that river just as well, she said. Without looking at him, Mercedes pushed away his arms and wiped away the sweat spots on the countertop. Those milling about the kiosk raised their brows.

—What a bit of money does to a little girl, ¿ah? ¡No more Sunday Mass or the love of Christ for this greedy merchant! Mustafá sure knew how to pick out his cow.

Desiderio winked at Mercedes and took off his hat before walking out of the kiosk.

—¡Get out of here if you're not buying! Mercedes yelled at the rest of the loiterers. Her hands had begun to shake, and she popped the cap off a bottle of beer.

· · · · ·

A few months later, Mustafá appeared at the kiosk, eyes sunken deeper into his face than Mercedes had ever seen. He had sent her a postcard announcing his imminent return, and Mercedes had read it with a mix of relief and disappointment. There was a purple nub where his left hand had been, and the gash on his crown was still moist.

She dared not ask about the wounds, knowing all too well that to do so would crush Mustafá's pride and compromise her position in the kiosk. Mercedes and Andrés had been running the kiosk efficiently—better than Mustafá and Adara ever had. They had re-arranged the products on the shelves and ordered more popular items. Mercedes had thought to fill old lard cans with flowers and line them up out front. Then she asked Andrés to build a deck with a thatched roof, where people could sit and enjoy a bite or a drink. Andrés also painted the kiosk a brilliant pink, and, like bees, peo-ple from nearby towns had begun to make the trip to shop there. Soon Yunco began complaining that he was losing customers from his local bar.

—You have taken over my business quite well, Mustafá said to Mercedes when they squared away the books and he saw that the profits had fattened. Mercedes could see his envy, his happiness, his anger, his hurt all trembling in the handless arm. She could not bring herself to ask how he had been enmeshed in the horror out west; the answer was painfully etched in his violet skin, in his in-ability to pronounce *parsley*.


It was during this time of prosperity and sadness that Mercedes felt the first fury of jealousy. All along she believed her hold on Andrés was secure, towering over him by eight inches, her success with the kiosk. She now noticed that he had added more gold fillings to his mouth, and that he laughed with increased aplomb. And then one day Mercedes caught sight of her competition.

The woman had waddled into the group that liked to sit under the thatched roof on Sundays while Mercedes took a break from her shift at the kiosk to attend Mass. As tall as Andrés, her abun-dance quivered behind her in the yellow skirts she liked to wear. Mercedes noticed that her tiny nails were painted, and her classy hats announced her arrival from miles away. La Vedette, she was called, for her warbling voice. On sticky Sundays, La Vedette would stand on the table and sing boleros that drew people in from the surrounding hills—and, to Mercedes' surprising dismay, pumped more money into the kiosk.

—¿But who doesn't like La Vedette? Andrés said with a twinkle in his eyes. And Mercedes felt a panic she had not felt in a long time.

When they made love, she wrapped her arms and legs around Andrés' entire body until he lost his urge to enter her. —¿What is it? ¿I'm not small and dainty enough? Mercedes sobbed in the dark. He feared that she would draw him completely inside of her, Andrés said with a laugh that made Mercedes sob even harder. She wished for shorter limbs, for a gelatinous behind, for that charming waddle.

But La Vedette continued to make her Sunday appearances with her entourage of admirers. Like a doll she was hoisted up to the table, and Mercedes wondered if they cranked her up, too. Her voice was a full-throated cry that ricocheted off the hills and turned Andrés' eyes into a cloudy green liquid. And then one day, after a yodeled lullaby, La Vedette asked no one in particular for a shot of rum with honey and a dash of lemon to condition her throat.

—¿You think that love potion will work, stupid? Mercedes said to Andrés when he ran to the counter to concoct the drink.

—I am only doing my job, he said.

When he ceremoniously offered the drink to La Vedette, she sized him up and gulped it down without batting her lashes. La Vedette stood up and sang the classic ballad about the jealous woman with the meat cleaver.

Mercedes had felt the familiar rush of rage in her chest, a pump that vacuumed out her sanity. It all happened so fast. Mercedes hadn't expected the shotglass to hit La Vedette. La Vedette's face had made a funny expression, her song stuck in her throat, and like a broken doll she fell off the table. Everyone crowded around her, Mercedes included, as La Vedette's eyes rolled to the back of her head.

—¡It was a mistake! Mercedes said as she wiped the trickle of blood from La Vedette's forehead with her own hands. She was truly sorry, especially after she saw how disappointment and embarrassment burned Andrés' face.

—Wish I had me a woman who loved me that much, one of the men said with a whoop as La Vedette was taken away, still faintly warbling her songs.

—¡At least I didn't throw the glass at you! Mercedes said to Andrés during their subsequent yelling match at home.

—I'm going to look at women until the day I die. And neither God nor Trujillo, woman nor shotglass is going to keep me from having my fill, he said.

Mercedes was free to carry on her little conversations with men at the kiosk, Andrés said, without him coming after them with shotglasses. Live and let live.

# ISMAEL · *1950*

Two decades after Graciela's death, Mercedes and Andrés conceived the son who would much later put them on a plane to a new country. Mercedes, at thirty-three, was overcome with joy when her body convulsed with nausea and she began feeling the sensation of ground glass in her breasts. Her twenty childless years with Andrés had been accepted by everyone without comment. And this silence was fine by Mercedes, because from the very beginning she had made her life with Andrés her own business. No one had dared ask Mercedes when she was going to bless Andrés with a son. The question would force them to imagine her and Andrés making love. When Mai was alive, however, she had been the only person to openly talk about children. With the boldness of age, Mai made sure on every possible occasion to express her relief that Mercedes had not let Andrés put an "odd" child in her womb; Mai was content with being a great-grandmother to Fausto's many scattered children.

The portrait of El Generalisimo Doctor Rafael Leónidas Trujillo Molina, Benefactor de la Patria y Padre de la Patria Nueva, hung at the entrance of the kiosk. A smaller one commanded a special corner inside, where Mercedes always kept its altar breathing with fresh white flowers, camphor water, and a white candle. La Virgen de la Altagracia and patron of merchants Saint Francis of Assisi completed the trio.

—¿Mercedes, you don't think one portrait of the General is enough? Andrés had told her many times.

—Andrés, careful with what you say about our Benefactor—especially here, she warned, a finger to her lips. The ears of the stockboy they had just hired were floating about. There were too many people eager to bring their prosperity down, especially after Mercedes inherited the kiosk from the late Mustafá. Some had tried, on more than one occasion, to knock down or deface the kiosk's main portrait; when this happened (always at night), Mercedes made sure to be seen lovingly replacing the portrait.

—If I take down Saint Francis, the business fails. If La Virgen goes, my belly goes. And if Trujillo goes, everything goes.


Daily speech was reduced to whispers to keep the skies from shattering, as the most trivial of exchanges could cause pieces of heaven to flake off and lose divinity.


Andrés stopped pestering Mercedes about the redundant portraits.

—Today I got a ride into the city from Dr. Ibiza, the one who came to see Graciela during . . . that time, Andrés said to Mercedes as they lay in bed.

—Lower your voice, Mercedes whispered.

Andrés said he did not know what made Dr. Ibiza trust him enough to inform him that one Doctora Angelina Torres had been the first of the professionals to disappear in the affluent neighboring town of La Cigüeta. She had treated the poor at no charge and was notorious for her double-talk and innuendo. She disappeared after telling patients that only by cleaning out their ears could they cure blindness.

And in the same town, architect Ricardo Perez vanished after he hosted a Sunday gathering for intellectuals who enjoyed food and drink and spoke excitedly of a futuristic notion called television. After one too many drinks, Perez criticized the aesthetic of the regime's public works.

Dr. Ibiza himself often treated the Benefactor's henchmen and their families without charge.

—I told you, it just takes the word of some scum for one of us to end up with our nails yanked out, Mercedes whispered back to Andrés in the dark. —We have to be very careful of what we say— even to that Dr. Ibiza.

—Yes, Meche, but I'm not going to live like a rabbit. I don't skulk around God, either, Andrés said, then reached under Mercedes' nightgown to feel her swollen belly.

. . . . .

Zinc roof and turquoise paint. Gold fillings and leather shoes. Sweet ham and blocks of ice. A car. Face powder and lavender soap. Eye kohl and bangles. A yellow lace hat and a purse to match. A washerwoman, cleaning woman, cook. Hair relaxers and bleaching creams. Biscuit figurines on the coffee table. Extra cabin and new latrine. A radio and electric light. A firstborn son, Ismael, named after the late Mustafá's prosperous father.

# AMALFI · *1987*

Amalfi told Mercedes and Andrés that she was a grown woman who could take care of her damned self and her daughter, if that lousy Porfirio Pimentel, Attorney at Law, would not. It was not the first time she had spoken to her mother with such looseness. What most surprised Mercedes, however, was that Amalfi had also directed her rancor toward Andrés, a man whose nasal voice and stubbornness compensated for his stature.

Amalfi said she would stay. She was not budging from her country.

—¿How can a single mother make do without her family around? Mercedes had sighed as she watched her older son, Ismael, bounce on an overstuffed suitcase to zipper it up. ¿Why did Amalfi have to throw a wrench in their plans? Most people would have scrambled at the opportunity to escape the village to a place like New York. Mercedes scratched a patch of dry skin on her cheek.

—I blame you, Mercedes, said Andrés, his eyes green-gray and bulging. —You insisted on that animal for Amalfi, as if you wanted him for yourself.

—Now he's left her spewing anti-American shit. Ismael chuckled. He knew about women like his sister, he said, who, after mouthing patriotic quips, ended up working in the industrial free zones. He spoke as if Amalfi were not in the room.

It was Ismael who had whipped everyone up into a frenzy about New York. He had single-handedly gone through the process of applying for visas for all of them, including baby Leila. And, as irony would have it, it was Amalfi's visa that was the first to be approved.

—Made me drive her all the way out to the airport. A waste of my time and money.

Mercedes watched Amalfi pick the pins out of the rollers in her hair.

—Please. You're all going to wake up the baby with your whining, Amalfi said.


At first, Amalfi had indeed run out with Mercedes and bought a set of luggage, filled it with her pastry bags, hair rollers, stretch jeans, and textbooks. For a while, Mercedes tolerated Amalfi's obsessive New York fantasies, her checking out stacks of relevant books and magazines from the library. Then a tiny seed of doubt appeared to sprout in all directions. Amalfi worried about having to quit her studies of cakes at La Escuela de Capacitación Femenina Maria Trinidad Reyes, the promise of a prosperous baking business aborted. And after telling Mercedes about a nightmare in which a plane they boarded crashed "like in the movies," Amalfi purchased from Andrés a lottery ticket numbered as the flight had been in the dream (567). Then she complained that her own skull was too thick to absorb a new language, another culture.

—¿Why go to New York? she would ask whenever the news reported snow in New York or the city's astronomical crime rate. And Amalfi told Mercedes about a fortune-teller who assured her that she would indeed travel, although the same woman had predicted a black president in the future of the nation.

.  .  .  .  .

Mercedes had given breath to Amalfi on the day of the assassination, in 1961, of El Generalisimo Doctor Rafael Leónidas Trujillo Molina. With fear like a vapor, the streets had been hushed with rumors of his death, yet no one dared to venture out in joy after three decades of numbing dictatorship. Mercedes had feared, instead, the labor with her forty-four years, feared that her second child might be the one to carry Andrés' gene for dwarfness. She was no longer worried about Ismael, then eleven years old, but her second pregnancy came with myriad complications.

In sea-white blinding labor pain, Mercedes had bitten the glass beads of her rosary and pictured her own transparent body, pulsating heart behind ribs, spongy brain tissue inside her skull. She had stared in disbelief at the tangle of her viscera, and the bulge where the child hid from the midwife.

—Push, goddamnit, said the midwife.

¿To curse God in the middle of a birth?

Mercedes pushed, tried to imagine her own hands massaging the bulge away from her heart. The pain had hurled her into a very real Russian-doll dream in which the child, sea moss encircling its neck, had another child writhing inside. And Mercedes dreamt that her own hands reached inside herself, then inside her child, between its mesh of bone and flesh, to pluck free a deeper child.

Mercedes awoke to the midwife's hand on her cervix, coaxing the elusive child. All Mercedes had to do was push, goddamnit, and let the child go. And alone—so alone—she pushed until a dot of blood tinged the white of her eye and her sphincter blossomed. The fury of her efforts made Mercedes feel as if she had just nudged humanity just a little further forward.

—A girl, said the midwife. —A normal baby girl named Amalfi, she yelled louder to the circle of people praying on the other side of the curtain.

. . . . .

And now, more than twenty years later, Mercedes finds that Dominicans flee the nation in hordes, feeding themselves to sharks living on both land and sea; that green has become the color of love; that tourism is the nation's new sugar—in the 1980s, anything is better than Home. The seesaw economy forces her and Andrés to close down the kiosk, after decades of business.

The dry patches of eczema on Mercedes' cheeks spread to the inside of her elbows in those tumultuous times.

—You're softening up on us, Andrés said when Mercedes quit trying to control their daughter. But what could Mercedes do when Amalfi, eighteenth student at the School of Capacitación Femenina Maria Trinidad Reyes, and thirty-fifth girlfriend to Attorney at Law Porfirio Pimentel, belittled herself by invoking every saint in the Haitian pantheon of gods to strike down that no-good son-of-a-bitch lawyer for having stirred up the honeycomb between her legs.

—Amalfi, this would be a good opportunity for you to start over, with the baby. Mercedes kept trying to make her change her mind about going to New York. Just weeks before, they had all sat in Ismael's Volkswagen bug on the way to see Amalfi off to the airport. Amalfi was to go first to try to find them all housing and jobs.

— Still can't believe it, Ismael had said, steering around pickup trucks heaped with people and fowl down the long row of broken palm trees.

— Don't be jealous, Son, Mercedes said from the backseat when she saw through the sideview mirror that Amalfi couldn't help smiling at Ismael's discomfort; Amalfi would be the first to pick gold from foreign streets. Her lacquered hair bounced, and she adjusted her tube top, which kept revealing a long line of cleavage.

— And you better call us as soon as you get to the airport in New York, Mercedes said to her.

Ismael spat out the window. Mercedes studied the sheen at the edges of her son's small afro and wondered how long it would be before he would leave, too.

— And you make sure the money I'll send goes solely to Leila's care, Amalfi said with an index finger pinned to her brother's shoulder. She turned around to look at Mercedes in the backseat.

— I know how much Isma likes to gamble, and how you and Papá can be too generous with other people.

— Ah, don't you worry, we'll camp out at the casino with your hard-earned cash, Mercedes laughed coldly.

In the distance Mercedes could hear the rumble of airplanes. The breeze blowing in through the window carried the pungent odor of burning trash and salty water. She also discerned the smell of cement from the many construction projects of the Blind President. Honorable Balaguer, that son of a bitch. But she was not about to get into yet another argument with hardcore-Balaguerista Ismael. Instead, she closed her eyes and tried to imagine New York through her nose. Fabric softener. Perfumed hotel lobbies. Pasteurized milk. When she opened her eyes, she saw a muscled man mixing something in a wheelbarrow growing smaller in the sideview mirror. Go ahead, blind pawn, add more cement and another shovelful of sand, she thought. Dip a finger in the batter, taste the brown sugar before pouring it into molds to make imaginary castles reaching to the clouds. Say goodbye, Amalfi, to perpetually incomplete construction projects.

—Mmm-hmmm, I worry about all the fun you'll have with my money, Ismael, Amalfi said, as Mercedes watched the skeletons of buildings whiz by.

—Please, let's not start another fight now, Mercedes said in a worn, maternal voice.

Ismael soon parked the car and with his usual industry pulled Amalfi's bags from the trunk. Amalfi readjusted her top and applied a fresh frost of lipstick. Mercedes wished they could have brought the baby to see Amalfi off. Had Leila's ear infection not made her so irritable . . .

The airport sweltered. Mercedes heard skinny busboys and shoeshine boys speaking the güiri-güiri she knew Amalfi had to learn as soon as the plane landed on the other side of the waters. Her own tongue slid around her dentures, and she found it hard to accept any other language forcing rubber balls into her mouth.

Mercedes could easily distinguish between the arriving tourists, pale-faced in Hawaiian-print shirts, and the departing ones, who wore guayaberas and crisp tans. There were tears, whole families embracing, lovers in long kisses (¿returning or departing?). ¿What would her own goodbye taste like? Her head hurt from the many kisses and hugs she had given Amalfi the night before, when she did not think she could stand going to the airport. She had sidled close to Andrés with sobs in the middle of the night. And she knew he was so afraid of acting the same way that he gave up his place in the car and encouraged her to go to the airport instead.

Inside the souvenir shops, Mercedes watched Amalfi run her manicured hands over little wooden ships and ceramics, nylon flowers and papier-mâché parrots. The smell of mustiness and sanded wood, of plaster and cheap perfume suddenly made Mercedes envious of her daughter. She wished she could have traveled sooner, especially in the days when the kiosk had afforded her and Andrés more luxuries. But in those times, Trujillo rarely let anyone of their origins out of the country, and besides, they had been swamped with the business, then she had Ismael, and then Amalfi . . .

They stopped at snack bars to buy fried cheese and fruit mints. Mercedes had never been to an airport, and now she stood at the gate, her breath racing at the prospect of her little girl being hoisted up into the skies by the silver beasts lined up outside the huge windows. Rumbling shook the ground and sped her heart.

Ismael kept looking at his watch. They had arrived two hours before the scheduled departure. —I'll be back, he said abruptly. Mercedes and Amalfi watched Ismael recede into the crowd with the overdignified walk of a sugar-mill employee who worked in the office and not in the mill or out in the fields.

He returned shortly, to their surprise, with three paper cups of limeade. They each savored the drink as if it would be the last time the sweet-sourness glazed the roof of their mouths. Mercedes removed a handkerchief from her purse and tenderly wiped the sweat from Amalfi's cheeks, along with the heavy foundation and lipstick.

—Not my makeup . . .

She continued to wipe.

—Drink your limeade.

—Isma, ¿can you imagine me talking güiri-güiri? Amalfi laughed. Her cheeks were apple-shiny where Mercedes had wiped. Ismael snorted and beat a pack of cigarettes against his palm.

—Let me smoke one, Amalfi said, to Mercedes' surprise. Ismael removed another cigarette from the pack and lit it for her. Amalfi, suddenly a sophisticated traveling woman shooting a straight line of smoke from red red lips. Mercedes watched her children inhale without coughing, then exhale long plumes of smoke, the twitch on their lips of worldly smokers.

—¡Amalfi! Mercedes said. —¿Who knows what else you'll want to try out there?

—Tía Odepia told me you first puffed at eight—so I'm late in the game, Amalfi laughed and fluffed her hair.

—Here, Mamá, just have one, Ismael said, thrusting a cigarette in Mercedes' lips.

—Ay, ¿do you want to send this old lady to an early grave? Mercedes said, but let Ismael light the cigarette anyway when she saw the gleam in Amalfi's eyes.

—Don't tell Andrés, Mercedes said, feeling as nauseous after the first drag as she had long ago. She was sad, trying to conjure the faded memory of Casimiro in the midst of Amalfi's departure. The cigarette flicked from her hand. Next to her, Amalfi was no longer smoking, and her crossed arms bunched up her breasts.

—You need to go, for us, the future, Leila, Mercedes said and rubbed Amalfi's back.

—¿All this sentimentality again? Ismael said.

Amalfi's voice cracked.

—¿Mamá, did you know about that civilization of Atlantis that disappeared a long time ago under the sea? she said, tears welling up in her eyes.

—¿What the hell are you talking about? Ismael said. He lit another cigarette.

—Yes, the whole continent disappeared, and they're predicting the same for this whole island, Amalfi said. Mascara streaked around her eyes.

—You read too many stupid magazines, Ismael said.

—I feel like I can't be a coward and leave. Someone has to stay behind and—

—Amalfi, stop this talk. Look, people are already lining up, Mercedes stood and pulled Amalfi's arm.

The PA system crackled with boarding instructions. As the crowd of passengers shuffled around them, Amalfi remained seated, her legs crossed. Ismael picked up her bags and headed for the gate.

—¡Come on, Amalfi! He stood in line, beckoning wildly. Amalfi remained seated while Mercedes, hot and nauseous from the cigarette, stood over her. She followed Amalfi's gaze to a woman in a sequined dress who was yanking her son by the arm because he refused to get in line; the little boy wore a gold chain around his neck. And she saw a man ahead pull out a miniature bottle of rum for a quick swig; a skinny girl, no more than fifteen, French-kissing the middle-aged white man who held their tickets. There was an elderly woman in a wheelchair with a long line of drool that her chaperone did not bother to wipe. One man frantically opened and closed a briefcase.

—I'm staying, Amalfi said, I'm staying right here.

—Amalfi, please, Mercedes said. All her tugging could not pull Amalfi from the bench. With the piercing sounds of airplanes tensing her own shoulders, Mercedes stepped back and stopped trying.

# NUEBA YOL · *1987*

While Amalfi resolved that it was in her cards to stay and make the Dominican Republic her Atlantis, Ismael's visa was approved. He made plans to move to the United States in 1986, then bring over Mercedes, Andrés, and Leila—with the easy approval of Amalfi— once he was set up. Through a complicated network of friends in high and low places, he had sped up visa approvals for the family, which was to become part of the largest immigrant group to settle in New York City during the 1980s. Ismael wasted no time in getting odd jobs painting and mold-setting, deep-frying and ironing, mopping and delivering. The numbers he saw in his dreams he played in the lotteries, both the legal and the illegal, from La Bolita to El Palé. A year later, with the money made from his sweat and his luck, he sent for Mercedes, Andrés, and baby Leila. Through yet another network of coworkers and friends, Ismael had secured his parents a small apartment in Washington Heights.

—Here, we'll show Amalfi that there's a better future, he said when the last of the suitcases were emptied.

Though they were happy to join their son a year later, New York City's vastness seeped gloom into Mercedes and Andrés. The conditions they lived in did not match Ismael's cheery descriptions. Now in their seventies, they felt as if they were starting from scratch. ¿And how were they to be grandparents on alien soil?

In the cramped airplane seat, her meal untouched, Mercedes had noticed how anticlimactic the sky was—mist outside the window was supposed to be a cloud. Unlike Mamá Graciela in her heyday, Mercedes realized she herself preferred private, internal journeys to external ones. No limit to the world inside our minds, Mercedes thought. She had watched a flap of metal stir on the wing of the plane, a wing that could take them only so far. Perhaps Amalfi had been right to stay behind, after all. Mercedes had closed her eyes to keep from crying in front of Andrés.

Small as he was, few things impressed Andrés—especially at his age. Mercedes always liked that Andrés was bigger than this world. He had stared out the window as the island shrank beneath them, and yawned as if he were accustomed to seeing his entire universe become a speck of green. He ate the tiny meals and had no problem asking the stewardess for seconds. Those who had the boldness to speak with him soon forgot their own discomfort. Unashamed of his dwarfness, comfortable in his skin: He was who he was.

Three-year-old Leila had slept in his arms while Mercedes wondered what future lay ahead for their granddaughter. She had wrested the responsibility of raising Leila from her daughter because in Amalfi she spotted the same absentmindedness that had made Mercedes distrust Graciela; it was the quickness with which

Amalfi agreed to part, even temporarily, with Leila. Mercedes' shaking hands clutched her glass rosary against the turbulent flight to New York. Looking out the window at the grid of lights under them, Mercedes could not have imagined integrating her life into that vast dotted network. As they landed, Mercedes cracked ice with her dentures, while Andrés calmly watched patches of ground speeding below them. When the passengers clapped in relief, Mercedes crushed the ice cubes in her mouth harder, until the chill ached in her mouth. She and Andrés hugged tightly, Leila struggling between them. At the airport, in the confusion of documents and inspections, Leila and luggage, Mercedes tightened the beads around her wrists. When moving stairs flattened under her feet, she screamed, vertigo brewing in her stomach. A stiletto heel had sliced into her canvas shoes like a knife into fresh bread, so that one of her corns felt like a separate toe. Ahead of her, a beefy woman had tossed a *sorry*.

—¡With *sorry* you think you fix everything! she cried, shoving the woman.

—God Almighty, Andrés, ¿what in heaven's name lies ahead of us?

It had taken Andrés' steady hands to calm her.

· · · · ·

Mercedes' amber crucifix dangles below her waist from a string. She stands over a steaming pot. Gray elbows block her face. In the other arm, Leila is perched, her face pinched in mid-cry. Mercedes' hips push the toddler away from the stove as she peers through the top half of her bifocals into the sancocho. Her tight hairbun makes up for lost glamour. The pristine white behind her is broken by a single wall calendar, compliments of Salcedo Meat Market. On the shelf in a wood frame, six da Vincian disciples look past her sancocho to where the scene ends, cut off at John, who leans almost amicably toward a leering Judas Iscariot.

*... that they should be with Him, and that He may send them forth to preach, and to have power to heal sicknesses, and to cast out devils.*

¿Why did Andrés always take pictures of her when she looked so shabby? Mercedes wondered after the camera's shutter clicked. Then again, he had better send that picture around, even though in this country they can take a child away from you for the smallest infractions. But yes, Andrés should send the picture back home so that Amalfi and Odepia could see how well they're all doing in New York, thank the Lord. Mercedes covered the pot and handed a screaming Leila to Andrés to disentangle her little hands from the crucifix.

Yes, she and Andrés may have been sharper twenty years ago, Mercedes thought; she with her accountant's mind and he with his uncanny ability with lottery predictions. But now she did not think it was so late to have come here. ¿Who said travel was only for the young? In fact, the move had reignited excitement between her and Andrés. They were content to share with each other the simplest discoveries: jackpot video games and the Puerto Rican lottery at the bodega, a chute in the hallway that swallows up the garbage, little black discs that magically destroy roaches, yet another Spanish-speaking channel on television. It was exciting to invent another lifetime together—and just when they thought they would melt away into the routine of old age, they were thrust into parenthood again.

# CIRCLES

Graciela's ghost is not a shadow, or a shiver, or a statue falling from an altar. It is not a white sheet with slits for eyes, or a howl in the wind. It is not in the eerie highlights of a portrait, or in the twitch of a nerve.

Her ghost is in the fullness of a frog's underbelly, in a cipher of pigeons, in the river's rush. It is threaded through the eggplant-and-salmon braid of birth.

· · · · ·

—Kiss this hand, Leila, and bid your defunct Graciela her blessings. "Blessings, Greatest-Grandmamajama-of-Them-All . . ."

—We're happy naked, Leila.

"My naked's too ugly, Greatest-Grandmama."

—Ah, and ¿who cares in this life?

"I wanna be a woman."

—Then, Leila, take off that skin.

"Get outta those clouds, Greatest-of-the-Grandmamajamas . . ."

—Take it off. To the bottom, disrespectful child.

"Such an apodysophiliac, with all this naked stuff."

—¡Ah! Don't talk to your elder of letters now.

"Everyone takes me seriously when I enunciate."

—Shed the troubles of life.

"What'll be left of me then?"

—Bones.

"A 206-piece skeleton."

—Break your skull.

"Will you put my ass back together again?"

—Of course.

"Look at me: just brains, guts, lungs, heart."

—Keep your heart. ¿What's inside?

"Ventricles and the venae cavas . . ."

—No—

" . . . the valves and aorta . . ."

—No, Leila, let's bleed your heart for truth.

# LEILA · *1998*

"Leila Pimentel."

"Present."

Leila sat in biology class, very much present. It was the only class that put an A on her report card and earned her new clothes. The rest of her classes could bust as far as she was concerned, she had told Ms. Valenza in a parent-teacher conference, minus parents. In general, she maintained, she was an epistemophiliac whose lust for knowledge had nothing to do with grades.

Today they were studying the circulatory system, following a month-long tour of the human body. Leila smiled when Ms. Valenza said that the heart was about the size of a fist. When Ms. Valenza asked students to check each other's pulses, Leila's study partner thought he had miscounted.

"Nah, I'm just horny," she said only to watch the blood rise in his face.

Ventricles, the venae cavas, the valves, and aortas. She liked
the v's and a's in her mouth, and repeated the words to keep from
thinking about Him. Miguel Ulloa Hernández: the bastard who
was straining the muscle that was supposed to beat seventy-two
times a minute for the rest of her life.

Privacy was luxury. Leila's bed was in the living room, and Mercedes and Andrés slept in the bedroom. In a corner between the
sofa and the armchair was a spot where on most afternoons the sun
made a rhombus on the linoleum.

Leila was still angry at Them for not letting her go out with
Mirangeli and Elsa. Mercedes and Andrés were good to her, but as
Leila got older, the generation gap caused them to shout across
canyons at each other. Her grandparents, no matter how strong and
lucid they seemed, were in their eighties, getting ready to step away
from life, while Leila was just beginning to get her feet wet. Her
Uncle Ismael came over often to listen to Mercedes and Andrés'
complaints, as well as to boss Leila around and give her an ear pull if
need be. Always trying to act like the father he ain't. Then he would
go right back to his life of money and women. Even the home attendant who cared for Mercedes and Andrés during the day was starting
to get too preachy with Leila. At times like this, Leila wished her
mother would not have stayed behind in DR like a goddamned coward, and that her father would not have been such an asshole.

·   ·   ·   ·   ·

Leila sat with Mercedes to write Amalfi a letter.

*Querida Amalfi . . .*

How difficult for Leila to turn Mercedes' ramblings into neatly
scripted letters. Mercedes dictated to Leila as if Amalfi sat right
next to them in the bedroom.

—This goes to greet you in union with your family, that you may be in good health . . .

—. . . and Amalfi, my love, I keep telling that home attendant to stop buying me more panties . . . up to my neck in them.

The Spanish trudged through Leila's weak short-term memory and slow hands; a script full of fat spaces and balled dots. In the beginning she faithfully included Mercedes' every "humph" and her occasional laughter (written as "ja ja ja" in comic-strip bubbles). The process: take in the words tumbling out of Mercedes, remember them, translate them into English for meaning in her own mind, then retranslate them into Spanish, and, finally, write them neatly and correctly on the page—all the while listening for the next barrage.

"Damn, slow down, 'Buela! What was that again?"

Mercedes craned her neck to listen, and responded in her usual delay.

—¿What do you go to school for? ¿Now how do I start that story up again?

Mercedes snorted, then picked up the fringes of gossip for Amalfi: more robberies in the building, a dream of lots of little rabbits, the fish special at Key Foods, your daughter who can't even write a decent letter.

" 'Buela, I said slow the hell down!"

—. . . tell Amalfi also that I send a champú with Isma to make her hair good and twenty dollars, not for any boyfriends to gobble it up . . .

Mercedes pointed to the loose-leaf notebook in Leila's lap.

. . . *for you only and not for whoever cunnilinguses you, Ma,* Leila wrote.

—I pray you're well, Amalfi. ¿How's the foot?

*Ma, when the fuck are you fucking coming to see me?*

—¿What are you writing there? Mercedes said, peering at the change in the pen's rhythm.

—Should've gotten the home attendant for this, Mercedes said and picked at her housedress.

" 'Buela, Ma doesn't care about us. This is a waste of time," Leila whined.

But Mercedes had been sending letters to Amalfi for ten years, despite Andrés and Leila's frustration, despite arthritis and bad eyesight. When Mercedes had arrived in New York City, she made it her duty to understand the business of sending letters. Though Amalfi occasionally sent them white frying cheese or luxuriant hair conditioners with acquaintances traveling to New York, everyone knew she would never join them.

Leila bounced back on Mercedes' bed with a cramped hand.

—¡Get those tennies off my bed, little girl!

Leila laughed at her alarm and kicked off the sneakers. She shot the balled-up letter across the room to the mirror. Mercedes narrowed her eyes and slowly shook her head.

—The things you do . . . she said, then removed her dentures and put them into a jar on the bureau.

Leila crossed her arms, then uncrossed them to rip threads from the curtains.

—If you don't want to do me favors, then go, Mercedes said with a wave of her hands. —And they killed the goat on you, look at those circles under your eyes, Mercedes blurted out.

"What?" Leila stopped unthreading the embroidered hummingbirds and ran to the bureau mirror.

—I know you have the menses, Mercedes said.

" 'Buela, how do you know?"

—I know more than you think, little girl.

Mercedes elbowed Leila out of the way and began opening the

bureau drawers and unwrapping tissue paper. Occasionally she made scratchy noises with her throat. From one drawer she pulled out a ball of tissue. Then she slid onto the bed, where Leila now sat, to undo the ball with her veined hands. An amber crucifix lay in the wad like honey candy anchored in gold. Mercedes held it to the lamplight for Leila to see the delicate mite limbs trapped in resin.

—From Puerto Plata, I think. Mamá gave it to me before she died, when I was around your age. But in those times we never really knew our ages, because parents would sometimes wait years before they officially declared your existence to the government offices. Yes, I must've been like you, maybe thicker, because I was thick, you know, like a woman even before my menses . . . had the sharpest mind . . . had all the menfolk coming to me, but I settled for Andrés because if there's one thing I know is to marry smart, get one who you know will never double-cross you. Early on, make sure to keep the kitchen knives hidden, so that he is the one who has to ask you for their use. You have to be smart, my sweet girl, you have to be smart in life.

Mercedes' eyes had grown milky and her lips without the dentures looked drawstringed. Leila hated when Mercedes got lost in her own memories.

"I am smart. Ms. Valenza tells me I should think more about a medical career 'cause I like biology. Can't I just be good at it?" Leila spoke even though her grandmother could not understand her English.

But Mercedes continued as if Leila had not spoken.

—Be smart, little girl. Here in this country, you can't be having too many kids, with no village around to help you raise them. Over there, anyone—the grocer, the butcher—had every right to box your ears if they saw you on the wrong path. But here, you're on your own. Everything you do alone in this country. That's why people get crazy here, forget the Lord. Remember, Leila, the Lord's eyes are big enough to see everything you do.

"Anyway, who gave Mamá Graciela the crucifix?" Leila had to ask twice, as Mercedes dug a fingernail into her own ear.

—A nun or a priest gave it to her, something like that. Mamá, I must say in this old age, was as smart as me to have had only me, so she could pick up and go at will—¿and did I tell you she had me with a fine man of the purest breed? Amalfi must have that picture . . .

A hollow noise came from Mercedes' throat as she inserted a hairpin to get at the inside of her ear.

" 'Buela, you're gonna destroy the stereocilia in your ear!" Leila said as she fingered the crucifix. It was perfect to wear over a messed-up heart. She wanted to pop the cross in her mouth.

"Wow. Looks like vitamin E."

—Real amber, sweet girl. It floats in the sea.

They were quiet for a while, admiring the tiny window in their hands. Mercedes told Leila how Graciela had admitted to almost eating the cross as well.

—Always remember the things I tell you.

"Nah, 'Buela, I live for the now. Everyone's either telling me to remember stuff I never lived, or to prepare for some who-knows future."

Mercedes yawned.

To Leila, those who carried the past carried the dead, and those who chased the future died of cardiac arrest.

—¿Can I wear the crucifix? she asked Mercedes carefully in Spanish.

—It's already yours, sweet girl.

. . . . .

—Late bloomers last longer, Andrés told Leila.

"But I wanna bloom now, man," she said under her breath.


Leila and Miguel were in the basement, hidden in the labyrinth of thick walls. He squeezed her flesh, searching for roundness that was not there. She moaned, afraid and excited that the superintendent of the building would catch them and trot upstairs to tell her grandparents. She imagined them racing down with her Uncle Ismael to beat up Miguel and then beat her with the belt, and Mercedes would then have the home attendant write a long I-told-you-so letter to Amalfi.

Leila felt a delicious rain of needles. Miguel's fingers were now drawing circles in her tightness. She was wet and swollen and full of water while sucking on his earlobe. He seemed nice, she thought, liking and wincing at the easy way his hand claimed the newest hairs down there. She tried to hide her smile when his other hand reached under her tank top and pinched her nipples, as if he were handling the married woman who had borne him three children. A rain of needles. Studying him through the peephole every morning as he left the building for work, she had initially thought he'd be more mysterious. But here, against the wall, his mystique reduced to his mouth smothering hers. They grappled against the wall until the creak of the elevator doors separated them.

A woman sang to her son on her way to the laundry room behind their wall. An echo of giggles. Leila was relieved, too flustered to continue. She really did not know what to do next. They could not do It in the basement. Once she had kissed a boy with soft hands named Danny at the YMCA summer camp, and one childhood summer in DR, she and her third cousin Alex had felt each other up under Mamá Graciela's cashew tree. Leila had decided she did not like to kiss, and, to her amazement, she had in fact read in a book that people like her were called philematophobes. This man here, did not seem to be curing her. But while smoothing down her hair and snapping her bra back into place, Miguel told her she was pretty—Mercedes' pigeon soup must be fattening her up so that it even made a man want to cheat on wifey. Miguel was flesh, more flesh than the Dannys and Alexes of her recycled fantasies. Next time, Leila would make him take her somewhere else. Not on the wall. She was about to ask him for his phone number, but he put his index finger to her lips. Shshsh. And before she slipped off ahead of him to ride the elevator back to reality, Miguel gave Leila his crisp business card.

Two years of Leila's life were missing from family albums; after her twelfth birthday, it seemed she disappeared. From then on she wanted no more birthday pictures. She saved her grandparents' public-assistance money by refusing to sit for annual school portraits, and shutterbug friends called her a vampire for her absence in their photos. When she saw herself in pictures, it was as if she were looking at someone else, not the person she remembers being at the time of the photo. But, as Elsa said, Leila's problem was that she was too "self-conscientious—just stand there and smile, stupid!"

On the morning of her fourteenth birthday, Leila looked through the albums. She peeled off the snapshots of her birthdays and lined them up on the floor to see how she had grown into the beanstalk she was now—despite platefuls of rice and beans, heaps of pasta, giant triangles of pizza. Her medical factoid book confirmed that she was planistethic, her chest flat as a board.

— Pigeon soup and malt extract should fatten you up good, L'il Greedy Gal, Mercedes said if a tank top highlighted the tiny knobs at Leila's chest.

Each successive snapshot captured Leila in front of the same cupboard and smiling to the world. She gathered the snapshots, the cheeky one-year-old in bright pink at the bottom of the pile, and, at the top, the twelve-year-old fatale with puffy bangs. Her fingers flipped through the twelve slices of her life. Back then, her stronger sense of self had allowed her to look straight into the camera. A toddler smiled in the opening frame where she reached toward a jeweled cake. Frame by frame, Leila stretched past Felíz Cumpleaños streamers (which become Happy Birthday by the sixth frame). With each frame, faces filled out, hairstyles flattened, and Mercedes and Andrés wrinkled, while the china cupboard behind them remained unchanged throughout Leila's growth and fading smiles. Each year, the cake was transformed into a doll, rabbit, heart.

The rhombus of sunlight had long disappeared. Mercedes and Andrés went to bed early, as usual. They slept snug and confident that their granddaughter was up late studying hard for her future medical career.

Leila curled up by the television, the volume on mute. Her thumb was poised on the remote's Off button, her ears cocked for the sound of creaking floor behind the bedroom door. She had wound and rewound the videotape Mirangeli lent her to That Part. That Part, where a multitude of naked bodies wriggled in oil like a pit of ravenous snakes. A woman with melon breasts slid under a man with a face like Miguel's and the butt of a horse. Leila had munched her nails down to tender skin.

Finally, after fast-forwarding through monotonous fellatio

scenes, the videotape stopped. Her heart pounded like a fist in her chest. Three floors above, Miguel was probably in bed with his wife, his three children sleeping soundly.

A child answered the phone.

—Good evening, ¿may I please speak to Mr. Miguel Hernández? Leila asked. She heard a cough, then the tiny voice yell out for Papi.

—¿Aló?

His phone voice was hoarser than she had expected. Leila pictured Miguel standing with a hand on his hip, maybe bare-chested and in boxer shorts.

—Meet me in the basement. Ten minutes.

Leila hung up the phone. Her tongue searched for her fingernail, then settled on cuticle.

As she stuffed her bedsheets with sofa cushions, Leila shook her head at the cliché. With rough strokes, she brushed her teeth and combed around the hairline of her ponytail. Lights in the living room went out. She muffled the noisy padlock with her arm and then the bright hallway stung her eyes.

Leila waited. Each time the elevator door opened in the basement, her heart rattled. After a while, the heat inside her began to fizz. She stood against the wall where they had last heaved, right where the gray paint had been chipped off by a vandal.

—¿How'd you get my home number?

Miguel wore red checked boxers and a V-neck undershirt.

—I have my ways, she said with a breath of surprise.

—I'm supposed to be throwing out the garbage, he said, then hooked his finger around the waist of her jeans.

His hips pinned her to the wall. His tongue was fatter than Leila remembered. His boxer shorts pointed forward against her belly.

—Suck it.

His hands pushed down on her shoulders. Suck it, she did. Close her eyes, she did. Enjoyed it, until she started to drown. No easy business.

Their eyes never met while Miguel wiped the corners of Leila's mouth with the heel of his hand.

—Don't call my house again, he said, I'll call you, ¿okay?

Leila nodded. Most of the heat had fizzled in her belly, but embers still glowed. A peck on her cheek, and with a swish of his house slippers, Miguel was gone as easily as he had appeared. Leila waited for the sound of the closing elevator doors, then bounded up the stairs to prepare for her biology exam.

Leila's heart is a pear-shaped muscle, slightly larger than a clenched fist. At the center of the circulatory system, it pumps blood through the body at a rate of about four quarts per minute. Her heart weighs eight ounces and beats an average of seventy-two times per minute. The closing and opening of its valves produce the "lub-dub . . . lub-dub" sound of a healthy heart.

DR · *1998*

The mass visit back to the Dominican Republic was conceived by Ismael with the same spontaneity that had originally swept them all to New York. He spent so much time traveling between Santo Domingo and New York, that Mercedes called him The Pilot. To satisfy his insatiable need for possessions, he worked hard at his landscaping job in Long Island, and in his apartment he built a glass shelf to display his sneaker collection. Temporary riches. With visions of buying a ranch in DR (house complete with fireplace and bidet), Ismael was also committed to the lottery—what he termed "high-risk investment." Rubbing silver-gummed cards with a penny, filling out sweepstakes forms at grocery stores, examining soda caps, and staring at overhead instant-lottery number screens at a local bar-restaurant gave him a shot at standing out from the rest. With his new money—when he won it—he could swallow the sick feeling of anonymity that plagued him. In the meantime, he settled for prizes of free packs of Coca-Cola, ten dollars here, a blender there.

He had fired up Mercedes and Andrés into joining him on his next trip—for Leila's sake; he felt she should see her mother.

—To fly backwards again, after so many years . . .

Mercedes worried and Andrés shook his head. Ismael insisted.

—Leila needs her mother. I'm warning you, kids in New York grow up wild.

As Amalfi had not been willing to come to New York in the eleven years since they had emigrated, then they would all have to go see her themselves, because, Ismael concluded, somebody had to keep this small family together.

Ismael secured a modest bank loan to drench himself in gold chains and silk shirts for his trip back. Leila watched him trying to pack the twenty Avon deodorants he planned to sell into a suitcase.

Leila buried her apprehension about meeting Amalfi again in the bustle of buying new clothes and packing and weighing suitcases. She did not want to deal with yet another authority figure— not to mention the remote possibility of bumping into her father.

—Tío, you look like a damn Christmas tree, she said, still angry at Ismael's insistence. Leila was, however, excited about riding on a plane. And the prospect of summer romance, her friend Mirangeli had assured her, was a given for any New Yorker returning to native soil. Fine older men who wore shoes with tassels and trousers, lots of cologne, men who had gravelly voices and mossy chests—tacky by New York standards, but Leila found it endearing.

Her passport picture revealed an incomplete smile, as if the camera had sucked up its other half.

. . .

It was not love at first sight. On the porch of a turquoise palmwood house sat a fat woman rocking in a chair of stretched plastic strips. As she fanned herself with one hand, and waved with another, the loose skin of her upper arms flapped. She was golden and plenty in a flowery housedress and flip-flops.

—¡Your hair, my love! You used to have such a pretty head of hair, were Amalfi's first words to Leila. And Leila cringed as her mother dug her fingers into the heavily gelled "messy bun" on top of Leila's head.

The ride from the airport on a pickup truck had been long and dusty. As the truck meandered through thick vegetation, the crimson dust made Leila coppery. She could touch the trees and feel the wind, and everywhere was the smell of burnt leaves.

What stained Leila's memory of that summer was the ubiquitous crimson dust and her incessant bickering with Amalfi. It had started with the distribution of gifts: pastry tools, candy, hair accessories, shoes, jeans, dresses. Amalfi crossed her arms when Leila spread an I-Luv-NY T-shirt for her on the bed.

—I probably made this myself when I worked at the free zone, Amalfi laughed, when she read the shirt's Made in Dominican Republic tag.

Leila, Mercedes, and Andrés looked on, horrified, as Amalfi went on to explain how she no longer felt like being exploited.

After quitting sweatshop work, Amalfi had started her own business. Thank God, she assured everyone, that she had chosen to stay in Santo Domingo. She had ultimately become Miriam de Gautreaux's best pastry student, which is why her body had expanded like bread, with the increasing success of her cake-making business. She believed that although everyone used the same ingredients, her cakes secreted a drug from the way her flour married the milk, her eggs hugged the batter, her rum kissed the sugar through the powerful forearms she'd developed. With that money, Amalfi showed them how she was able to remodel the old kitchen cabin: put in electricity, a stove, a refrigerator, the rooster motifs. Always she stressed that she believed in progress. Also in the name of progress, Amalfi had purchased a scooter to deliver her cakes.

Then there was the murder of Leila's beloved—a chicken that had taken to following Leila about from the very day of her arrival. Weeks later, Amalfi stewed it and served it alongside rice, beans, and salad. Only after Leila had eaten it with relish, did Amalfi giggle and tell her she was in the process of digesting her "summer boyfriend."

There was the avocado fight.

—¿Avocado a fruit? Look, my love, don't come strutting here from the lap of imperialism and take me for a fool, Amalfi had said as she stirred a sancocho. And then and there, Leila decided she hated sancocho, hated having to sip the thick liquid and gnash the starchy roots like a hog. Hog food, that's what it was. Slave food.

" 'Buela, thank God you rescued me early from that crazy-ass bitch," Leila murmured under her breath.

—Stay with me here, love, Amalfi said.

Leila felt betrayed when Mercedes complained to Amalfi about the deterioration of Dominicans living abroad, especially that of the youth, who were living out of wedlock and dressing like common hookers—including the boys. And they've forgotten Spanish and stopped combing their hair and become Negros who bop their heads to that awful awful music.

—You wanted me to live out there, raise Leila there, speak a language that sounds like people chewing rubber bands, Amalfi said.

. . .

Leila had fantasized running down beaches and dancing merengue into the night for the five weeks, instead of sipping limeade on the porch while dust-stirring scooters screeched on the main road. No, she was not allowed to ride her mother's scooter into town. Ismael had taken her out for Bon ice cream one night, but spent most of his days stuffing the eyes of gold-digging, chrysophiliac, nymphomaniac, anisonogamist girls, most probably her own age. There she sat with guava-scented skin, the fluorescent porch lights buzzing with unfamiliar insects. Her grandparents were already in bed, her mother baking magic in the kitchen. Leila wished she had a big family of cousins her age she could hang out with, like Mirangeli did.

Other days she watched the clouds form mounds in the sky. Besides some hills, it seemed the sky was all there was. Once she saw a gargantuan woman rolling across the sky. A woman with massive thighs that dissolved under her belly and became arms, then a second head, until she was a dragon, then a car, then a sheet of milk. No way in hell was Leila going to leave New York and come and live with that corpulent woman who smelled like doughnuts in a country as boring and backward as this one. Not one cute guy in sight—and she knew the papis had to be somewhere on this half of the island. Leila lowered her head and cried out of sheer boredom.

—¿Why do you write those awful things to me in your grandmother's letters? Amalfi asked Leila one night while teaching her how to squeeze icing out as flowers.

The icing was supposed to curl out as even, white rose petals on top of the cake. It was a practice cake, which Amalfi had turned over to Leila. Leila's flowers came out wilted and uneven.

—You plant your feet on the ground, keep your elbow firm. It's a good life lesson, love, Amalfi said.

"I suck at this stupid shit!" Leila said and squirted the icing all over the cake.

—Not that güiri-güiri talk again, Amalfi said. —Answer my question . . .

—Answer why you never write back to us, then, Leila said. Her fingers destroyed the even flowers Amalfi had started her out with.

Guilt. And pride. Simple, yet complicated answers.

—I always felt like such a coward for not going along with everyone else, for having the will. And now here we are, you, already a woman . . . Time doesn't forgive. Here I am, making T-shirts that get sold right back to me, making cakes from sugar that we make and isn't even ours.

—¡But why don't you write back to us!

—Ay, Leila, ¿what can I tell you? 'Hi, I'm doing great here baking, and I'm happier than ever, thank you very much.'

Leila saw her mother's chin quiver just like hers did when she was about to cry.

—Let's not make a practice cake. Let's make a real one together, you and me, Leila said. She put her arms awkwardly around Amalfi and they held each other, briefly.

# GARDEN
## (OF DE-LIGHTS) · *1999*

—Late bloomers last longer, and with that Mercedes and Andrés once again foiled Leila's plans to go out with friends. Leila regretted asking permission before the dishes were stacked clean and dry in the cupboard. She gritted her teeth to rein in the back talk searing her tongue.

—Just remember, not too long ago I wiped that skinny behind, Mercedes said when she heard slight teeth sucking.

Leila clinked the final dishes in their "bedroom," as she had called the cupboard in happier, less complicated times.

—At fifteen, you should have more respect for yourself, Mercedes added. —Don't think we haven't heard about you and that louse from 4B.

—¿What are you talking about? Oh my God, I don't even know who lives in 4B. Leila pulled the dishrag taut between her hands.

—Now that's a beast, pretty-faced as you see him, and the day I hear your name and his in the same breath, so help me God Almighty I'll call up Ismael and you'll find yourself back on an airplane, Mercedes said, one fist jabbing the air. Then she shook the eucalyptus tea leaves she had been rinsing at Leila, who rewiped the stove and the counter until old starches and grease bubbles disappeared. After boiling tea for Andrés, Mercedes turned off the kitchen lights, leaving Leila standing there with the dishrag balled up in her hands. Nine in the evening, and already lights were going out in the house. Leila's birthday gift still lay unopened on the table. She knew it was a pair of tacky shoes her grandparents had bought from the woman who sold stolen clothes on the fifth floor.

Leila stomped to the living room and turned off the television. She did not feel like watching a transvestite spill her life story, or the soapy premiere of *Pobre Maria, Rica Maria*. Friday night. She could hear a staccato baseline thumping somewhere out the window. Heels clattered across the pavement outside.

Neatly folded clothing she had placed in her plastic wardrobe and a spotless coffee table had failed to earn her permission. She had made her bed, washed the soiled panties hidden under her pillows, and had lined up her stuffed animals among the cushions. And she had completed all her schoolwork during the day.

"The fuck you looking at?" Leila snapped, slapping a piggy, which landed on her pile of books on the floor. *Biology Lives— First Edition* and curled romance paperbacks were stacked in a milk crate at the foot of her bed. Leila huffed with boredom and self-pity. She briefly considered rereading one of the paperbacks' prefolded pages, the one in which the wanton Athenian girl, in preparation for marriage, is inducted into the world of love.

Leila sprang up and grabbed her backpack. A red satin bra and bikini went into the pencil pocket. The woman on the fifth floor had smuggled a dozen underwear sets for Leila from a sweatshop. The plastic wardrobe shook as Leila searched for a pair of black (cat) leggings and the sequined (punk rocker) bustier—remnants of very deliberate Halloween costumes. A toothbrush and black-coffee nylons rolled in the underwear, and Leila was ready. Piggy stared at her from a missing eye.

Leila examined the bathroom mirror. Hair had started to kink up at the roots and she cursed her genes again. Her eyebrows stretched when she pulled all the thickness into a ponytail at the top of her head. With veteran hands she pinned the mass into a ball and pressed down the stray hairs near her temple with petroleum jelly. Once Leila had clasped the gold hoops to her earlobes and smoothed some more jelly on her widow's peak, she smiled indulgently at the picture she had created. Profile. Front. Back. A pretend laugh. An arched eyebrow. A lick of seductive lips. Dance steps.

Leila jumped when she heard Andrés cough in the bedroom, where she knew Mercedes was lulled by television. *Pobre Maria, Rica Maria* had thirty more minutes of airtime to introduce its poverty-stricken, yet bewitching Maria, who will find love and riches in another 120 episodes.

Leila turned off the lights in the living room. In darkness, she sat on the bed and once again stuffed the bedsheets with sofa cushions.

The air outside was unseasonably warm. She saw Miguel leaning against the front of the building with his hands in his pockets as if he had been waiting for her all along. Leila had not seen him since The BJ Episode many weeks ago.

—¿Where you going? he asked. Only his eyes moved.

"Look, I don't have a dad, okay?" Leila said. A smile trembled in her voice.

Miguel kept quiet with half-lidded eyes that made Leila feel words gurgle in her throat.

"The Pavo Real. Meet me there," she said, then winked with both her eyes. Washington Heights, New York City, the world, heaved ahead. Crowds eager for spring hovered on stoops and street corners. The music of the plum sky made Leila drunk with freedom. In the distance she could see the glitter of the George Washington Bridge. Streetlamps shone where there should have been stars. Leila looked up and felt the span of wings. She sprinted the ten blocks to Mirangeli's house.

"You made it, shithead!" Mirangeli popped her gum ecstatically. Elsa was there, too.

"You should've seen me! I just fucking walked out," Leila said snapping her fingers. "Just like that."

The three hopped about like bunnies.

"Shoulda done it a long time ago." Elsa blew on her wet nails.

"Next time my parents go to DR, let's do this again. Like a tradition," Mirangeli said.

They compared outfits. Mirangeli's miniskirt and tank top garnered applause. Elsa's little black dress and knee-boots drew ooohs. Leila's bustier and flared leggings got Diablo's. Except for the shoes.

"No wonder that guy broke up withchoo," Elsa said as she pulled on a stiletto boot.

"And no wonder Shorty fucked you up in gym class for talking so much shit," Leila said.

"They're kinda cute, okay?" Mirangeli said when she saw Leila bite on her lip.

"I mean, they're okay. I just wouldn't wear 'em." Elsa slipped a little dress over bulging breasts.

"Whatever," Leila said, stuffing napkins into her bustier.

Then all three collapsed on the bed, cackling. Mirangeli blasted the latest merengue from the stereo and she brought out beers.

"So, Leila, have you seen your old dude?" Mirangeli asked before tipping her head for a long swig from the bottle.

"Nah, he's too busy providing for his family to be polyamorous," Leila said with a wink.

"You're so corny," Elsa said.

"Shut up, El," Mirangeli said, then turned to Leila. "But you never showed me how good he kissed."

Leila went over to Mirangeli, pulled back her head, and gave her a long and deep kiss.

"Y'all so damn nasty!" Elsa said, throwing a boot at them.

"You're just jealous 'cause you're not sexually liberated," Leila said while reapplying lipstick. It was not the first time she had kissed Mirangeli.

"How're we getting to the club, stupids?" Mirangeli quickly changed the subject.

"Cab. I ain't rippin' my pantyhose on the train," Elsa yelled from the bathroom.

Mirangeli undid Leila's bun and fought Leila's hair with great vengeance. "Sometimes, Leila, you just gotta make your forehead bleed to get this shit straight."

Mentholated cigarettes. More makeup. Some rum. Practiced dance moves. Cheerios. A quick communal budget. One crank call. Another for a cab to the Pavo Real.

. . . . .

The Pavo Real: a meeting of peacocks. The neon sign of a peacock in his splendor had enough plumage to keep the line growing outside its doors. Bouncers were busy, as were the bartenders. Air conditioning fought to dissipate the steam of sweat, peppermint breath, and mingling fragrances. The cult of the body was celebrated with vehemence as everyone drank the brassy imported liquor of the latest music bands.

Leila screamed when she saw the flashy vocalists. The three girls had shimmied their way through the crowd to stand at the edge of the raised platform. From their vantage point, they could see the sweat spots on the singers' canary suits. Leila and Elsa grabbed Mirangeli's arms tight when the vocalists rammed their groins at the fluttering crowd. *Ay, ay, mi negra. No borrowed women, I like no borrowed women.* Mirangeli cocked her head and a lazy smile stretched across her bubble-gum-blowing lips.

A finger brushed Leila's shoulder and she turned around, syrupy as syrup. Her heart pounded against the sliding wads of tissue paper. Silk tie and navy blue blazer. Miguel! But when Leila looked up at the face, the nose broadened where she had remembered it narrow, the jawline softened, the hairline curved where it had been square, and hair curled neatly into a mustache. Miguel? Leila hadn't expected him to come at all, dressed to the tens, boxers and house slippers blasted asunder.

Miguel danced well, smoothly maneuvering her body. Leila controlled her turns to keep her bustier in place. She could smell the soap of his skin and the spearmint of his breath. By the way he looked aloofly past her, she decided he was much older than she had first thought, maybe he had some money and had arrived in a nice car and — the merengue ended with an avalanche of piano trills.

They separated. He thanked her as if his fingers had never pinched her nipples, walking away with an arrogance that excited her. When she returned to Mirangeli and Elsa, they were sipping colorful drinks and whispering to two boys who looked slightly uncooked.

"You got drinks and everything!" Leila said after Mirangeli and Elsa refused to dance with the boys.

"Those idiots?" Elsa sucked her teeth.

"Yeah, but you were guzzling that drink like it was cum." Leila liked to show them she could be just as foul-mouthed, just as coprophemiatic.

"That's the guy you said you broke up with?" Elsa asked Leila.

"Yup, but we're back together now, so don't mess things up with those big tits, you bathycolpian."

"If you had him so good, you wouldn't worry, geek," Elsa said and jiggled her breasts.

Onstage, the band burned. The trombones and saxes seemed to swallow up the lungs of their players, and the keyboard chewed on fingers. The gyrating lead vocalist had the hard, fluid body of a swimmer—and was bucktoothed. He instructed the musicians to kill all instruments, except bass, tambora, and güira. To the beat of the chorus he threw off his vest, hips rotating to a much slower tempo. Women shrieked. Men watched with arms crossed. Elsa and Mirangeli lowered their drinks, Leila bit her lip.

—¡Ladies! ¿Enjoying yourselves? and the singer held out the microphone to amplify the "¡Sí!" and he wiped his forehead and he tapped his foot to the unrelenting tempo.

—¡They say we men fall in love with our eyes, and women with their ears!

The microphone picked up static.

—Well, tonight Banda Canaria makes everyone fall in love. ¡This is for the women! ¡Un! ¡Dos! ¡Trés!

Leila jumped to life, caught in the spirit. The music spread her wings wider. A few feet away, Elsa looked miserable, pressed up against a bug-eyed dancer. Mirangeli's orange lips were wrapped around another plastic cup and she was murmuring to a man with overgelled hair. Leila scanned the surrounding bodies around her for the unmistakable navy blazer.

—¡Now it's time for the men to fall in love!

The microphone hummed.

—¡We need a bold girl to come to the stage and chew at a few hearts! ¿Who wants amooooooor?

Leila strained her hand to the vocalist and he plucked her up onto the stage.

—¿Your name, muñequita? he cooed into the microphone.

—Cherry, Leila cooed back in a voice far away from herself. She looked at the singer's bucked teeth and caught a whiff of halitosis.

—¿Anyone here you want to enamoooorar, Cherrisita?

Sweat dotted his cheeks. His eyes were dull.

—A certain Miguel out there, Leila heaved into the microphone.

The music slowed as the lead vocalist invoked the classic merengue of the jealous woman with the meat cleaver. When it was time to pound, to beat, to mash, to bash the meat, Leila gyrated as she had practiced at home. With the growing chants, her hips ground the tangle of wires on the stage floor.

Soon a doughy hand touched her back.

—Gracias, Cherrisita. ¡Look at all the carnage, all those broken hearts out there! ¿Do we have another heartbreaker?

And Leila was led off the stage.

Below, Leila got shy. Mirangeli and Elsa surrounded her as if she had just conquered the world.

"You so crazy!" Mirangeli pinched her.

"Your napkins fell out." Elsa lolled her head, then turned around and tripped.

Leila caught sight of Miguel leaning against the bar, and she deserted her hiccuping friends. Her gait was long-legged, high-headed, loose-hipped. Walking past him, she noted his brief glance amidst his haze of cigarette smoke. She asked the bartender for a Presidente and he winked at the stage with a smile of recognition while sliding her the beer, without a glance at her bandless wrist. Miguel watched the bottle tip to her lips.

—Hola, Cherry, he leaned over.

—¡Oh! ¡I was just looking for you! Leila said, quick as a reflex.

—I was right here, waiting all this time.

He took a long drag, closing one eye as Tío Ismael did during domino games. Leila took another swig to forget her uncle.

—Last time we were together I was doing this . . .

Leila took a long, bitter sip from the lip of the president.

—¿Your grandparents know you're this naughty? he asked.

—¿Wife and kids know you're this bad? she shot back.

Miguel folded his hands. He looked impatiently around him.
—¿Who you here with?

—Oh . . . nobody. Just me.

Her beer was like pop.

—Such a young and pretty . . .

—¿ . . . girl like me all by myself?

Miguel's eyes narrowed.

—So, you're one of the smart ones. Okay, I see now.

He had glassy eyes in which Leila, with tingling in her cheeks, saw herself reflected as a baked chicken. And she laughed because his eyes twinkled like diamonds, really.

—¿Laughing at me? he asked, apparently amused by the way her bustier shifted each time she leaned forward.

Leila's bottle was empty.

—Just laughing. Señor Miguelito, ¿you know that I like presidents?

—No, no, no. No more Bill Clinton politics today, not here, he waved his hands.

—Pre-si-den-tes. Cold green presidents . . .

Leila's voice warbled.

—. . . and earlobes. I vote for those, too. Ooh, she felt so witty.

Miguel ordered another round of beers from the winking bartender.

—You could've just asked me for a drink. I'm direct, not too poetic, he said.

—With me you get más, mucho más, she drawled, running her fingers over her lips, like the popular beer commercial. Then she added her own lick of the bottle—before dropping it to the floor, where it shattered.

—Oops.

The band had left for their next gig; a deejay spun for the thinning crowd. Mirangeli and Elsa, through their own haze, found their missing friend. They stood at a distance from the bar, mouthing lewd messages. Leila gazed past them. Her friends danced some more in the waning crowd, before getting on the long coat line. Leila was on her own.

. . . . .

—You can call me Migo. As in your amigo, Miguel had said to Leila at the bar.

—Or Me-go, as in me go with you . . .

And that was when Leila knew there was no turning back. She was on her queasy own to lean over and kiss Miguel full on the lips, though bile bittered her throat. Conversation, the coat line, a chilliness outside the Pavo Real, the stagger to Miguel's car: it all happened fast as catechism filmstrips, where the entire meaning of the Body and Blood flashed in frames.

"Children of light, come and sing with me!"

Her hair was mussed, the petroleum jelly in it having attracted lint. She sang loud and out of tune in Miguel's sedan.

—You into young girls like me, ¿right? she said, then held up a finger and said, —Don Miguel, latex and gentooments, is an ephebophiliac . . .

—Loca, loca, loca. Miguel pulled her shoulders away from the dashboard before igniting the engine.

Leila sang the "Children of Light" tune again.

Miguel's free hand snapped at her leggings.

Leila watched the streetlights speed by. Buildings came and went like monotonous cartoon backdrops. She wanted to slow down, for there to be a beep, then the next frame. Beep, the Chalice and Bread. Beep, her body stretching past a Happy Birthday streamer. Beep, the quickly changing traffic lights speeding them from Manhattan to the Bronx.

What would Mirangeli and Elsa say now?

—¿Is your wife Carmen nice?

—Mm-hm.

Miguel returned his hand to the wheel to make the tight turn into the Jardín Motel's parking lot. His hand had been massaging Leila's shoulder, but she did not yet feel the same throbbing she had felt with him in the basement. A dog barked in a faraway lot, with the crunch of gravel beneath them. Jardín Motel, she mouthed the words.

—Get out of the car, Cherry, Miguel said.

A dumpster in the parking lot sobered her.

No gardens inside the Jardín Motel. Plastic vines hung from paneled walls. The bald man at the desk gave them a key attached to a lilac keychain, and Miguel promptly paid for the room.

"What about the free gift after four A.M.?" Leila pointed to the sign above the bald man. Miguel pulled her shoulder.

"Only with the newspaper coupon," the desk attendant said,

eyeing Leila's thin limbs. Then he shrugged and slipped them a vial stuffed with a condom.

"Enjoy," and he dipped back into his newspaper.

Room 32 was dismal. A lumpy bed. No sample-sized lotions or soaps for Leila to pocket, and certainly no Bible inside the night table.

—I bet hotels in DR are better than this. Leila sucked her teeth and picked loose yarn from the withered bedspread.

Miguel lowered the venetian blinds. When Leila got up to explore the closet, he pulled her to him by her shoulders and threw her on the bed.

—¿Why you always pull me by my shoulders?

—Take off your clothes, slut, he motioned and smacked her thighs.

Smiling, Leila kissed him, but he turned her on her stomach and pulled off her shoes. They flew into the bathroom and cracked the mirror.

—Migo, please kiss me at least, Leila whimpered into faded flowers.

Her leggings cut into her legs as Miguel rolled them off. He turned her around to dig into the crook of her shoulders and the hollow of her bustier.

—¿Paper? he snorted when she shivered in the naked gloom of lamplight. The wads lay flattened on the carpet and Leila covered her nipples.

—Fake, he said, spanking her. —¿What other lies have you told me, Carmen?

—¿Carmen?

Miguel straddled her while fumbling with the rest of his clothing. Leila remembered once rushing up to a silver dollar on the pavement that turned out to be a circle of spittle. Miguel was in his boxers, tugging at the pins in her hair. She fought him, until all that was left of her was panting and thoughts of Mercedes lovingly combing out her knots by the one-eyed piggy.

—I thought you said you could give me más, mucho más, Miguel growled into her armpit.

A fog. Not tears. She would not cry. Instead, her legs widened and Leila dug her nails into Miguel's back. When he pushed past her tightness, Leila felt herself turn to rubber. The free gift remained untouched on the nightstand, while the headboard banged into a groove that had worn through the sunflower wallpaper. Leila saw them. She witnessed the man on top of the girl, her legs twisted under him, her brand-new breasts crushed. She winced with the digging of his feet into the mattress at each thrust, the horse-buttocks tightening, the shock in her own eyes, then her face extinguished.

—Go to hell, Carmen. The man lay still over the girl, sobbing quietly behind the heaving of his climax.


—I like you. You're tough for a skinny little thing, Miguel said, later that night while fingering one of Leila's nipples. —I could kill you in here, ¿you know? Get a hanger from the closet, wrap it around your neck, and spill you on this bedspread.

Leila wanted to go to the bathroom. When she had come to, Miguel had been propped on his elbow, playing with her hair. The way he had sobbed earlier scared her more than empty threats.

—I could throw you out the window the way that German did to a cuero back in Boca Chica, he said and pulled her sparse pubic hairs.

—We're on a third floor, she managed to say, really focusing on the wedding band for the first time. It was an ugly ring—

lackluster gold. The little fear left in her she wiped off on the back of her hand. —Plus, this place is so cheap it don't even got hangers.

—Tough, tough, tough, this one. Miguel rolled over on top of her. His teeth were sharp on her shoulders, though Leila remembered them small and round like a five-year-old's.

—¿What now? It's still dark outside, he said, then bit her, this time softly. Gaining her trust with gentle kisses, he was soon rough again. His cries were guttural, as Leila floated back to the ceiling and waited by the curtain rods.

Afterwards, she wiggled from under his snores. In the cracked bathroom mirror, the fluorescent light revealed a splintered face with green around the eyes and purple blotches on the neck. The hair was yarn. Leila washed away the clotted blood. Then she dug her index finger deep into her throat, but none of the poison she felt churned her belly. She wondered if Mercedes and Andrés' spirits were watching as their bodies lay asleep at home. But her grandparents were probably too entertained in the dream world to spot her dry heaving in a Bronx motel. It was then that Leila really began to cry.

Spicy videotapes in the wee hours. Curled romances on her bookshelf. Lunchtime braggadeering. Cheated, she felt, and she hated Mirangeli and Elsa for their stupidity about It, and cursed Ms. Valenza for teaching It, and damned everyone else for celebrating.

Leila dressed—five minutes to reconstruct the outfit that had originally required so much primping.

Miguel was sprawled on the bed, wrapped in sheets. Leila got a glimpse of his belly button, which protruded like a purple olive—nothing immediately scary about him, despite his large frame and wide jaw. If she had the strength of a bull to strangle him, would she? She had more of an overwhelming desire to stick a long needle into the middle of his chest, where his wife seemed to have already. Ease into his heart, still and patient, until his heart valves creaked like the gears of a broken clock. He would flinch once. Die slowly. Then, vamplike, Leila would walk out of the Jardín Motel.

Leila sat on the bed to see if Miguel would stir. His snores eclipsed that of the garbage trucks outside. The morning was wet, yet surprisingly peaceful after the night she had endured. Even days have their sleepy side, Leila thought, the safety pin from her makeshift breasts buried in the tougher skin of her thumb. The swishing of early cars cut into the quiet; the morning light was silver in the hollow of Miguel's chest. Carefully, Leila ran the pin along the hollow, remembering the unopened condom vial and wondering if a little virus was already multiplying in her own cells (or was it just her cypridophobia?).

Miguel jumped awake.

—¿What? ¿What is it?

He scratched his chest as he sat up.

"I want to go now," Leila said, arms folded.

—¿Ya? ¿So the fun is over?

He yawned, too sleepy to resist. He rinsed his mouth in the bathroom like a gentleman (as Leila would later recount) and dressed with as much care as she imagined he had the night before.

—You're not mad at me . . . he said once they were in his car.

Miguel squeezed her cheek with tenderness. Leila looked out the window: bodega gates groaned at every other corner. She wondered if Mercedes was already out of bed, waiting for the woman who brought her blessed Communion host on Sundays—but no, today was Saturday. For Leila, it was as if the whole weekend had already ended.

—By the way, Carmen already knows about you, so don't

bother trying to cause me trouble. Now, in your house, that's a different story.

His bottom lip curled as he shrugged.

—Just take me home, already, Leila mumbled.

Miguel dropped her off two blocks away from their building. When the car door slammed behind her, she felt her hangover grip her head and spin her in circles.

. . . . .

"Diablooo!" Mirangeli said when she opened the door. Her eyes were swollen with sleep.

"Where you been, slut-face? I was praying for you."

"Lemme use your phone," Leila said. It took a few rings before Andrés' scratchy voice answered. That she'd risen very early to go to the library to finish a project for school—Leila rushed through her excuse—and she'd be home later in the afternoon, and please tell 'Buela that she would clean the rest of the apartment as soon as she got home.

—Devil knows not 'cause he's Devil but 'cause he's old, Andrés said in a tone Leila had never heard before. —I may not talk much, but I'm not to be fooled with, ¿you hear? Come home now, you shameless little—

Leila hung up. She wasn't afraid of her grandfather—hell if her own absent father can say shit to her. Really, would Andrés kill her if she got pregnant? It's what all his fears ever seemed to amount to with her. Of course, he was probably also worried that she had been kidnaped by some rapist . . .

There was no way Leila was going back home any time soon.

Over bowls of cereal, Mirangeli slowly came back to life.

"When are your parents coming home?" Leila asked.

"A week. My grannymama called ten times to make sure I wasn't doing the nasty."

Mirangeli seemed so simple.

"Where's Elsa?"

"Hungover. Threw up all over my quilt, that pendeja. So show me, Leila, how did he kiss?"

Mirangeli's morning voice sounded like a man's. Her eyes were no longer bloodshot. They now brimmed as they did the time she had asked Leila for a sampling of her Danny-and-Alex episode.

"You didn't even brush your teeth, and now you got all that cereal in your mouth . . ." Leila mumbled. More than anything, she wanted a good lung-cleansing cry on Mirangeli's lap.

"What the fuck happened, then?" Mirangeli said, still chewing.

After the Pavo Real, Miguel had driven Leila to the Mariott Hotel out in Westchester. He kissed better than any *guy* she'd ever kissed: slow, tracing her teeth and lips with his tongue, sucking on her lips, nibbling her chin. At the hotel, room service was excellent: they ate warm bread and sipped real wine while watching steamy cable movies he wasn't too cheap to pay for. They had a bubbly bath, where Miguel combed Leila's hair into fluffy white volumes.

"But what about this?" Mirangeli got up to gyrate wildly in her polka-dot pajamas. It was she who had once proudly broken the Santa Claus myth to Leila.

"It was good," Leila answered, the uneaten cereal soggy in her bowl.

"Oh, come on!"

Miguel was a'right, but not as good as YMCA Daniel with the twenty-inch you-know-what.

Each detail widened Leila's ulcer of disgust.

"You lucked out, girl," Mirangeli said, without noticing the twitching of her friend's mouth.

. . .

Under a comforter scented by Mirangeli's bubblegum, Leila tossed about the bed. Mild cramps kept her from sleep, reminded her of the previous night. Leila closed her eyes. She let her breath reach into her belly until the flush of oxygen put her to sleep. Her dreams were a collage of confounding images: two copulating lizards . . . cumulonimbus clouds shaped like ships . . . small brown hands paring an apple . . . the map of the world on a face . . . La Virgen de la Altagracia without a face . . . a peppermint stick inside a coffee cup . . . lavender tangled in pubic hair . . . a hatbox . . . mercury-stained skin . . . an uncombed baby under a chair . . . a thorned and bleeding plaster heart.

After a week's stay at Mirangeli's, Leila awoke one afternoon with cereal still lodged in her teeth and the taste of sour milk clinging to her throat. Mirangeli snored next to her, her hair a splash of matted curls on the pillow. Television blared in the living room, the radio babbled in the kitchen, and Leila also found that Mirangeli had left all the lights on in the apartment, despite the daylight. How she missed the order of her own home, the soothing murmur of her grandmother's Christian radio show. Her grandfather was probably still curled up in a ball on the bed, always covered entirely, except for his feet. When Leila finally found her coat in the pile of Mirangeli's dirty clothes on the sofa, she zipped it up so fast that it made a nick in the center of her chin.

# REUNION · *1999*

Mercedes and Andrés received Leila quietly, almost matter-of-factly, as if they had known all along that she would come home a week later with the faithfulness of a boomerang. In Leila's rush to meet her friends the week before, she had left her keys behind and was forced to ring the doorbell. When Mercedes looked through the peephole, she was relieved to see a convex Leila, looking like a circus pinhead, tongue stuck out and eyes crossed, without a care in the world. By the time Mercedes undid the top chain, unlocked the middle padlock, and then unlatched the long steel pole, she was frazzled. But acting as if Leila had not been missed seemed to a weary Mercedes to be the best punishment. The years had eroded Mercedes' need for revenge; she accepted that the justice of God the Lord Her Savior would always be infinitely more poetic than her own. Andrés himself considered flicking Leila's ear between his fingers, then giving her a beating to prove he still had it in him. But in Leila's face he saw that life had already done the job.

Leila explained nothing of her absence to her grandparents. For weeks she bid her blessings to them, when she hadn't always before. In the evenings, Mercedes was amazed to see a pair of freshly washed panties dangling over the tub like a flag of truce. Mercedes and Andrés were sure Leila had carried some kind of cross to Calvary and back.

. . . . .

The day Leila finally decided to return home from her week-long stay at Mirangeli's, she started out early. Andrés and Mercedes had been calling Mirangeli's house, but after a few days they had given up scolding Leila and her no-good, so-called friends on the answering machine. Their last message threatened to call Ismael, and even to call Amalfi in Santo Domingo, if Leila did not return by the end of the week.

When Leila woke up at Mirangeli's that Saturday, the city was bathed in light. Through the dingy windows of the train that sped Leila downtown, she could see Manhattan sprawled beneath her. The rumble of the tracks gave her an unusual comfort. Buildings flashed across the reflection of her nose. When her home station sign whizzed across her mouth, Leila did not feel like standing up. She let her stop come and go across her frown. Later, a brilliant mosaic dotted her eyes, and on impulse Leila stepped out of the train.

The Museum Gift Shop was nestled in a glass box under the arches of the museum. By the door, a mechanical parrot in a bamboo cage graciously shrieked evening "Good mornings" and morning "Good evenings": an attraction that sold souvenirs and tourist trinkets faster than museum tickets.

Leila stood at the threshold, afraid she would brush up against an antique-looking globe and have it come crashing down to knock over onyx chess sets, to break open vials of colored sand, to crush I-Luv-NY top hats, to put out Tiffany lamps with Victorian girls lounging in their glass, to free naked Tahitians from Gauguin mugs and scatter the postcards of nymphs like a game of spades gone sour.

No way could Leila ever bring Mirangeli or Elsa to a place like this, where she won a game of chess against herself on a too-expensive set, flipped through gargantuan coffee-table books about dinosaurs, and tried to solve a mind-bender puzzle on display. Finally, after an hour of browsing, a hyper-polite clerk asked Leila if she was sure she did not need any help.

"Look, bitch, I'm not gonna steal nothing, okay?" Leila said with a deadly roll of her eyes. She decided she just wanted to go home and curl up on her little sandwich bed with a candy bar in one hand and the remote control in the other, with Mercedes listening to the radio in the kitchen and Andrés reading in the bedroom.

The train had just left the station as Leila paid her fare and stepped onto the platform. The echo of her cough rang hollow, and only one man stood across from her, on the downtown side. The sound of dripping somewhere lulled Leila as she paced between one end of the platform to another. She tried not to think of what she would tell Mercedes and Andrés about her absence by reading the movie ads and the profane handwriting scribbled over celebrities' faces. Life-size ads told Leila about how she could fix her credit, where she could find a mortgage, a great place to study the culinary arts, a new AIDS drug that invigorates the T cells of attractive people, an MTA appeal urging her not to throw her gum wrapper on the train tracks, a blank wall.

A hot breeze picked up and the platform shook with the coming roar. Dust flew in her eyes. Leila stepped into the last car of the train and looked out the door window into nothingness.

The Feeling started up again. She smiled. It had been a while since she'd had it. The familiar flutter center-left of her chest got warmer . . .

*Waited on a long line to get born. Still, life dealt me a shit deal. Don't listen to whoever invents magics about me. Always tried to live what I wanted. Never pretended to be a good woman. Never tried to be a bad one. Just lived what I wanted. That's all my mystery. Forget dirty tongues. They're next door, in the soup, even in your own head. Some weak soul always trying to slip their tongue inside your mouth, clean as a baby's pit. You, listen. My life was more salt than goat. Lived between memory and wishes . . . but ¿how much can a foot do inside a tight shoe? Make something better of it than me.*

Leila missed Mercedes and Andrés, Ismael and Amalfi, and even the great-grandmother she's never met. She unpinned Mamá Graciela's amber crucifix from her bustier and put it in her mouth and was overcome with a desire to love them, to make their lives happy before they all turned to leather, then ash underground.

## ACKNOWLEDGMENTS

Acknowledgments to all the Saints:

Always first and foremost to the Creator and to the Ancestors. 'Ción Abuela y 'ción Abuelita. A mis padres Israel (natural aristocrat) and Isabel (ravenous bookworm), for Vida, for passing on your love of travel and knowledge through literature, and for continuing to teach me the importance of education, as well as integrity. To the rock-solid siblings, Maria Isabel (always encouraging, Womanda of the hour), Israel, Jr. (the realist, lil' bruh I look up to), and Alexander (art soul, me as a dude)—you all ground and inspire me with your unique gifts. Cuz Alexandra, keep keepin' it gangsta. John Olmo: for witnessing and supporting my work's metamorphosis from the git-go, for your luv/creative lessons, for OMO. Jackie Estevez, for fueling me with your joie de vivre and wayback, genuine friendship (plus, the photocopies!). Sheron Johnson, creative-genius-in-crime, for paving us forward with pen and camera in hand. Annecy Baez, for your friendship and for exhibiting the many creative possibilities of Woman. Josefina Baez, ¡mujer!, for your spirited guidance and delicious wickedness. Angie Cruz, "the other fish," for your gift of Women in Literature and Letters (WILL) and joined-at-the-fin sisterhood. Juleyka Lantigua, keep stewing in your talents—the time'll come.

The Williamsburg, Brooklyn, community (Southside, y'all!)—especially Transfiguration Parish—for your village-hand in raising me. Williamsburg Public Library, flying me to other worlds since my first library card twenty-six years ago. El Puente, for the sweet smell of teen spirit. Gerard Moss, remember way back when you stuffed me with books? Ms. Heinlein, who believed me a writer. Elzbieta Ettinger, you showed me how to give wings to pain. Decima Francis, Brenda Cotto-Escalera, Maureen Costello, Bruno Aponte, for exposing me to the wonder of the stage. Marie Brown, thanx for inducting me into New York's literary community and for your warm smile. Thank you, Fred Hudson, Martin Simmons, and the Frederick Douglass Creative Arts Center, for the magical things you're doing Uptown and all around. Arthur Flowers, you're the green-thumbed gardener who tilled the soil when this joint was just a seed. Daisy Cocco De Filippis, madrina de nuestra literatura, your wand keeps sparklin'. A las mujeres de Tertuliando and to the WILL warriors, for those midwife hands. Silvio Torres Saillant (and the CUNY Dominican Studies Institute), for paving so many roads. Carolina Gonzalez, you're the woman. Maureen Howard, your perceptiveness, your faith, and your generosity have brought me far. Helen Schulman, always honest, always on-point, always firm. Jaime Manrique, oh, the power of a Colombian writer's syllabus! Magda Bogin, we language-hoppers and luvin' it. Beverly Lowry and Patricia O'Toole, for teaching me how to dig thru history. Richard Peña, for your tour of the Latin-American silver screen. Romulus Linney, you opened my characters' mouths. Meri Nana-Ama Danquah, you helped me pick up my pen again. Andrea Greene, Victor LaValle, Matt Johnson, Doug Jones, Touré, Amy Barnett, Cristina Lem, and Cristina Chiu for the advice, the laughs and for warming up the Columbian tundra. Junot Diaz (bad-ass extraordinaire) and Edwidge Danticat (quill sistren), for joining our countries' hands through your creative and public works. And always gratitude to all my writing students for being my teachers.

Columbia University, for its invaluable resources, including the Hertog Fellowship and all my writing peers. Marita Golden and the Zora Neale Hurston/Richard Wright Foundation, who with seven hundred dollars and a dream started stirrin' up the Diaspora's scribes. Lenora Todaro and Joy Press at the *Village Voice Literary Supplement*, for the faith (and the books!), and thanx to the staff at the National Book Foundation for surrounding me with inspiration.

The National Hispanic Scholarship Fund for making two years of grad school easier on my pockets. The National Arts Club, for honoring my work. To the Van Lier Fellowship at the Bronx Writers' Center (Leslie Shipman and Laurie Palmieri!) and the Money for Women/Barbara Deming Memorial Fund: you all kept a pregnant woman fed, writing, and sane. Thanks to International Residencies for Artists (IRA) funds, I can, in turn, thank La Fundación Valparaíso for allowing me a month of unhindered creativity in Spain. The Authors League Fund for its generosity. Sherine Gilmour, Eileen Lamboy, and Dawn Lectora, you wondergals watched my back and kept the cash flowing.

Thank you, gracias, merci, Gloria Loomis for being the sweetest, smartest, most sensitive, most encouraging bulldog around.

## ACKNOWLEDGMENTS

Katherine Fausset, for all your patience and characteristic grace at the Loom. Jenny Minton, literary personal trainer, thanx for your keen eye, quick wit, and belief in the book when others said nay (and that title!). Adam Pringle and Megan Hustad, y'all got patience!

This book is dedicated to Olivia Monet Olmo, who will forever teach me the true meaning of Creation.